A PUREE

OF POISON

*Also by Claudia Bishop
in Large Print:*

Fried by Jury

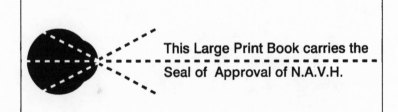

This Large Print Book carries the
Seal of Approval of N.A.V.H.

A PUREE
OF POISON

CLAUDIA BISHOP

WHEELER
PUBLISHING

Published in 2004 by arrangement with The Berkley Publishing Group, a member of Penguin Group (USA) Inc.

Wheeler Large Print Cozy Mystery.

The text of this Large Print edition is unabridged.
Other aspects of the book may vary from the original edition.

Set in 16 pt. Plantin by Christina S. Huff.

Printed in the United States on permanent paper.

Library of Congress Cataloging-in-Publication Data

Bishop, Claudia, 1947–
    A puree of poison / Claudia Bishop.
      p. cm.
    "A Hemlock Falls mystery" — T.p. verso.
    ISBN 1-58724-684-8 (lg. print : sc : alk. paper)
    1. Quilliam, Meg (Fictitious character) — Fiction.   2. Quilliam, Quill (Fictitious character) — Fiction.   3. Hemlock Falls (N.Y. : Imaginary place) — Fiction.   4. Women detectives — New York (State) — Fiction.   5. Historical reenactments — Fiction.
    6. New York (State) — Fiction.   7. Sisters — Fiction.
    8. Cookery — Fiction.   9. Hotels — Fiction.   10. Large type books.   I. Title.
    PS3552.I75955P87 2004
    813'.54—dc22   2004043782

For Bob, once more

As the Founder/CEO of NAVH, the only national health agency solely devoted to those who, although not totally blind, have an eye disease which could lead to serious visual impairment, I am pleased to recognize Thorndike Press* as one of the leading publishers in the large print field.

Founded in 1954 in San Francisco to prepare large print textbooks for partially seeing children, NAVH became the pioneer and standard setting agency in the preparation of large type.

Today, those publishers who meet our standards carry the prestigious "Seal of Approval" indicating high quality large print. We are delighted that Thorndike Press is one of the publishers whose titles meet these standards. We are also pleased to recognize the significant contribution Thorndike Press is making in this important and growing field.

Lorraine H. Marchi, L.H.D.
Founder/CEO
NAVH

* Thorndike Press encompasses the following imprints: Thorndike, Wheeler, Walker and Large Pr int Press.

CAST OF CHARACTERS

THE INN AT HEMLOCK FALLS

Sarah Quilliam . . .	the manager and owner
Margaret Quilliam . . .	her sister, and head chef and owner
Doreen Muxworthy-Stoker . . .	the head housekeeper
Dina Muir . . .	a graduate student and receptionist
John Raintree . . .	the business manager
Kathleen Kidder-meister . . .	the head waitress
Peter Hairston . . .	a waiter and sommelier
Mike Santin . . .	the groundskeeper
Devora MacIntyre . . .	a waitress
Donna Olafson . . .	a guest
Brian Olafson . . .	her husband, also a guest, and insurance broker
Azalea Cummings . . .	a guest, and a filmmaker
Ralph Austin . . .	a guest, and a filmmaker
Warrender Hack-meyer . . .	a guest, an insurance broker, and a Civil

War reenactor

Malcolm Fetter-
man . . .   a guest, and a Civil
War reenactor

John Paul
Coolidge . . .   a guest, and a Civil
War reenactor

Max . . .   a dog

Various waiters, waitresses, maids, chefs, and
dishwashers

RESIDENTS OF THE VILLAGE OF HEMLOCK FALLS

Myles McHale . . .   the sheriff, and a
                          private investigating
                          consultant

Davey Kidder-
    meister . . .   the acting sheriff
Elmer Henry . . .   the mayor
Adela Henry . . .   his wife
Howie Murchison . . .   the town attorney
Marge Schmidt . . .   a real estate broker,
                          insurance broker,
                          and entrepreneur
Betty Hall . . .   her partner
Harland Peterson . . .   an Agway president
                          and dairy farmer
Derwent Peterson . . .   his uncle
Alicia Nickerson . . .   the wife of Nicker-
                          son's Hardware
                          Store's owner
Nadine Nickerson . . .   her mother-in-law
Freddie Bellini . . .   a mortician
Mrs. Bellini . . .   his wife
Miriam Doncaster . . .   the town librarian
Carol Ann Spinoza . . .   the town tax assessor
Esther West . . .   the owner of West's
                          Best Dress Shoppe
Harvey Bozzel . . .   the president of
                          Bozzel Advertising

Betty Peterson . . .   a nurse
Andy Bishop . . .   an internist

PROLOGUE

It isn't as hard to kill, the second time. That's the conventional wisdom, isn't it? Everyone knows the first one is the hardest.

So just relax, think the next one through, forget about the night terrors, the nausea, and the sudden dizziness after the first one died. Plan the next one calmly.

An air bubble in the IV, same as last time? Untraceable as a cause of death, right? So much less risky than a car accident or a gun or poison. As long as the poor son of a gun stayed in the hospital, it'd be all right. It'd be okay. It'd be easy.

And the third time would be easier still.

CHAPTER 1

"I don't see how Andy can blame himself," Sarah Quilliam said. "All doctors lose patients, Meg."

"Spare me the conventional wisdom." Her sister, Meg, ran her hands through her short dark hair. They sat in the dining room of their Inn at Hemlock Falls. They were at the table nearest the Falls overlook. Outside the long windows, the water was a tumbled silver under the hot June sun. Inside, the last of the breakfast crowd was trickling slowly out of the room. It was midmorning, and both Meg and Quill were taking a break just after the breakfast rush. "It's just the two deaths so close together. Nadine Nickerson and then poor Freddie. And the same cause, Quill. Infarcts, both of them. Andy says neither of them were that sick."

"Infarcts," Quill repeated with a knowledge-able air.

This didn't fool Meg for a minute. "Myocardial infarctions. You know, a heart attack."

"Andy's one of the best doctors around, Meg. But he can't save everyone. Freddie Bellini had a dicky heart for years."

"I know." Meg sighed and twirled Andy's large diamond around her ring finger. "But Nadine Nickerson didn't have a dicky heart."

"She was eighty-six years old, and frail," Quill said. Even the best doctors overlooked diagnoses. But if she said that, Meg would have her guts for garters, or something similarly unpleasant. Quill wasn't in the mood for a fracas this morning.

"Anyway, Andy needs a break. Between the consulting job at Cornell and the clinic here, he's just been run off his feet. He hasn't said so, Quill, but he thinks he's been making mistakes. So he needs to get away for a while."

"Oh, dear. Right now, you mean? This week?"

"Right now as in this afternoon," Meg said.

"And you need to go with him. Well, we can manage. Don't worry about a thing." Quill put her hand over her sister's. "Bjarne will be back from vacation on Friday and we'll find some way to staff the kitchen until then. If push comes to shove, the sous chefs and I can handle things?"

"Oh, *right*," Meg said. "Just like you handled it the last time I had to leave? It was a disaster."

"The last time I helped out in the kitchen, you didn't 'have to leave,' " Quill pointed out with spurious patience. "You walked out in the middle of a huge lunch. Bang. Just like that. And I did just fine. As a matter of fact, I did better than fine."

"If Banion O'Haggerty hadn't stepped in to help, the state could have declared us a disaster area. Besides, you've had your hands full just managing the Inn since John dropped back to one day a week."

"There were excellent reasons why John dropped back to one day a week. His consulting business is paying him far more than we could ever pay him, and we don't need a full-time business manager. Those courses I've taken at the Cornell Hotel School of Management are really paying off, Meg. This new W.A.T.C.H. program is fabulous."

Meg made a noise like *"Phuut!"* and laughed rudely.

"What do you mean by going "phuut!" And why are you laughing? This new program is wonderful. I know it's ruffling the employees a little, Meg, but every time a good manager institutes change, somebody's not happy. Not right at first."

"Is that according to the Immortal Professor Wojowski?"

"Well, yes." Quill settled her coffee onto the saucer in a dignified way. "Everyone will come around, you'll see."

Meg said, "When pigs fly," and kicked the legs of her chair. Her socks this morning were a shrieky orange. This was not a good sign. Orange was an irascible sort of color. Meg's mood almost always reflected the color of her socks. She was the best chef in the northeastern

United States, in Quill's unbiased opinion, but she was temperamental.

Quill wound one finger around a strand of hair and tugged it hard. It was a beautiful morning. The Inn was booked through the end of summer and business was doing fine, despite the media talk about recession. She and Myles were as happy as they'd ever been. Her new process improvement program was going to make dramatic changes in the Inn's profits. Life was, for once, serene, and she wasn't about to puddle the waters with a stupid argument with her sister. She tucked the strand of hair behind her ear and said, "What if I ask Betty Hall to pinch-hit for you while you and Andy take some time off?"

"Betty Hall?" Meg sat up, her lower lip at a belligerent angle. "Betty knows as much about gourmet cooking as I know about gene mode therapy."

"Betty's an expert at American diner food and she knows how to run a professional kitchen. She can supervise the sous chefs. Honestly, Meg. Don't worry about it. You can't be here twenty-four seven. Go away with Andy for a few days."

Meg's sigh was deep and martyred. "It doesn't matter. We have the Civil War re-enactors coming in this weekend."

"That's not until Friday. Bjarne will be back from vacation by then."

"And the Short American Film Festival

people are beginning to come in this afternoon. We have a cocktail reception for them this evening."

"Are they?"

"Are they what?"

"Short. I mean they call themselves the Short American . . ."

"And you wondered if they are all under five foot two?" Meg grinned reluctantly.

Quill relaxed a little. She wasn't quite sure how to handle Meg in this spiky mood. "And the full contingent won't be in until late this week, either."

"The Civil War reenactors want an authentic 1860s menu for the banquet," Meg said. "Who's going to handle that if I'm not here?"

"Miriam Doncaster's researching recipes for you. She said that's what town librarians are for. She said the domestic recipes are astoundingly straightforward, so I don't see why Betty Hall and I can't —"

"I wasn't planning on going anywhere with Andy." Meg's interruption was abrupt. Her eyes were a clear, aggressive gray.

"Oh," Quill said. She bit her lip so she wouldn't say any more.

"What do you mean by 'Oh'?"

"Not a thing," Quill said hastily. "What do you mean by that?"

"What do I mean by what?"

"You know exactly what I'm talking about." Quill allowed herself a moment of exasperation.

"You're giving me the bug-eyed 'what's it to you' look. I don't deserve it. What I do deserve is to be told what's going on. I'm your sister, for goodness' sake. Are you and Andy getting along? Does he want to get away from you or from the clinic? Is that because you don't want to go or because he doesn't want you to go or because he wants to go alone? Pick one. Pick two. But pick."

"I think he wants some time to himself."

"But that's just fine, Meg. You don't need to spend every minute with each other."

"Do you know how many minutes we've spent with each other in the last three weeks? Would you believe five, maybe? Or ten? We never spend any time together. Between the clinic and the kitchen . . ." Meg pushed herself away from the table and stood up abruptly. "Never mind. I'm fine. He's fine. We're fine. Don't worry about it. I just wanted to let you know that Andy's going to take a weeklong break from the clinic and the five or ten minutes that I would have spent with him are now at the disposal of the Inn at Hemlock Falls. *Along with the rest of my life!*" Meg wheeled and marched across the deep maroon carpeting to the kitchen doors, whacked each of the swinging panels with an open palm, and disappeared. A loud "clang" some seconds later told Quill that one of the (fortunately) inexhaustible supply of eight-inch sauté pans had been flung against the slate floor.

"Whoa," said a familiar voice behind Quill. "Is she, like, having major PMS, or what?"

"Hey, Dina." Quill turned in her chair and looked up at their receptionist.

Dina was somewhere in her midtwenties and a grad student at nearby Cornell University. She had recently started putting purple and green streaks in her glossy brown hair. Quill rather liked the effect. Dina herself, however, looked somewhat truculent. Quill didn't like that effect at all. "Whatever it is, it'll pass. It always does. Do you have the W.A.T.C.H. Report for today?"

Dina scowled and waved her clipboard in the air. Then she said, "Ur." The institution of the W.A.T.C.H. Report had not gone down well with the staff, and she held it just out of Quill's reach. "Talk at the Croh Bar is that Dr. Bishop's losing it." Dina sank into Meg's abandoned chair and regarded the W.A.T.C.H. Report with what only could be described as a sneer. "They say there's no way poor old Mr. Bellini should have kicked off the way he did, just like that!" Dina snapped her fingers. "But what I say is, you never can tell. So it's no wonder Meg's losing it, too. It's like, symbiosis. Which is when paired organisms' behavior affects each half of the pair."

"Thank you for that compelling piece of information," Quill said. Dina was a graduate student in limnology, which was fresh water pond ecology to those uninitiated in its mysteries. "And you might let the guys at the Croh Bar know that Dr. Bishop's not losing a thing. I don't need to tell you, as a scientist, that death is a natural part of life. And it's very sad about Mr. Bellini. Now, about the W.A.T.C.H. Report . . ."

Dina held it just out of reach. "And who's going to bury people, now that Mr. Bellini's gone? That's the one thing the people at the Croh Bar are worried about. I mean, think about it, Quill. They say that with no one to run the mortuary, bodies'll just stack up and stack up and goodness knows where things will end. Carol Ann Spinoza says that there's some kind of law against not burying bodies right away and that Mrs. Bellini's going to run into a whole pile of trouble with these body ordinances if she doesn't get someone in to take care of it immediately."

"Stop," Quill said. "Just think about it, Dina. Number one, when has anything Carol Ann Spinoza's said or done made any sense whatsoever?"

"Carol Ann got her job as tax assessor back. She can raise everybody's taxes if she wants to and everyone in town is dead spit scared of her," Dina said. "She makes a lot of sense to me."

Quill ignored this, "And two, is Bellini's Funeral Home the only mortuary in Tompkins County?"

"Well, no, I suppose not. But Mrs. Nickerson's body is already there, Quill, because she died just before poor Mr. Bellini did, and what are they going to do, just ship Mrs. Nickerson and Mr. Bellini off like that to someone else?"

"Yes," Quill said.

"Poor Mr. Bellini is going to be buried by the competition? That has got to be so hard on poor Mrs. —"

"Dina," Quill said firmly. "Give me the W.A.T.C.H. Report and go away."

"Fine," Dina said. "Just fine. I mean, if you just want to totally ignore what people in town are saying, all I can say to *that* is that Hemlock Falls is just like the life cycle of the copepod, where what happens in one part of the pond affects what happens in the other part of the pond and you ignore stuff like that at your peril. Stuff like this" — she waved the clipboard in the air — "is, on the other hand, like, *hooey!*" She dropped the clipboard on the table with a bang. Then, like Meg, she wheeled on one foot and stamped out of the dining room. There were no doors to bang open at the arches leading to the reception area, so she smacked the maître d' stand instead.

Quill looked at the report without reading it and thought about standing on her head. It was supposed to be good for the circulation and it might clear the incipient headache at the back of her neck. Then she wondered why Dina was so hissy about the W.A.T.C.H. Report. Then she wondered where the bodies of poor Mr. Bellini and Mrs. Nickerson were going to be sent because the Inn always sent flowers to the funerals of people from Hemlock Falls. She took her sketch pad out of the pocket of her skirt and scribbled a note to herself about the flowers. Then she picked up the W.A.T.C.H. Report.

The acronym stood for Where Are The Customers Hiding? The WR (as Quill fondly called it) was the result of her latest evening class at the Cornell School of Hotel Management: Profit Master! Getting Control of Your Business Through Process. Quill liked the topic and all that it implied. She'd get control of those functions of the Inn under her direct supervision. She'd present a methodical and businesslike front to their business manager, John Raintree. She would appear competent and executive-like (two qualities that had not characterized her personal management style heretofore) to interested observers.

The Profit Master system was designed to let a manager know where every employee was at any moment of the work day. The W.A.T.C.H. Report was in two parts: The first was to be filled out from forms submitted by employees and it documented what the employees had actually done, rather than what their assignment duties were. The second part of the report — the important one, as far as Quill was concerned — had to do with the guests at the Inn.

Professor Wojowski had helped her design a system just for the Inn. She'd listed all of the major functions of the Inn — number of meals delivered, number of towels and sheets consumed, number of rooms cleaned, grounds maintenance, current bookings, future bookings, and the like — into a neat grid. Dina had filled all these numbers in her neat, precise handwriting, sevens crossed, nines rounded, fours open and clear so there was no mistake about what was what.

Following the grid was a large space for guest AttaBoys. The Cornell adjunct professor (a laid-off Xerox manager from nearby Rochester, working for two thousand dollars a semester) had defined an AttaBoy as any customer praise, written or oral. The Profit Master (Quill herself) made a list of all of the AttaBoys and then delivered reward and recognition to the Inn employee responsible for the good work.

This space was also nicely filled with the results of the collected survey cards left in every room. Quill and Meg had put survey cards into each of their twenty-seven guest rooms when they had opened the Inn ten years ago. Quill had designed them herself, with a pen and ink sketch of the copper-roofed Inn on the top. They'd collected only a handful over the years. The adjunct professor had suggested a larger format, free of 'extraneous clutter' and 'less complex to fill out,' and it appeared to have worked. There were lots of comments. The guests loved Meg's food, the lavender-scented sheets, the view from the suites over Hemlock Gorge and the waterfall, the wait staff, the grounds, and even Nate the bartender in the Tavern Bar.

Quill's incipient headache vanished. She sat back in the chair and smiled benignly at the view outside the window. Late June was a time when the rose garden on the front lawn was in full flower. The deep golds, peaches, and pinks of the roses accented the lush green of the neatly trimmed lawn. The sides of the driveway, just barely glimpsed from this end of the Inn, almost vibrated with contrasting silver and purple of the alyssum and lavender that Mike the groundskeeper had planted there.

Quill bent over the sheets of the report once more. The AttaBoy space was followed by a second grid, listing breakage, lost items, and food returned to the kitchen.

There was a lot. John Raintree had kept track of these in the past, and Quill had never paid them much attention before. The grid had a space to describe the damaged item, a space for the room number, and an area for comment. An unusually high number of lost towels were followed by Dina's scribble:

All towels missing — 221 stole?
Damaged sheets: 324 don't ask — disgusting!!!!
Broken glasses: couple in 228 — divorce! (I think.)

Quill reviewed this information with decreasing enthusiasm. The Inn was a microcosm for the real world. And there, short of murder, it all was.

24

The space beneath LOST, DAMAGED, AND STOLEN was for employee complaints. They were different from the customer comments. These complaints were collected from the forms called WhyNots. Quill had placed stacks of WhyNot forms all over the Inn and they were offered to guests and employees alike. They were bright red and about the size of a postcard.

The number of WhyNots was dismaying. After ten years of innkeeping experience, Quill was familiar with complaints. It was just depressing to see them written out and collected in one place. She sifted through the usual and expected:

Housekeeper threatened my son!
(Doreen, her mop, and the bratty little kid in 314.)
WhyNot have her arrested?

Drinks watered??
(The red-nosed salesman in 225.)
WhyNot make them stronger?

And Is Your Receptioniss (sic) a commie? Tell her to wash her hair!
And Receponiss (sic) RUDE AND ABUSIVE!
WhyNot Fire Her!

So that last comment was why Dina was grouchy. She was the receptionist, and a very good one, too. Well, at least she hadn't thrown it out. A lesser woman would have. There was no room number listed — typical, she thought, of the nastier type of complainer. She rose to her feet with a sigh. She would have to talk to Dina. The adjunct professor had been most firm on this point. Complaints had to be addressed immediately; both the complainee and the complainer had to be dealt with in as firm and focused a manner as possible. The matter had to be investigated with fairness. Then all the facts could be laid out and a Corrective Action issued if necessary. Quill wasn't precisely sure what a corrective action was, since she'd had to miss that week's class. She wasn't certain she wanted to know anyway.

Dina sat hunched behind the mahogany reception desk, her nose buried in a textbook titled *Recent Genetic Modifications to the Copopod.* The foyer was exceptionally pleasant on this June morning. The big oak door was open to the outside and fresh sweet air wafted in. The two Chinese vases by the cobblestone fireplace were filled with late iris and peonies.

Quill waved the W.A.T.C.H. Report at Dina in a vague way. "Do you have a second?"

Dina's eyes went to the file in Quill's hand. She turned bright pink and gave Quill a ferocious scowl.

Quill said weakly, "I mean, if you're busy . . ." She stopped herself. This was *not* the way to management effectiveness, nor to becoming a

Profit Master. Quill said firmly, "In my office, Dina. If you don't mind, that is."

Dina slammed the text shut and preceded Quill into her office.

Quill loved her office. The ceiling was tin. It dated from the early nineteenth century, when the Inn was a small wayfarers' stop on the route to the fur trade up north. The leaded windows looked directly out over the koi pond and the small statue of Niobe that stood in its center. Her desk was made of warm cherrywood, and the couch against the far wall was covered in bronze chintz printed with white spider chrysanthemums.

Dina thumped down on the couch, her face pink.

"Well," Quill said.

"Before you start, about the communist stuff. I think it was this complete and total jerk that just walked in and demanded a room, and when he heard the rates, he stomped out again. *He* was a communist, if you ask me. I mean, who else would complain about prices that kept the quote 'little guy' unquote from this 'artsy-fartsy Inn'? I'm quoting again," she added hastily. "And if it wasn't him, it was this totally revolting couple with fake Vuitton luggage that would have skipped out on their bill if I hadn't practically grabbed them by the scruff of the neck and had to practically hold them at gunpoint to get their credit card off of them. And if it wasn't them, it was this —"

"There's more?" Quill asked, startled.

"This isn't the easiest job in the world, you know."

"No, it isn't," Quill said, thinking of really tough jobs like fire-fighting, terrorist-capturing, police work, and baby-sitting some seven-year-olds. "I sympathize. I really do. I mean, when we first opened up, I was the receptionist. You're right. Customers can be complete and total jerks."

"You bet I'm right."

"We don't know, however, if this customer is a complete and total jerk or if he has a legitimate complaint." Quill faltered. She didn't think a complainer whose complaint was that her twenty-two-year-old receptionist was a communist had any degree of legitimacy whatsoever. But the adjunct professor had been quite emphatic about the need to Follow Up. "Dina, this must have been someone who stayed here after a, um, disagreement with you. The man that came in and left wouldn't have had access to a WhyNot card. And the couple that tried to skip out on their bill wouldn't have gone back and filled out a card after you caught them."

"They might have carried it with them. And mailed it. For revenge," Dina said.

"Perhaps. You can't think of any other person you might have inadvertently annoyed?"

Dina's face became pinker. Her large brown eyes welled up.

"Or maybe someone who was under stress?"

28

"Just the people who came here for Mrs. Nickerson's funeral. It was canceled, you know, because of poor Mr. Bellini being dead and nobody to bury the body. They were kind of upset. But I don't think they were upset at me, although I couldn't help hearing what they were saying about Mrs. Nickerson because they were saying it right here in the lobby and I was sitting right where I was supposed to." Dina leaned forward. "I had no idea she was worth that much money! And her relatives got it all! That Alicia Nickerson was really happy about it."

"Never mind, Dina," Quill said as repressively as she could. "You know that people who come to hotels want the staff to be anonymous. Anything else? This would have been yesterday."

"I kind of accidentally bombed into Mr. Olafson's room, which upset him and Mrs. Olafson because I fell against the door and it opened and Mrs. Olafson was in her slip and Mr. Olafson was naked. But they just sort of yelped, if you know what I mean. They weren't mad."

The Olafsons were new to Hemlock Falls. He was a wealthy insurance broker. His wife was busily constructing a huge new house at the edge of town. They stayed at the Inn when the Sheetrock dust became too oppressive. Donna Olafson was drop-dead gorgeous and didn't seem the type to be worried about communists. Or maybe she was. Mr. Olafson had to be pretty wealthy to drape her with all the jewelry she wore.

Mrs. Nickerson's relatives were known to Quill too. The old lady had been quite a tarter while she'd been alive, and her three sons and their sons had been firmly under her thumb. Had one of the family cracked under pressure? Quill thought not. They all seemed like stable, responsible citizens of Hemlock Falls. Besides, after Freddie Bellini died yesterday afternoon, they had gone back home to wait for the funeral.

"I think we should just forget it," Quill said. "I mean, this person didn't even fill out a room number?"

"Right."

"There's no name, no address. Just spite. Maybe it's someone's idea of a bad joke." Quill had a feeling that the adjunct professor would not approve of the way she was handling Follow Up. So she said sternly, "Just in case, Dina, let's make sure that the guests who stay here have as good a time as possible. We have to be professionals about this."

"Mm."

"Okay?"

"Mm."

"And," Quill continued recklessly, "while we're at it, being professional means being on time, every time. I've noticed from the W.A.T.C.H. Report that you tend to come in just a little bit later than nine o'clock when your shift starts, Dina. Nine o'clock is nine o'clock. Not nine-twenty." Quill tapped her forefinger on her desk and repeated the adjunct professor's aphorism on the subject of timeliness: "When you're on time, you're ahead of the game. And the game is professionalism, Dina."

Dina rolled her eyes, exhaled loudly, and looked at her watch.

"Is there anything else?" Quill asked a little frostily.

"You're twenty minutes late for the Chamber of Commerce meeting."

"That's today?"

"It's the fourth Monday of the month," Dina said. "The Chamber meeting is always the fourth Monday of the month. As a professional employee, I make it a point to know what day of the week it is and this is Monday."

"Thank you," Quill said. "Thank you very much."

"You're welcome," Dina said smugly.

Quill abandoned dignity and ran down the flagstone hall to the conference room. The door was open and she paused for a moment before she went in.

Mayor Elmer Henry stood at the head of the long mahogany conference table. To his left were his wife, Adela; Howie Murchison, the town attorney; Miriam Doncaster, the town librarian; and Dookie Shuttleworth, minister of the Hemlock Falls Church of the Word of God. To his right were Marge Schmidt, the richest citizen in Tompkins County; her partner, Betty Hall; and Mark Anthony Jefferson, who'd just been promoted to executive vice president of the Hemlock Savings and Loan Bank. Esther West, owner of West's Best Dress Shoppe, and Harvey Bozzel — president of Hemlock Falls best (and only) advertising agency — sat hunched together farther on down. There was an empty chair next to Harvey, with a sheaf of white lilies laid on the seat. Poor Mr. Bellini had sat there in happier days, which were, Quill recalled, just last week.

There were two new members at the table as well: Mr. Olafson, the insurance broker whom Dina had interrupted in the hotel room, and Carol Ann Spinoza. Quill's eye slid over Carol Ann Spinoza the way one's eye shies away from a dead skunk in the road. The snaky, horrible, mean, and spiteful Carol Ann had somehow weaseled her way back into the job of town tax assessor. And it looked as if she had weaseled her way into membership in the Chamber of Commerce, too. Quill gave Carol Ann a smile as sociable as she could make it. Carol Ann blinked lazily, like a cobra in the sun, and turned the corners of her mouth up in a smirk.

"Where have you been, Quill?" Mayor Henry said crossly. "We've been waiting." Normally a cheerful soul, the mayor looked like a hot and bothered baby. "Can't get started without those minutes of the last meeting and Miriam here can't make head nor tail of 'em. Even," he added obscurely, "if she is a librarian."

"Sorry," Quill said. She slipped into the

empty chair between Marge and Betty and smiled apologetically. "Is anyone taking the minutes right now?"

"I am," Miriam said.

"Since you've already started taking notes, Miriam, why don't you —"

"No. You're Chamber of Commerce secretary. I'm not." Miriam tossed over the minutes book. Quill kept the book in the conference room because she tended to lose it, otherwise. "The only notes I've started taking have to do with trying to read last month's minutes. It's not your handwriting, Quill. Goodness knows it's pretty enough. The notes just don't make any sense. The drawings are nice, of course. Ever think of doing it professionally?"

Quill's national reputation as an artist was a source of pride to Hemlock Falls (except for Carol Ann Spinoza, who thought Quill was overrated). Quill acknowledged Miriam's slight dig with a rueful shake of her head.

"It doesn't matter about the old business anyway," the mayor said tolerantly as Quill riffled through the minutes book. "What matters is the old new business. We just want to be sure we got the old new business right because of what's happening right now in Hemlock Falls. You want to read us the old new business, Quill?"

Quill found the NEW BUSINESS heading from the prior month and peered hopefully at it.

Ju (Hackmeyer reanct) 12–18 plus F? (EH to ask)
Whose Reb? Meg y/n re men?

She pulled at her lower lip. At the less exciting Chamber of Commerce meetings, she tended to nap, and a month later, even she couldn't decipher her minutes. "Well, of course. It's all about Warrender Hackmeyer and the Civil War reenactors."

Elmer nodded in suppressed excitement. Warrender Hackmeyer had been at the Inn only last week, setting up preparations for the reenactment event. He had spent a lot of time with Elmer. He was also the only insurance broker to be listed in the Fortune 500 list of the wealthiest men in America. He was Elmer's kind of guy.

"Mr. Hackmeyer booked the Inn for the first four days in July. You all know by now he's the leader of a group of Civil War reenactors. I gave him Maureen Peterson's name at the Town Hall so he could ask about using Peterson Park for some of the reenactment and you, Mayor, were going to call him to see just what the reenactment was going to entail. I think the F is for fight. They're going to reenact a battle and we didn't know if they used real artillery."

"What's that about Meg and men, then?" Esther West demanded. Esther, owner (and chief customer) of West's Best Dress Shoppe, smoothed the Peter Pan collar of her summer

34

print dress. "Are she and Andy splitting up?" she added hopefully.

"It's not men, it's menu," Quill said. "The reenactors asked about having an authentic 1860s banquet here and I was going to ask Meg if she'd be willing to do it. I did," Quill added proudly, "and she will. Miriam was going to research some recipes for her."

"I've got those right here," Miriam said. She lifted a folder off the table and dropped it again. "Loaded with carbohydrates, of course. Lot of cornmeal and yams. It might be fun, though. There's something called a raspberry syllabub that sounds delicious. On the other hand, the barley puree sounds revolting."

Elmer waved the recipes away with an impatient hand. "Forget the food," he said. "I got a meeting set up with Mr. Hackmeyer right after we're finished here. And I want to be able to present my idea —" Adela, who was half a head higher than her husband, and whose chest was considerably broader, rapped her knuckles on the table. "Sorry, dear," Elmer said, "I want to present my good wife's idea to us Chamber members here, and if we approve, well. All I can say is Hemlock Falls won't see the like of *this* again."

"The like of what?" Marge Schmidt asked suspiciously. Her beady (but undeniably intelligent) eyes narrowed in on the mayor like tank artillery training in on a doghouse. "I remember all too well what your ideas come to, Elmer Henry. First we had Hemlock History Days, guaranteed to turn the village into a tourist attraction second only to Disneyland. Result? Three corpses. Then there was the Jell-O Architecture Society competition. Result? Two corpses. Not to mention that champion idiot idea of the year, the Texas Longhorn Beef–eating contest. Result?"

"Just hang on, now," Elmer interrupted. "Each and every one of them — I mean those — municipal occasions ended up in a tidy profit for this town."

"If it wasn't for the fact that we got one of the best investigators in the country living right here, it could have been a disaster," Marge said flatly. "If we hadn't gotten those murders solved, you can bet your butt the town wouldn't have ended up with a profit. And it was no thanks to you and your loony ideas, Elmer."

"Good heavens." Brian Olafson's interruption was almost involuntary. "My wife and I had no idea there had been so many murders. We moved here from Syracuse to get away from crime." The insurance broker was a tall, mild-looking man in his early sixties. He removed his wire-rimmed glasses, wiped them carefully with a tissue, and put them back on again. "How many unnatural deaths did you say?"

"Not that many," Elmer said hastily, "and like Marge here says, we got crime well in hand here in Hemlock Falls. Each and every one of them — those — murders was solved."

"By whom?" Mr. Olafson demanded. "You

can't possibly have funds sufficient to retain an entire police force. The village isn't that big."

"We don't need a big police force," Elmer said. "We got . . ."

Quill patted her unruly hair to smooth it, and prepared to smile modestly.

"Myles McHale," Elmer finished. "Retired from the NYPD, Mr. Olafson. And he was a pretty big deal there, in his day."

"In his day?" Quill said, her tone a little chilly. "At forty-nine, he's not exactly over the hill, Mayor."

"No, no. He retired at a fair young age, that's true."

Quill smiled reassuringly at Mr. Olafson, "My sister Meg and I are pretty fair hands at crime investigation ourselves. We had quite a lot to do with solving several of those crimes. As did Sheriff McHale."

"Still," Brian Olafson frowned, "it seems strange, from an underwriting point of view. Perhaps Donna and I should have searched a little more carefully for a place to retire."

Elmer shot a venomous glance at Marge of the See-what-you-started! variety and rapped the official gavel on the table. "Point of order. Point of order."

"Will you *stop* whacking that thing, Elmer," Miriam said irritably. "You're going to dent Quill's table one of these days. I just know it."

"Point of order!" Elmer said loudly.

The room quieted.

"All right then." Elmer brushed his hands over his thinning hair. "Where were we? Quill? Read me back what we were doing before all this hoo-ha commenced."

Quill bent over the minutes book (which had nothing whatever written on it — if she started recording the Chamber's collective squabbles, her hand would have had permanent writer's cramp) and said, "Umm. We were discussing Adela's great idea." She looked up and smiled at the mayor's wife. "What is your great idea, Adela?"

Adela took a majestic breath and stood up. She was an imposing woman, with a decided chin, a prominent nose, and a preference for large, flowery hats. Although she wasn't wearing one at the moment, she carried herself as though wearing one of the smaller crowns belonging to the House of Windsor. "Those of you native to our town," she said, "are well aware of my family's past. But our newest members" — she nodded genially in Brian Olafson's direction — "may not know that I am a direct descendant of the Civil War General C. C. Hemlock."

Brian Olafson looked from side to side, saw that Adela's pinioning glance was indeed directed at him, and then nodded politely.

"You do know the general," Adela continued. Her voice had taken on a timbre more appropriate to Westminster Abbey than to Quill's twenty-foot-long conference room.

"Ah. Well. Actually." Brian Olafson's Adam's

apple moved nervously up and down his skinny throat.

"The granite tribute to him in Peterson Park?" Adela showed her teeth in a chilly smile.

"The statue of the old bird on the horse in the park, Olafson," Marge said. "Get *on* with it, Adela."

Ten years of innkeeping (and five years as the Chamber of Commerce secretary) had allowed Quill to perfect the art of attentive inattention. She turned to a fresh page in the minutes book and did a brief sketch of Myles McHale in three-quarter profile. This brought a slight lump to her throat; a part-time consultant for Global Investigations, Myles was out of town for several weeks. Then she did a sketch of the statue of General Hemlock in Peterson Park. The piece had been commissioned in the late nineteenth century. Something had happened to the temperature of the bronze during casting. As a result, the general looked as if there were something very uncomfortable on his saddle.

". . . The general trained the troops responsible for the victory at the Battle of Hemlock Falls," Adela said loudly.

Quill gave the general a big smile and Teddy Roosevelt teeth.

"He had married my great-grandmother, Bethesda Lucille . . ."

Quill added a wedding veil to the horse's head, and sketched a bouquet of rose between its teeth.

"Directly descending to me." Adela sat down.

Esther West clapped in a tentative way, then stopped.

Elmer got to his feet and placed a fond hand on Adela's meaty shoulder. "So what we are proposing here is a kind of celebration. This is, after all, the one hundred and thirty-third-year celebration of the battle. I've talked to Hackmeyer about actually re-creating the Battle of Hemlock Falls. He's agreed. So I'd like the town to join in with a nice little celebration. I was thinking maybe a rededication of the statue of the general, with Adela here accepting the blessing, so to speak, and then maybe a variety show."

Quill put her pencil down. She raised her hand. "A variety show?"

"It's historically authentic," Esther West broke in. "Adela and I have been all over the back shelves of the library, looking at the most fascinating issues of the old *Hemlock Falls Gazette*. And yes, it's a historical fact. The town celebrated the Battle of Hemlock Falls with a variety show. And we thought we'd re-create it. With town talent."

There was a puzzled, if appreciative, silence.

"A variety show," Miriam Doncaster said. "Hum. I have to say I don't recall a variety show as such from the village records. Now, minstrel shows, yes. I'm afraid we were all too prone to those, up until the early 1930s if I'm not mistaken."

40

"I suppose you could call it that. A minstrel show," said the mayor with a defiantly innocent air.

Mark Anthony Jefferson cleared his throat in a highly meaningful way. There was a ferocious scowl on his face.

The silence was deafening.

Nobody looked at Mark Anthony Jefferson.

"A minstrel show?!" Meg dropped a sieveful of wild blueberries into the prep sink and stared incredulously at her sister. "I don't believe it." She folded her arms and leaned back against the sink.

Quill swung on top of the stool at the birch work counter and looked back at her. The kitchen was relatively quiet, although it was past twelve o'clock and the lunch hour was in full swing. Monday lunches, even in high season, tended to be lighter than other days of the week. The kitchen staff worked busily around them, but there was none of the frantic, stroke-inducing stress that frequently surrounded Meg when she cooked.

"What did you say? You couldn't just sit there! And what about Mark Jefferson? What did he do, the poor guy?"

"The mayor said he was sure that Mark wouldn't have a problem with black face because all that stuff — and by 'stuff' I guess Elmer meant racism — was in the past and nobody thought anything these days of black folks and white folks working together."

"Oh my God," Meg muttered. "They didn't ask him to sing 'Ole Man River,' did they?"

"No, they asked Harvey Bozzel to sing 'Ole Man River.' And Mark said no, he didn't have a problem as long as he could do 'Putting on the Ritz' in white face. And then Marge Schmidt started to laugh so hard I thought she was going to have a stroke and the moment, as they say, passed."

"Yikes," Meg said.

"Yikes doesn't begin to describe it. The new guy, Brian Olafson, thinks we're all lunatics."

"And what did you do in all of this? You struck a blow for *egalité, fraternité,* and what's the third thing? I always forget."

"Liberty," Quill said.

"Oooh, yes. Liberty. You know why I forget that word so often, Quill? Because I don't have any. Because instead of taking the next few days off to be with the man I am going to marry, I am chained, chained to this bloody stove." She reached over and gave the Aga a smack.

Quill was unmoved by this evidence of her sister's illogic. If Meg wanted to deal with the separation from Andy by claiming a sacrifice to duty, that was fine. Just fine. "I just pointed out that we would no more want to put on a minstrel show than do a diorama of Andersonville. There are some parts of our history not fit for celebration. So everyone voted to have an 1860s talent show and rededication of the statue in Peterson Park. It is, after all, the one hundred

42

and thirty-third anniversary of the Battle of Hemlock Falls. This is after the reenactment. Or before the reenactment. Or during the reenactment, if the reenactors don't agree to participate."

Meg digested this. "You know," she said, "I don't get the whole reenactment thing. I mean, it's hot here in July. And these guys wear heavy wool uniforms. And sleep in teeny canvas tents, on the ground, on straw with fleas in it. And they reenact killing other guys in equally hot scratchy uniforms."

"Well, we won't be in hot scratchy uniforms," Quill pointed out. "It might be fun. And if it isn't fun, it'll be profitable for the Inn, at least, and that will make John happy. Can I have some of those blueberries?"

"You cannot. They're actual early wild blueberries that Mike carefully collected this morning and there's only enough for garnish. I'm not wasting them on my crazy sister."

"I am more than just your crazy sister."

Meg raised a skeptical eyebrow.

"I've been appointed an official member of the Hundred and Thirty-third Festival Subcommittee," Quill said loftily. "And that should come with blueberries, shouldn't it?"

"Depends on what it means."

"What it means," Quill said, "is that I've been co-opted to serve on the planning committee for the one hundred and thirty-third anniversary celebration of the Battle of Hemlock Falls. My

43

first duty is to sit down with Warrender Hack-meyer, the guy in charge of the reenactment; the mayor; Mark Anthony Jefferson; and Laughing Marge Schmidt. God bless her, to make sure that we don't tick off a paying guest. That happens in" — Quill consulted her watch — "ten minutes. It's a working lunch. My second duty is to make sure I don't have to picket the Hundred and Thirty-third Festival myself for egregious insults to the fifteen percent of American citizens whose ancestors were dragged unwillingly to these shores hundreds of years ago. All this by the weekend. If anyone deserves those blueberries, I do."

Meg picked the colander out of the sink and presented it. "You are absolutely right."

Quill had asked Kathleen Kiddermeister, head of the Inn's wait staff, to set the first lunch of the 133rd Festival Committee on the terrace off the Tavern Bar. There were several reasons for this: First, the June day was splendid — "rare" as in perfect, indeed, and perfect weather predisposed almost everyone on the planet to good humor, and second, if anyone ended up throwing crockery at Elmer Henry, it would bounce off the lawn and she wouldn't have to add to the breakage section of the W.A.T.C.H. Report.

Mark was seated at the table when she arrived, deep in conversation with Marge. Elmer and Warrender Hackmeyer were nowhere in sight. Marge broke off in midsentence and greeted her with a sharp nod. "You're early," she accused. "You're never early."

"I can go away again," Quill offered. "Maybe to Seattle?" She unfolded her napkin and took a sip of water.

Mark smiled at her and rumbled, "It wouldn't be half so much fun in Seattle."

Quill knew enough not to apologize for the events of the Chamber meeting. Instead, she signaled to Nate the bartender, whose duties covered the terrace on weekdays, to bring the menus.

"You're being a good sport about that minstrel show crap," Marge said to Mark in an approving way. "What the hell. It takes all kinds. Thing is, I think the next generation's gonna know better."

Mark shrugged. Quill, who knew there was nothing to say, merely mentioned that the fruited pâté was exceptionally good today and that she had met Warrender Hackmeyer only once, when he'd stayed at the Inn the previous week.

"You're about to meet him again," Marge said. "And there's Fudd with him."

"Fudd?" Quill said as she turned to see the mayor escort Warrender out onto the terrace. "Oh. As in Elmer. Oh, dear."

The two men seated themselves, expressing great satisfaction with Quill's proposed meal of pâté, grilled pork tenderloin, and seasonal greens.

"Warrender here was just telling me that he and his men do these reenactments all over New York State," Elmer said. "Tell Quill what you said when I asked you how often you have to practice, Warrender."

"*Practice* shooting people?" Warrender Hackmeyer sent a bored smile in Quill's direction. His teeth were artificially white in his bearded face. He was a strongly built man with that indefinable patina of prosperity that the wealthy and successful seem to have.

Elmer laughed sycophantically. Mark smiled politely. Marge, who was never under any compulsion to be polite, sipped her iced tea and burped.

Quill herself was fascinated with Warrender Hackmeyer's teeth. Warrender's long, scraggly beard and droopy mustache were constant visual reminders that he was a Civil War reenactor. Real Civil War soldiers didn't carry Crest Whitening Strips into battle and most of them chewed tobacco. If Warrender were truly committed to the authentic, he should have stained, cavity-filled choppers clenching the stump of a cigar. On the other hand, deodorant hadn't been invented in the midnineteenth century, and soap was at a premium then, or so she believed. She rather liked the scent of bay rum and Ivory Soap. All in all, she decided, the dental anachronism was justifiable. Aesthetics weren't everything.

"The Fourteenth Regiment's had years of

practice shooting people," Elmer continued. "Haven't you, Hack?"

"Indeed." Hackmeyer turned the pâté over with his fork and let it drop back on his plate. He stared meditatively into space.

"I'll just bet you boys are a dab hand at war," Elmer said eagerly. "Now, if we can just get a real clear idea of what the old Fourteenth wants from Hemlock Falls, why, I'll present the whole picture to the rest of the Chamber in about" — he consulted his Timex with a flourish — "three hours, when we reconvene this month's meeting."

Warrender's thick eyebrows contracted with annoyance. "I hope you're not telling me there's going to be any objection to the Fourteenth Regiment's restaging the Battle of Hemlock Falls, Mayor?"

Elmer sank his rather substantial chin into his neck. "If there is, General, I want you to know that I will do everything in my power to make sure that those objections disappear like that." He snapped his fingers.

"There aren't any objections," Marge said. "Fudd here's just puffin' himself off."

"Fudd?" Elmer said.

Marge assessed Hackmeyer coolly. "The town's just fine with the reenactment. What we want to know is if you fellows will give us a hand in the whole celebration."

Hackmeyer's thick eyebrow went up. Quill decided he'd seen too many John Wayne movies while he was growing up. "What whole celebration, ma'am?"

"What d'ya mean, 'Fudd'?" Elmer said indignantly. "You mean like that cartoon character? I . . . hey! That's not funny, Marge."

Marge gave Elmer a lethal look. Then she delivered a succinct, if somewhat flat, summary of the village's plans for a talent show, a rededication ceremony, and a celebratory banquet after General C. C. Hemlock's victory in the Battle of Hemlock Falls.

"Victory celebration?" Warrender said. "Your Chamber of Commerce is arranging a victory celebration?" He grinned, rather nastily.

Elmer snapped his fingers, then rose to his feet and placed his hand solemnly on the table, to the imminent danger of the Dutch iris arrangement in the middle. "The Chamber knows I know what's good for Hemlock Falls, all right. Thing is, General, you got no worries when you're dealing direct with me."

Nominally, at least, the mayor was chairperson of the subcommittee. Since Elmer tended to a rather endearing self-importance only when his wife Adela wasn't around, Quill forgave him the bluster. But she mentally added a Napoleonic tricorne to Elmer's bald head.

"He's not a general, Elmer," Marge said, who never forgave anybody anything. Marge was the real chairperson of any committee she attended, and both Quill and the mayor knew it. "You're a major, if I got that right, Hackmeyer."

"Honorary major," Hackmeyer said in a deprecating way. "The men insisted, I'm afraid. But I don't use the title, of course."

"Right," Marge said with satisfaction. "Told you, Elmer. Not a general."

"The Fourteenth doesn't have a general yet?" Elmer asked eagerly.

"It's a regiment," Hackmeyer explained. "Yankee companies are headed by captains. There are one hundred and one men in a company. There are any number of companies in a regiment. And majors and captains head regiments. There are up to ten regiments in a battalion. Battalions are headed by generals."

Elmer stroked his chin. "Battalions, huh?"

Marge, who hadn't become the richest citizen of Tompkins County without a shrewd understanding of her fellow men, snorted, "Forget it, Fudd. From what I know about the Battle of Hemlock Falls, there wasn't a battalion within a hundred miles. So you can take off your general's hat and sit on it. Adela," she added with brutal honesty, "wouldn't let you get away with it anyways."

"What'n heck do you know about history, Marge Schmidt?" Elmer demanded.

"A sight more than you do, Mayor," Marge said. "I know a sight more than you about —"

"Mr. Hackmeyer," Quill interrupted loudly, "I'm fascinated by the whole idea of re-enactments. Just what are your plans?"

"Good question," Elmer said, abandoning the

fight with Marge with relief. "I'll tell you anything you want about reenactments, Quill. Fact
is, I've been a pretty fair student of Hemlock
Falls Civil War times —"

"Since when?" Marge demanded.

"Since a long time," Elmer said. "Warrender
here called me to consult about this reenactment, if you remember right, which you
hardly ever do."

"Warrender called Quill, because he wants to
use that five acres next to the Inn for the Battle
of Hemlock Falls," Marge said. "And also because the Inn is famous all over the United
States of America for its food."

This admission, given that Marge and her
partner Betty Hall ran several successful com-
peting restaurants of their own, threw Quill for
a loop. Marge was on Elmer's case, for some
reason.

Marge continued with the brutal directness of
a howitzer at the Battle of the Bulge, "Then
Quill called you and *you* called Major Hackmeyer. So don't you go puffing off about how
you were the one that got the Fourteenth to
come in for the reenactment." Marge jutted her
chin out, increasing her uncanny resemblance
to General Donitz.

"So *you* say," Elmer muttered.

"Yeah. And it's the truth. Right, Major?"

"Major Hackmeyer knows what's true and
what's phony as a three-dollar bill, right, Major?"

Warrender Hackmeyer looked bored, which

didn't, Quill thought, augur well for any nimbleness in battle, reenacted or otherwise. On the other hand, he didn't say anything at all, which was pretty smart.

Quill prided herself on her social diplomacy, honed by more than ten years bobbing in the tricky waters of innkeeping. It almost always sank before Marge the battering ram, so she didn't regret that she'd offered her purported fascination with reenactments as a tactical diversion. She did regret that she hadn't picked up on the more than usually aggressive sniping between Marge and the mayor and guided the conversation into safer channels sooner. "I know that your, um, avocation must take a great deal of your time, Major. Does it take much time away from business, being a reenactor?"

"Course it does," Marge said. "Elmer knows all about that, too, don't you, Elmer? Warrender here must have told you all about it when he called you to pick your amazing and profound brain about how the Civil War was fought?"

"Insurance," Elmer said triumphantly. "Owner of the biggest insurance business in America. Marge, he's got lots of people to take care of his affairs. So he can spend all the time he wants on the Civil War. I got your card right here, Hack." Elmer patted the breast pocket of his seersucker jacket. "You want any customers here in Hemlock Falls, you come straight to me."

Hackmeyer glanced at his watch. Quill, on the other hand, had begun to see where Marge was

51

headed. Marge had owned her own insurance company for several months now. And most of the citizens of Hemlock Falls had policies with her.

"We all know he's an insurance man." Marge sucked her teeth. "Well, an insurance salesman is as good as any other job, far as I can see, and a darn sight better than some." She raised one gingery eyebrow. "So, Major, I know your companies specialize in casualty and surety. Any advice for a small-time owner like me?"

"Give 'em your card, Hack."

Warrender slipped two white pasteboard cards from the pocket of his blue linen blazer — the gold buttons embossed with the emblem of the Union Army — and laid them before the two women. HACKMEYER & ASSOCIATES, Quill read, *Investments, Securities, Viaticals.*

"Viaticals," Marge said. "Well, well. Haven't had too much to do with them myself. Heard there can be a tidy profit in them. Is that right?"

Quill sneaked a quick glance at her watch — five more minutes until she could plead other duties and escape. The insurance agents she knew could fill up five minutes with the most socially innocuous chat in the known universe. "Viaticals," she said. "I'm not at all familiar with that term, um, Warrender. Is it life insurance?"

Marge shifted her substantial bulk and tipped backward in her chair. Her small chilly eyes regarded Hackmeyer with the disapprobation of an Enron stockholder at a post-2002 share-holders meeting. "More like death insurance, Major?" she said genially.

"What are you on about, Marge Schmidt?" Elmer said crossly. "Goodness' sake, the man's in investments. Thing is, Warrender, Marge here's been dabbling in insurance in a little bitty way herself over the past couple months . . ."

"I wouldn't call Schmidt Casualty and Surety little bitty," Marge said. "Not five million dol-lars' worth of policies in two months, I wouldn't. On the other hand, now that I have some competition in town, you might be right, Elmer. Yes, you just might be right, it might re-duce itself to dabbling at that."

So that was it, Quill thought. Not Hackmeyer himself, then. It was Brian Olafson and his in-surance business that irritated Marge. And Elmer had actively recruited the man's mem-bership in the Chamber of Commerce.

"Whatever," Elmer said airily. "Anyways, she could probably learn a lot from you, Warrender."

"That does it, Fudd." Marge's voice was as le-thal as a stiletto.

"Stop calling me Fudd!"

Quill's gaze met Mark Jefferson's. Mark coughed heartily into his napkin. Quill pinched her leg hard and said, "You know, we really haven't gotten to the point of this meeting. What we are proposing, Mr. — I mean Major — Hackmeyer, is that we take advantage of the in-terest in your reenactment and expand the weekend to include some other activates of, um, historical interest."

"My wife," Elmer said with spurious modesty, "is a direct descent of General C. C. Hemlock himself. And since it's the one hundred and thirty-third anniversary of the victory . . ."

"But that's just it," Warrender Hackmeyer said. "It wasn't a victory. The general lost the Battle of Hemlock Falls."

CHAPTER 2

"We *lost?!*" Elmer looked as if a building had fallen on his head. Even Marge was taken aback. Quill swallowed a tactless laugh and said warmly, "It's too bad, Elmer. I'm so sorry." Mark Jefferson, with a banker's predilection for certainty, said, "You're sure about this, Mr. Hackmeyer?"

Hackmeyer stroked his beard. His boredom was gone. "There's a great deal of documentation about the larger battles of the Civil War, 'course. We have photographs, eyewitness accounts, diaries, and newspaper articles. And admittedly, the *Hemlock Gazette* of the time claimed a victory for the Union troops. But I've uncovered some dispatches from the Confederate side that tell a different story from the official account. I'm planning on writing a paper."

"The Rebs," Elmer snorted. "What do they know? Of course the buggers wouldn't want to report back home that old C.C. trained troops that outmaneuvered them. Just like those guys at Enron, lying to Kenneth Lay like they did. I don't believe a word of it."

"We don't know what 'it' is, yet, Mayor,"

Mark said. "Although you make a good point. Where did you find these dispatches, Mr. Hackmeyer? And who sent them?"

Hackmeyer's eyes glittered. It was clear he didn't care for a challenge to his expertise. "The skirmish —"

"Skirmish!" Elmer said indignantly. "I don't know from skirmish. What with the blood of our boys in blue staining the meadows of Hemlock Falls . . ."

"There were no actual casualties, Henry," Hackmeyer said. "No recorded deaths, that is. Now the skirmish . . ."

Elmer laughed loudly, "Now that's a darn lie right there, about no casualties. My good wife's very own second cousin lies in Peterson Cemetery, rest his soul. And the date on that tombstone is July eighteenth, 1864, the very day of the Battle of Hemlock Falls."

"That would be Rufus Stottle," Hackmeyer said testily. "Rufus never actually got to the skirmish, Mayor, although a number of his no-good relatives fought in the skirmish itself. Rufus never made combat due to an unfortunate altercation with the mule pulling the cannon. His actual cause of death was a kick in the ass."

Elmer's face fell. He realized at the same moment that he was arguing with a very important man. Quill, who had rather admired the mayor's spunk, waited for the inevitable cringing apology.

"Quill?"

Quill turned. Dina waved at her from the

French doors leading to the tavern and called her name again. Quill jumped up with relief.

Dina shook her head. "No, you don't have to get up! I just wanted to tell you —"

"I'll be right there!" Quill called. "I'm sorry, gentlemen. Urgent Inn business. You'll excuse me."

"I don't think you should go and just leave us, Quill," Elmer said pathetically. "We've got a pretty big problem here."

"That message came in?" Quill called to Dina. "The one I've been waiting for?"

"Huh? What message?" Dina started across the flagstone terrace. "It's no big —"

"Wait right there!" Quill shook hands with Hackmeyer, touched Mark lightly on the shoulder, and smiled warmly at Marge. "Please let me know how this turns out. If it weren't critical business . . ." She shrugged. What could she do? She avoided Hackmeyer's sardonic squint.

"I told you. You didn't have to get up," Dina complained as Quill came up to her. Quill shoved her gently back into the Tavern Bar. "It's not all that big a deal."

"Getting out of that lunch is a big deal. I owe you one."

"Really?" Dina looked pleased. "Then do you mind if I come in a little bit late tomorrow morning?"

Quill stopped. "That's what you wanted to tell me?"

"I figured that part of the reason you get, like, peeved if I'm the teeniest bit late is that you don't know I'm going to be late. So I was sitting there, checking the film people in, when it hit me. Like, wow. She doesn't know it's going to be, like, maybe a quarter after nine before —"

"The film people are checking in?" Quill started back through the Bar, threading her way through the tables. Dina followed like a little duck after its mother.

Dina's voice sounded doubtful. "Well, they were. But you and I just had this talk about how the best run inns offer quality service every time, and quality, you said, means predictable. So if you *know* I'm going to be late . . ."

"Did you check all of them in? The film people?"

"Pretty nearly. They were busy getting their luggage and stuff out of the van, and that's predictable, too. I figured it would take a predictable five minutes or so for them to get the luggage out and that I'd be efficient — because that's the other thing you said, it's important to be efficient, and so I efficiently used those five minutes to come and tell you . . ."

Quill lengthened her stride and arrived at the reception desk slightly out of breath. The foyer was filled with battered black cases, tripods, duffel bags, and two very thin impatient people dressed in black. One was tall with short brown hair in a bowl cut. The other was shorter, with short brown hair in a bowl cut. Both wore black turtlenecks and black Gap jeans. A herringbone tweed sports coat hung over the taller one's arm. The leather patches on the elbows were new.

"How do you do?" Quill said. "I'm Sarah Quilliam. Welcome to the Inn at Hemlock Falls."

"We've been waiting to get checked in," the smaller impatient person said. "So it's not much of a welcome, is it?" She stood with her arms folded across her inadequate chest. Her fingernails were tipped with black polish.

"I'm so sorry." Quill moved behind the mahogany reception desk, flipped open the registration book, and took a wild guess. "You must be Azalea Cummings. And you're Ralph Austin?"

"It's pronounced Rafe." His tone of voice added, *These yokels!*

"Rafe," Quill repeated with every appearance of pleasure. "I'm so glad you arrived safely. Will you need help with your bags?"

"Well, ye-ah," Azalea said in the way that kids said *D'uh!*

"We're exhausted," Ralph said, in what might have been an apology. "And there's so much to do before the others arrive."

Azalea wandered restlessly around the foyer, hands behind her back. She kicked idly at the cobblestone fireplace, cocked her head at the creamy magnificence of the Oriental carpet, then twitched a piece of eucalyptus out of the tall Oriental vase at the side of the leather sofa. "Not bad," she said. "Not bad at all. What do

59

you think, Ralph? Good background for the revelation scene?"

Ralph made a square with his thumbs and held his hands in front of his eyes. "Maybe. Maybe. It has just the right too-too-ness of the middle class."

"We'll see." Azalea tossed the eucalyptus to the floor. Quill bent and picked it up. "You did see to the theater arrangements," she said to Quill.

"I did," Dina volunteered. "Everything's cool at the high school. Norm Pasquale said you could do your screenings every night this week but Thursday. The Ladies Auxiliary's called to reserve the auditorium for their rehearsals Thursday, and Norm couldn't say no because they do a fund-raiser for the soccer team every year and he has an obligation."

Azalea and Ralph stared at Dina. Both were expressionless.

"It must be, like, so cool to make movies," Dina added.

Somehow they managed to convey weary contempt. Quill counted backward from ten, and mentally recited the First Rule of Innkeeping ("Don't Belt the Guests"). "So the arrangements for your screenings are all set, then. I take it you're taping a new piece while you're here?" She offered the registration card and a pen to Azalea, who filled it out, lips pursed, with meticulous attention to her handwriting.

"We're always working on a new piece," Ralph explained. "In our line of work, the arts, you never stop working. Outsiders rarely understand. It's not likely that I can enlighten you." He scanned the foyer as if it were a particularly unappealing planet. "Cool," he repeated. He smiled wearily at Dina. "I suppose to you it is cool. To artists . . ." He shrugged. "How can I make you understand when there are no artists here? It's unlikely that I can."

Dina opened her mouth, looked at Quill, and then shut it.

"It must be quite out of the ordinary," Quill agreed. She selected their keys from the cubbies that lined the wall in back of the desk. "And here you are. Dina's put you into Suite 214. It has one of the nicest views of any of our rooms."

"Views." Azalea rolled her eyes. "Oh my god. Views."

"And we'll take care of the luggage," Dina added. "In our line of work, you never stop working, either."

"I'll show you up," Quill said. She eyed the largest cases dubiously. They had to be four feet long, at least, and just as wide. "And Dina, why don't you get Mike in here to give you a hand. There's too much for one person to handle."

She led the way up the curving staircase to the Provençal suite. This was one of her favorite rooms at the Inn. The balcony opened out directly over the Falls. The drapes, bedspreads, and linens were a marvelous combination of sunshine yellow, peacock blue, and small scarlet flowers. The small fireplace was made of river rock from the Gorge. She opened the double doors to the suite and let Azalea and Ralph precede her. Azalea wandered to the French doors and looked out at the waterfall. "Glaciers passed through this part of New York State hundreds of thousands of years ago," Quill said in a conversational way. "They left behind ravines like the one you're looking at now. That's Hemlock Gorge. The colors change all the time, depending on the light and the season."

"The water's green," Azalea said. "Polluted, I suppose."

"Actually, no. That's a natural algae. Hemlock Stream pools just above the Falls and it's quite shady there, so we tend to get that golden green in spring and summer. Especially when it's been warm. It makes a lot of fodder for the fish. We have poles and bait buckets in the garden shed if you'd like to try your luck."

Azalea shuddered delicately.

"You don't fish?"

"It's barbaric," she said shortly.

"Zale's first award-winning piece was a five-minute short of the world from the viewpoint of a trout," Ralph said. "She shot the whole thing from the bottom of a bucket. The climax was a close-up of a bloody hook coming down down down into the camera's eye. And then . . ." He chopped his hand decisively. "Quick cut to black."

"And the scream," Azalea prodded him in a murmur.

"The scream of the dying fish," Ralph confirmed. "Dying away into the infinite. And then? Nothing but the sound of the water running out of the bucket. Knocked the audience just flat on its ass."

"Award-winning?" Quill prompted obediently. "Which award was it?"

"BP's BEST OF THE LEAST." Ralph shook his head in admiration. "The LEAST is BP's award for films ten minutes and under."

Quill decided not to ask what organization the initials "BP" represented. She could look it up on the Net if she had to.

"So, no. I don't fish." Azalea ran black-tipped nails through her hair. "And I wouldn't be so sure about that algae if I were you. I spent a year of my life scouting streams for the right trout and what I don't know about polluted streams isn't worth knowing."

"Well, if you have any questions about the stream, Dina's the one you should talk to. She's in the final stage of her doctorate in limnology. That's fresh water pond ecology," she added.

"I see." Azalea drew the drapes across the view and said, "Ah, what's your name, Quill? You have any rooms a little less . . ."

"A little less . . ." Quill prompted.

"It's rather . . ." Ralph grimaced. "I wouldn't want to use the word 'twee—' "

Then don't, Quill thought.

"Bright," Azalea said in the manner of someone attempting to be tactful.

"There's the Shaker suite, of course. That has a quieter palette of colors. It has a view of the herb and vegetable garden. You can look at the Brussels sprouts and the broccoli. And I can replace the quilts with plain comforters."

Azalea tossed her backpack onto the bed. "Never mind. We'll live with it. It's just that my vision, Quill, my artistic vision, is stark. Stark. I work only in black-and-white film. Only with those extremes that you don't find in what the rest of the world laughingly calls nature. God. Why am I talking to you about this? It's like this: This kind of room is an assault to someone of my sensibilities."

Quill firmly repressed any idea of assaulting Azalea and said aloud, "I'll check on the plans for your reception this evening. You wanted hors d'oeurves and wine for twelve people? Around seven-thirty?"

"I think everyone will be in by then, don't you, R? And it's to be billed to my university, Quill. This whole festival is supported by an arts grant. It took me a goddamned year to get the funds from those jerks in Admin, and it'll probably take you a whole goddamned year just to get paid. But that's the system. Get used to it. Anyway, in the meantime, is there anything at all happening around here? Part of the grant's supposed to be used for a film I'm shooting, and I'd better get some background work in or the assholes in Admin are going to think of another reason to jerk me around."

Nature was out. Azalea had made that pretty clear. And the pretty cobblestone buildings of Hemlock Village would send her into a snit. "What about war?"

"War? Yeah, I can live with war. Are the farmers around here picking off the townies?"

"Slaughterhouses," Ralph said, brightening. "What about slaughterhouses?"

"Too colorful, don't you think? I mean, all that red. You shoot in black and white, don't you? We don't slaughter here at the end of June. Maybe next week." Quill was careful to keep her expression hospitable. "We do have a group of Civil War reenactors here at the end of the week. Some of them are setting up part of the encampment already. It's in the field right next to the Inn. You might get some good footage of people working in wool uniforms in the hot sun."

"Maybe." Azalea yawned heartily. Quill snatched at the chance to leave, and handed over the room keys.

"So what happened up there?" Dina asked as Quill came down the stairs a few moments later. "You look, like, discomfited."

"Sometimes I think I should have gone into a different profession. Like hermiting. I could have been a hermit."

Dina gazed up the stairs. "They think we're a bunch of hicks, don't they?"

"I suppose so. Who cares?" Quill drew in a deep breath, caught the expression on Dina's face, and exhaled sharply. "Don't even think about it."

"About what?"

"Don't bat those baby blues at me. About sabotaging those people in some way."

"Who, me? And my eyes are brown, if you haven't noticed already. But of course you have. I remember that last review from the Arts and Leisure Section of the *New York Times* — 'Sarah Quilliam's sensitivity to and use of color places her at the forefront of —' "

"Cut it out, Dina. And I don't want any complaint cards from 214 about the service here, okay? They're obnoxious, but we're used to obnoxious."

"It's not me you have to worry about. They run into Doreen, you better believe you're going to get complaint cards."

Quill suddenly remembered the other comment card, the one involving Doreen and the bratty little kid in 322. "Where is she anyway? I haven't seen her all day."

"I wondered if you were going to pick on me and nobody else," Dina said. "I mean, I didn't whack a six-year-old with the business end of a wet mop."

Quill closed her eyes and opened them again. "No injuries, I take it."

"Doreen's never actually hurt anybody," Dina said. "For goodness' sake, Quill. You shouldn't take those stupid complaint cards seriously."

"If I took those complaint cards seriously. . . ." She stopped herself in midsentence. "Never *mind*. Darn it, I would like to end one day, just one day, in this job without being driven stark staring bonkers."

"You shouldn't let yourself get upset," Dina said virtuously. "And do you want your messages?"

"What? Yes, of course I want my messages. You didn't tell me I had any messages."

"You didn't give me a chance," Dina said pointedly.

She picked up a sheaf of pink slips lying next to the phone and handed them over.

She'd missed a call from Myles, darn it. And there was a call from Elmer asking her to be sure to attend an emergency session of the 133rd Festival Committee later in the day. She'd rather have all her teeth pulled. "Andy called?" she said as she came to the last slip. "He's still in town?"

"Apparently. At home, though. Not the clinic."

"You're sure this isn't for Meg?"

"Nope. He would have called her on the kitchen line."

A little puzzled, Quill went into her office.

Her dog Max lay upside down on the couch, front paws over his face, feigning sleep. Quill regarded him with exasperated affection, and shoved him gently off the couch and onto the floor. Max's only distinction in the canine world was his ugliness. He had floppy ears of two different lengths and his coat was an unpleasant mixture of muddy browns, dirty gray, and yellow-white. Quill loved him dearly.

Max landed with a thump, gave her a baleful glance, and trotted out of the office with a resigned sigh. Quill closed the door after him and sat down at her desk.

Andy didn't answer his phone. Quill called the clinic. He wasn't there, either. And his cell phone was turned off. Quill started to flip through her Rolodex, searching for someone to call who might have seen him. Was he at Nickerson's Hardware? Marge's Croh Bar? She shut the cover on the file with an exasperated snap. Once, in a rare moment of genuine irritation (as opposed to the ordinary affectionate kind), Meg had said: "You never know when to just quit. You come across as vague and kind of funny but you never just quit! Will you just give it up, once in a while?"

Maybe this was one of those times when she should just quit. There was a tap at the door, and before she could call "Come in," Andy walked through the door and sat down on the couch.

"Hey," Quill said.

"Hey." Andy was fair, with light brown hair, light blue eyes, and of a little less than medium height. He was well knit, with the build of a tennis player or a long-distance swimmer. Quill liked him a great deal. He provided a sober, steady focus to the vortex that was her sister. He was naturally reserved, with a precise, compassionate intelligence that made him very popular with his patients. "Can I take a few minutes of your time?" he asked.

"Of course. Would you like some tea or coffee while we talk? I can get the kitchen to send some in."

He shook his head and smiled. Faint bluish shadows were under his eyes.

"You look a little tired." Then, Quill added, "Meg said you might be going out of town for a while. She thought you needed a break."

"I was planning on it. But I don't think I want to take the time off just yet."

"You don't need to," Quill said kindly. "I mean, I know you lost those two patients, Andy, but as I told Meg this morning . . ."

"Three," Andy said.

"Three?"

"Derwent Peterson, just this afternoon."

Quill ran a rapid review of the numerous Petersons in Hemlock Falls. Old Harland Peterson was the most visible member of the clan; he owned the largest dairy farm within a hundred miles of Hemlock Falls. But he had eight brothers and sisters, all of whom had married and borne an incredible number of children. "Derwent is . . . was . . . Harland's oldest brother," she said. "Isn't he, I mean, wasn't he in his seventies, Andy?"

"Seventy-eight."

"I'm so sorry. What was it?"

"The pathology, you mean? Multiple myeloma. That's a disseminated skeletal cancer. Very ugly. Very nasty way to go."

"I'm sorry," Quill said. Then tentatively, "But it was expected, wasn't it?"

"No," Andy said roughly. "It wasn't. I mean, you can't tell a thing about cancers. And this part of the country, Quill — maybe it's the pesticides or the fertilizer or gamma rays from the moon, how the hell do I know? — but the older generation, the old farmers, they're prone to far too much cancer. Cancer of all kinds. There are seven small dairy farmers on Bear Creek Road. Each of them has come down with bladder cancer within the last ten years."

"I'd read that," Quill said soberly. "Doreen's husband wrote an article about it in the *Gazette*. Elmer had a fit."

"Yeah, well, you play the hand you've got." Andy rubbed his face hard with both hands. "Anyway, old Derwent should have lasted a few years longer. Myeloma's manageable in the early stages, Quill, and the spread of the lesions just wasn't that significant yet. He was admitted to the hospital with complaints of a headache, diarrhea, and dizziness. None of which made any sense at all, given his condition. I put him on an IV, as a precaution against dehydration. And then — he just died —" Andy cut himself off and slumped back on the couch.

Quill regarded him with sympathy. "Maybe you should take a break. You've just had a run

70

of bad luck. And it can happen to anyone. You know that none of these deaths say anything about you as a doctor."

"Oh? How would you know, Quill?"

"How? Well, because you're a terrific doctor, that's how."

"I want to marry your sister, and I know you approve of that. And I seem like a pretty nice guy, right? But how do you know I'm any good as a doctor?"

"You're a terrific doctor," Quill said indignantly. "You were terrific to me when I was your patient. Last year, when I thought I had — you know — that dread disease . . ."

"I'd forgotten about that." He regarded her sternly. "You did throw out the *Merck Manual*, didn't you? I'm telling you, when that text gets into the hands of patients, it gives them the craziest ideas. I had one patient last year, younger woman, I think, thought she had amyotrophic lateral sclerosis. Or maybe it was an astrocytoma."

"That," Quill said coldly, "would have been me."

"You!" He laughed, his head thrown back. "So it was. Oh my, sorry. I see so many people, I forget."

"Good. Forget it again."

"It's a deal." His smile died away, to be replaced by sober worry. "None of this is the reason why I dropped by today."

"I'm sorry," Quill said. "You look as if it's serious. What can I do?"

He hesitated. "It's a little tricky." He rubbed his forehead indecisively. Quill had never seen Andy look indecisive. Physicians weren't supposed to be indecisive. It was very unsettling. "It's about these deaths."

"I'm so sorry, Andy. But you simply can't blame your—"

He held his hand up. "Hang on. I don't, you know. Blame myself. Don't you see? Mrs. Nickerson and Derwent Peterson were admitted with the same kind of symptoms. Headache, dizziness . . . if they'd been younger, or if there hadn't been an underlying disease process in each of them, I would have sent them home with an aspirin. I prescribed the same palliative treatment: an IV, a little antibiotic for Derwent's eczema and . . ." He threw his hands in the air. "Gone. All three of them."

"Myocardial infarction," Quill said.

"Meg's spoken to you, then. I've been over and over the charts and I didn't miss anything at the hospital. I'm sure of it. But there's one thing that Nadine Nickerson, Derwent Peterson, and Freddie Bellini had in common. And I need your permission to go ahead with it."

"All three of them had something in common? What was it?"

"They all came to the Inn last week. On June twelfth. They stayed overnight. They ate here and slept here. Isn't that right?"

Quill stared at him for a moment. "Well, yes, but . . ."

"It was very out of the ordinary for all three of them, wasn't it? And Quill . . ." He leaned forward, his face somber. "Three of them. Three. It's too much of a coincidence to ignore. I think there may be something dangerous here."

She took a deep breath. She reminded herself that this was her sister's future husband. That there was no reason for him to want to destroy the Inn. "Well, yes, but there were perfectly good reasons they stayed here — as unusual as it was. There was a one-day meeting of the Upstate Morticians' Association. Freddie's a member. He stayed over because he had a little too much to drink and didn't want to drive home. He and Mrs. Bellini live out on Route 15 and Davey Kiddermeister's been cracking down on DUI, not that Freddie would have driven under the influence anyway, I mean he is, was very respons—"

"Quill . . ."

Aware she was defensive, and running on feverishly, Quill said, "And Mrs. Nickerson was here because it was her eighty-sixth birthday and the daughters-in-law all got together to give her a night away from home because she never gets out of —"

"Quill!"

"And we let poor old Derwent stay here overnight because he got dizzy when he and Harland dropped by the Tavern Bar after the Future Farmers of America meeting at the high school and he was such a frail old guy that we wanted to keep an eye on him, and if you're going to find something, I don't know, murderous about that —"

"*Quill!*"

"What!?"

"Please don't take this amiss."

Quill tugged at her lower lip.

Andy shifted uncomfortably on the couch. "This is hard for me . . ." he began.

"What exactly is it? That's hard for you?"

"I have to know what happened. I have to know the cause of death."

Quill recognized the thoughts chasing through her brain as unworthy. But she thought them anyway: Any other busy physician would let matters rest as they were. Mr. Peterson had a terrible cancer. Mrs. Nickerson was eighty-six and frail. And Freddie's heart problems were well known to Hemlock Falls.

Then she said quietly, "You're right, of course."

"Even if I weren't county coroner . . ."

"It's okay, Andy. Truly. I just panicked for a minute. I temporarily lost my sense of, I don't know, rightness. It's right that you be concerned. It's right that you look into it. And anything I can do to help . . ."

"Thank you."

"Where should we start?"

Andy looked a little bemused. "Well, I'm not sure. I thought perhaps that you might know what to do. I mean, after all . . ."

Quill brightened a little. "You mean, because of all the other cases I've solved?"

"That's not exactly . . ."

"That's true. I guess I do have a small bit of a reputation, don't I?"

"Perhaps it's a little more to the point that you manage the Inn and that you'd know where to start to look at the food they ate, the rooms they slept in, the air-conditioning system. That sort of thing."

"Andy? Can the county coroner formally request that I investigate?"

"Formally request?"

"Yes. You know. Write up a letter asking me to review the activities of the deceased, et cetera, et cetera." She waved her hand airily.

Andy opened his mouth, shut it, opened it again, and then lapsed into silence. "Look," he said. "I suppose unofficially I could. But one of the reasons I'm asking you privately — actually, it's *the* reason — is that I don't want to have to order an official investigation. You'd have county inspectors crawling all over the place."

"We've had county inspectors here before," Quill said bravely, although her stomach clenched. "Okay, an unofficial official letter, then." She rubbed her face and settled back in her chair. She couldn't suppress a small, but significant sense of satisfaction. This would be her first official unofficial case, as opposed to her other ten cases, which she supposed she could call inadvertently unofficial. Myles had once

75

said she was intrusively unofficial, come to think of it, so she'd be better off bagging her adverbs altogether and just call it her first official case.

Andy threw out his hands in what looked (suspiciously) like surrender. "Okay. Fine."

"You're going to hire me to investigate the deaths of Nadine Nickerson, Derwent Peterson, and Freddie Bellini?"

"Hire," Andy said. "Sure. Sure. Why not?"

Quill dismissed any tinge of resignation in Andy's voice as the product of her imagination. "May I have a letter? And would there be . . ." She cleared her throat and said too loudly, "A consulting fee? No. Never mind about the fee."

Andy nodded. "A letter I can handle."

There was a short, uncomfortable silence, in which Quill, dismayed (as usual) by her customary impulsiveness, wondered what she was getting herself into and what to do next.

"Any ideas on what to do next?" Andy asked.

"Yes. Of course." Quill rummaged in the top drawer of her desk and withdrew a fresh scratch pad. "We'll make a list. And a chart."

Andy eyed the pad. "Meg says you buy those a dozen at a time."

"I love them." Quill smoothed her hand over the first page. "There's something about the scent of the paper and the texture of the weave that's very . . ." She searched for the right word. "Appealing" was much too wimpy. "Sensual" was more like it. ". . . nice about them," she ended lamely.

"But you draw on those," Andy said. "You use those for your preliminary sketches."

Quill nodded. "I always carry one in my pocket. That's one of the reasons I always wear long skirts. They have nice big pockets."

"Perhaps this isn't a good idea, Quill. You have those dozens of pads to fill with drawings and Meg says you're at work on a series for a gallery in Manhattan . . ."

"Which isn't due for another six months," Quill said.

"And you have an Inn to run."

"I have an excellent staff," Quill said. "I have plenty of time for this." She closed the pad. "You're backing off, aren't you?"

"No. Not at all."

"You trust me to find the truth, don't you?"

His face cleared. "Of all the people I know, Quill, you're one of the most trustworthy. If you find that there's a slow unknown poison in the air-conditioning system, or a lethal strain of bacterium in the kitchen, or a homicidal staff member lurking in the broom closet, you'd stand up and announce it to the world. But I'm not even certain what we're looking for here. The only reason I'm looking at the Inn is because I literally can't find any reasonable explanation for why three patients under my care died in the same week. Did all three of these people come in contact with someone carrying a lethal, as yet undiscovered, virus? Was it mere circumstance? I have no idea what I'm looking for." He rose abruptly and walked to the window. "Damn it. Damn it."

"Well," Quill said gently, "you must have some idea of what you need."

Andy turned to look at her. The sunlight from the window was at his back and his face was in shadow. "I'm treading a fine line here, Quill. I don't have a solo practice anymore — not since the clinic has grown. I have responsibilities to my partners now. At the same time . . . I need to know what, if anything, happened to these three patients." He made an abrupt, fierce gesture with his fist. "I can't stand this," he said in an undertone. "And I have a responsibility to the families. It can't be right to just let this whole thing alone, Quill. I know it's not right if it's the expeditious thing to do. But what if it's the compassionate thing to do?"

Quill wondered how much needed to remain unsaid. Andy practiced medicine in a litigious age. He was a man of integrity in a culture that had lost belief in integrity. And he was a man who hated any sort of compromise, especially when the compromise was between his commitment to knowledge and his compassion.

"Are you asking me for an opinion?" she asked tentatively.

"Yes. No. I suppose so."

"We're looking at what may be dreadful coincidence: three deaths without a definite cause in a

78

week. Let me look at the records for last week here at the Inn — where and when these three people were together, if at all, what meals they had in common, that kind of thing, and if there's a second coincidence — well, at least we'll know that there's a higher degree of probability that something's odd." She smiled warmly. "The methodical, scientific approach. We can make another decision when the first set of facts are in."

There was still a lot of tension in Andy's shoulders. "That sounds reasonable. But how long is it going to take? I have to formally request an autopsy on Mrs. Nickerson, and I don't have much time. I released the body for burial, and if Freddie Bellini hadn't died, she would have been buried by now. I need at least a nominal reason for upsetting the family. And I can't order a full forensics scan on all three of the bodies without having some justification. The county's really monitoring funds this year. And how transparent is your investigation going to be? If I had a preference, it'd be for discretion." He paused, Quill presumed, to take a breath. He looked at his clenched fists in some surprise. "I'm sorry," he said eventually, "I'm more wound up about this than I thought."

"It's okay. Really." Then hesitantly, Quill said, "Is there something else? Other than the obvious, I mean."

"Something else?"

"Andy, for heaven's sake. You've been practicing medicine for how long? Ten years at least.

You seem more . . ." Quill searched for a gentle word, and failed. "More upset than the circumstances call for. It seems to me that any physician who can't handle, well, setbacks . . ."

"Failures," Andy said tightly.

"You don't know that these cases are failures."

"What I do know is that I'm convinced that whatever killed these patients originated here. At the Inn." Quill's face grew warm. Andy gave a laugh that was half groan. "There. You see? You didn't say a thing but I can read your face, Quill. You're angry. Defensive. You have every right to be. And it's worse. Headache? Diarrhea? Low blood pressure? Don't you see? The likeliest cause is the food."

Quill took a very deep breath.

"You see?" He struck his palm with his fist. "You see the problem? You're a fair woman, Quill. And if there is a problem here, you won't like it, but you'll handle it. And you won't blame me. But . . ."

"Meg," Quill said.

"Meg."

"You already sound defeated, and we don't have any facts yet." Quill leaned forward and looked at him intently. "She can't blame you for something that isn't your fault."

"She's a chef. As you're an artist. As I'm a doctor. What if something Myles did destroyed you as an artist? And fair? Would you call Meg fair?"

Quill decided not to answer this. She loved

her sister dearly. Meg was volatile, loving, passionate, opinionated, whimsical, and a great deal more. But she wasn't especially fair. Not right off the bat. But she could be convinced to be fair. Quill was sure of that. "She's honest and she loves you."

"She's honest, at least," Andy said. His face closed.

"You're leaping to conclusions, Andy. That's not like you. As a matter of fact, none of this is like you. Maybe you should go out of town as you'd planned. Take some time off. Leave this to me for a few days."

"I can't. I can't leave now. Meg and I had a dilly of a quarrel this morning. It takes her a few days to cool off. I'd rather be here when she does. Not five hours away in the damn mountains. And what am I going to do up there by myself? I'd just want to be back here."

Quill, smart enough to recognize this last as a piece of (understandable) self-pity, didn't rise to the bait. "Let's leave it at this. I'll do what I can."

"That's all anybody can ask." He nodded sharply. "Right. I'm going back to the clinic then. I'll hear from you soon?"

"As soon as I can," Quill promised. "The first task is to find out where each of them was when they were here, and what they ate. We'll be able to narrow the focus a bit if they all ate the same thing. And I can do that with an amazing degree of precision, Andy."

"You can?"

"I don't believe it, but it's working," Quill said more to herself than to Andy. She glanced up at him. "I finished this course at the Cornell School of Hotel Management a month ago . . ."

"So I heard."

"Has Meg been grumbling about it? I told everyone the changes might be a little uncomfortable at first, but the new process plan has only been in place a few weeks, and it's already helping. I mean, I'm going to be able to track the last days of each of these poor souls, Andy."

"You are?" There was more than a little disapprobation in his voice; Quill was about to defend her plan when the office door flew open. Meg stamped in, eyes a grim gray in her flushed face. "Okay. Fine. What the hell is going on with you two?!"

CHAPTER 3

"I thought you were on your way to the Adirondacks by now!" Meg planted herself squarely in front of Andy; her furious gaze raked him up and down.

"I've decided to put the trip off a bit." Andy started to edge past her. Meg grabbed his arm. Andy put his hand over hers and said, "Later, Meg. I've got to get back to the clinic."

"For what?" Meg demanded. "I thought Paul Lyell was covering your cases for you. You said that was all taken care of."

Quill rose from her desk chair. It seemed prudent to beat a quiet retreat.

Meg whirled. "And where are you going?"

"I have to see Dina about something," Quill said feebly.

"You sit down!"

Quill sat.

"Weasel, weasel, weasel," Meg raged. " 'I've decided to put the trip off for a bit.' 'I have to see Dina about something.' Don't you people ever get specific?"

"Not now, Meg. Please." Andy reached the door. "I'll call you later, all right?"

"When?" she demanded. "Later tonight? Later tomorrow? Later next week? Why don't you make it easy on yourself and not call at all?"

"Meg," Quill said. "Really, if you'd just calm down a —"

"Don't you tell me to calm down!" She bared her teeth in a really scary smile. "I am perfectly calm."

"Good!" Andy said heartily. "That's all right then. Meg? Call me when you're ready. Any time. I love you. Goodbye for the moment."

He shut the door gently behind him. Meg sat down on the couch and burst into tears. Quill tugged at her hair and sat next to her sister. Then she got back to her feet, reached for the box of Kleenex she kept in her top drawer, and sat down again. "Men," she offered, along with the Kleenex. "They're idiots."

"That," Meg hiccupped, "is a gross over-simplification." She scrubbed at her face with the tissue. "Not all men are idiots."

"That's true," Quill said agreeably.

"That man." She waved the sodden Kleenex in the direction of the office door. "That man is an idiot."

"He has a lot on his mind," Quill said vaguely.

"You know, if I cooked like that, I'd be out of business in a week."

"Cooked like what?" Quill looked at her in alarm. Meg wasn't an eavesdropper; she'd bet her life on her sister's lack of sneakiness. Of all the things she was, Meg was most of all direct and unambiguous. But could she have over-heard Andy's suspicions?

"Cooked like you're talking. Vague, impre-cise, and cliché-ridden."

"How can you cook in clichés?"

"Easy. Plunk almonds on every vegetable in sight. Cover every egg in the known universe with Hollandaise. And bake your potatoes. There's nothing more cliché-ridden than a foil-wrapped baked potato." Meg blew her nose. "Oh, screw it all anyway."

Quill patted her back. It was hot and sweaty beneath her thin T-shirt.

"So what is on his tiny little mind?"

"Whose? Andy's?"

"Yes. You said he had a lot on his mind. What, exactly?" She glanced at Quill sidelong. "Does he want to break up with me?"

"Of course he doesn't want to break up with you! Why would you think that?"

"We fight," Meg said dismally. "We fight all the time."

Quill had witnessed Andy's basic imperturb-ability with enormous respect for years. As a matter of fact, that same sort of rock-solid, even-tempered attitude had been an appealing charac-teristic of Meg's first husband, who had died in a terrible automobile accident some years before.

"What do you fight about?"

"What do you mean, what do we fight about?" Her reddened eyelids enhanced the ferocity of Meg's glare.

"I don't know." Quill had always known the value of the vague and imprecise when dealing with angry people, especially her sister. She tugged at her hair and considered modifying her Rules of Innkeeping. Rule One — Don't Belt the Guests — was inviolable. But Rule Two could use some work. Rule Two could be, for example: Bemuse to Defuse.

"Quill!"

"What?!"

"I hate it when you drift off like that. And you drift off like that whenever I ask you a perfectly reasonable question."

"What was the question?"

"Cut it out!"

"All right. Sorry. I'll cut it out." She paused for a moment, considering. For the first time in her life, Meg was in her way. She didn't count the times as "in her way" when they both were little and four-years-younger Meg hung around the back deck bugging Quill and her friends. Meg was in her way because she had to do something that might hurt her. Quill wanted to burst into tears herself, but she swallowed and said, "What I was after was this: If you and Andy fight over the Big Three, that's one thing."

"Big Three?"

Quill ticked them off on her fingers: "Money. Children. Fidelity. Substance abuse."

"That's four. And substance abuse is just ridiculous. You've been watching daytime television, obviously. And don't you dare tell me you're in therapy again. I thought you had enough of that. I mean, you're still paying off those therapist bills because Blue Cross Blue Shield wouldn't take "totally confused" as a genuine psychiatric illness. I mean, why would anyone in their right mind think total confusion is a legitimate medical claim? A crazy person would, that's for sure. Have you tried getting them to pay the bill because you think they should, and that's just nuts? Have you tried —"

"Stop."

Meg stopped.

"The Big Three is what couples fight about. Couples with relationship problems, I mean. And I'm not in therapy, as you put it."

"How else would you put it?"

"And I don't watch daytime television unless I have the flu. The thing is, couples with relationship problems —"

"I don't have relationship problems! Andy has relationship problems."

"Right. Anyway. If you're not fighting about really significant issues, deal breakers, so to speak, maybe you two can work it out."

Meg's glare decreased in wattage. "And?"

"And you two could go to a couples therapist. Maybe you just need a better way to talk to each other."

"I don't need a therapist. I don't have time to go to a therapist. And Andy doesn't either."

"Andy was going off to the Adirondack

Mountains for a break. You were going to go with him. You've both arranged backups. Why not?"

"We haven't agreed to have someone take over for me in the kitchen."

"We'd started talking about it, hadn't we? Look. This is a light week as far as the gourmet end is concerned. Bjarne can handle that. The Inn is full of the reenactors, and they're cooking their meals over campfires in the side meadow. And the banquet at the end of the week consists of recipes that any good cook will have to learn, even a great cook like you, and Betty Hall is a good cook."

"Betty Hall is a great cook," Meg corrected. "She makes the best American diner food in the known universe. But don't tell her I told you."

"Of course I'll tell her you told me. I'll have to come up with some reason why she should agree to run our kitchen instead of the Croh Bar's, but you let me handle that."

"Hmm," Meg said.

"Just hmm? Not, 'What a marvelous idea, sister dear'?"

"Maybe."

"Track Andy down. Make some appointments."

"With whom? There's nobody here in Hemlock Falls, not since that shrink Dr. Whosis left."

"Syracuse," Quill said promptly. "You should go to Syracuse for the week. Andy's bound to know a good referral there. And that will get the two of you out of the . . . I mean that will give the two of you a chance for some really intense, really worthwhile conversations."

"No."

"That means you'll think about it."

"Maybe. Maybe I'll think about it."

Quill glanced at her watch. "Andy said to call him when you were over your snit."

"I was not in a snit."

"Then you can call him."

Meg heaved a deep sigh, with a catch in it. Quill hugged her, hard. "And I have to talk to Doreen and then John, so I need to get going. Okay?"

"Is it about that stupid W.A.T.C.H. Report? That has the staff in a genuine, no-holds-barred uproar, Quill. I mean, all that record keeping is a royal pain. You tried this kind of thing eight years ago, remember?"

"Vaguely. But this is much more efficient. Much more — professional."

"Uh-huh. You try running this Inn when every single human being walks out of it from sheer exasperation with your managerial tactics."

"As long as they don't have to walk out because we're closed."

"Closed!"

"Never mind. Just a joke. A bad one. I'll walk out with you. Dina probably knows where Doreen is."

★ ★ ★

"I have no idea where Doreen is," Dina said when Quill came out of her office and asked after her housekeeper. "It's Monday, and the laundry guys have been here, so maybe she's out counting sheets and towels. Of course, you could always check the sign-in sheet."

"Why would Doreen be on the kitchen sign-in sheet?" Meg asked. "That's my sign-in sheet. For my staff. Doreen's housekeeping and she has a sign-in sheet too, but she's not on it because she knows where she is all the time. And she wouldn't be on the wait staff sign-in sheet because —"

"Stop!" Quill said.

Dina peered at Meg over her large horn-rimmed glasses, making a point to avoid Quill's gaze. "You don't know about the Neo-Nazi sign-in sheet? The W.A.T.C.H. thing? That's this big mother of a sheet right here" — she pulled a large pad of oversized paper from underneath the reception desk — "that pin-points with unerring accuracy where every op-pressed worker is in this place every darn minute of the day."

"Dina!" Quill said. "Neo-Nazi! I ask you!"

"Well, it was designed by Nazis, if you ask me, and since all the original ones are dead, it has to be new ones, ergo —"

"Wait, wait, wait." Meg put the tips of her fin-gers to her temple and closed her eyes. "I see," she said in a faraway voice, "I see a tall, slim

90

redheaded woman in a classroom. I see a pot-bellied guy with a gray beard waving a sign that reads PINHEADS FOR PROCESS. He's waving a watch in front of the redheaded woman. He's . . . he's hypnotizing her!"

"I thought you had a phone call to make," Quill said coldly.

"I do. You know, I'm glad I'm getting out of here for a few days." She twiddled her fingers. " 'Bye, guys."

"How come Meg doesn't have to use this stupid thing?" Dina's wistful gaze followed Meg's progress through the archway to the dining room and beyond to the kitchen.

"Because she'd scrawl rude words over it." Quill looked at her nice neat W.A.T.C.H. Sheet with pleasure. The professor of her Profit Master class had said clearly and unambiguously that good business was managed business. Just like the better-run manufacturing companies, a service business like the Inn could be run well only when each step in the process of delivering great service was known to all. Hence, the W.A.T.C.H. Sheet, which divided each hour of the eight-hour day into tasks for all employees at the Inn. Theoretically, you could look at the sheet and find anyone at the Inn at any time.

"It doesn't work," Dina said.

"Because Meg doesn't know about it? She's always in the kitchen except when she's not supposed to be. So that's what I've put down. Of course it works."

"Not only is it demeaning to have to account for every minute of your day like you were a little kid or, worse yet, a robot at the Honda factory in Marysville, Ohio, it doesn't work."

"It'll work if you use it, Dina. Look. Here. You were right. About laundry day. Here's Doreen's task for three to four in the afternoon: linen count." Quill checked her watch, "It's three-thirty. Now rather than run all over the Inn trying to find her, I just — ding-ding! — buzz her on the house phone and *voila!* I find Doreen in the linen room." Quill held the receiver to her ear.

Dina muttered; Quill may have caught the word "amok" — she wasn't sure. Then she said loudly, "Doreen answering that phone yet?"

"Doreen?" Quill said into the receiver. "Hi. How's the linen count going? Really? That many? Good. Good. No, I can tell you're busy, so . . . Dina!"

Dina punched the speakerphone button. The annoying beep-beep-beep of an unanswered phone filled the lobby air. Quill slammed the receiver down. "Fine!" she said crossly.

"It doesn't wor—"

"It would if everybody used it!"

"Let's see . . ." Dina settled her glasses firmly on her nose and ran her finger down the page. "S.Q. That's you, Quill, although it always makes me think of the Roman Empire and SQPR, which stands for —"

"It's SPQR."

"Sarah Quilliam's Process Rampage? Anyhow, here's you. Three to four P.M. Hundred and Thirty-third meeting, conference room."

"Nuts," Quill said.

"If you just used it . . ." Dina began sweetly.

"Well, I forgot."

"Now. As I understand it, if you screw up and aren't where you're supposed to be, you're supposed to fill out a WhyNot. Right? I like that phrase. A WhyNot. Cute. And this WhyNot gets sent to the supervisor and then the supervisor issues a Corrective Action Report and you get whacked by the big bosses. Right?"

"You do not get whacked, as you phrase it. And we do not have big bosses here. I loathe that phrase. I'm trying this out so we can make a genuine attempt at profit sharing. But to do that we have to maximize profits first. It may be necessary to change the process itself, Dina. This sheet is not a Big Brother sort of thing. It's proactive. It benefits worker and manager alike."

"Nothing benefits worker and manager alike. They are antithetical. Just ask that liar Jeffrey Skelling. And everybody else at Enron. On the other hand, I might believe you a little bit more if you filled this out and told on yourself." Dina waved the red WhyNot slip in the air.

Quill grabbed it, scrunched it into her pocket, and took off at a rapid (but dignified) trot to the conference room. The buzz of a contented, productive committee met Quill when she slipped into the conference room. Adela Henry and Esther West sorted through filmy dress material. Harvey Bozzel stood in front of the white board, making out a schedule. Miriam Doncaster had her glasses shoved up onto her head and listened intently to Donna Olafson, the insurance broker's wife. Carol Ann Spinoza (as usual) sat off to one side, exuding the clean scent of shampoo and an air of venom in equal measure, but then, Carol Ann exuded shampoo and venom on every committee, and on those Sundays when she attended the Hemlock Falls Church of the Word of God. Quill nodded to everyone and said to Donna, "I didn't know that you were on this committee, Donna. It's nice to see you here."

Donna Olafson was one of the most perfectly groomed women Quill had ever met. She had glorious creamy skin, a cascade of perfectly styled, chestnut-colored hair, and impeccable taste in clothes. Even nonspiteful women felt abashed in front of Donna Olafson.

"Nobody asked her," Carol Ann said spitefully. "She just showed up. You told me, Adela, that you had to be invited to be on this committee and that membership was closed anyway. It's a good thing that I reminded Harland Peterson about that assessment problem with his new barn or I wouldn't be here myself." She regarded Donna with a steady, unnerving stare. "So she just comes in here and sits herself down and nobody says boo about it."

A profound silence greeted Carol Ann's observation, since nobody wanted to point out that the only way Carol Ann got on any committee, ever, was if she blackmailed someone. Quill felt a sincere sympathy for Harland Peterson and his unexpected tax problems.

Marge Schmidt sat with her arms folded, scowling as Quill sat down next to her. "Are you ever on time?" she demanded. "We've been here half an hour waiting for you. I got people to see and places to go."

"This is Quill's third meeting today," Donna Olafson said sharply. "Isn't it, Quill? She can be forgiven a little tardiness, I think."

Quill blinked, taken aback at this sudden defense on her behalf. And how did Donna know she'd had three meetings that day?

Donna smiled nervously at Quill. She had a full, sensuous mouth. Every time Quill became aware of her mouth, she wondered about Brian Olafson, who was calm, restrained, and a little dusty. There must be more to Brian than anyone suspected, since they had seemed devoted to one another.

She didn't know Donna at all well; she'd engaged in the conventional courtesies when Donna and Brian had stayed at the Inn off and on while their house was being remodeled, but no more than that.

"I was just wondering if you wanted to do something about your complexion."

"My complexion?"

"Donna represents a line of makeup and skin cream," Miriam said from across the table. "It's wonderful stuff. We've all bought some."

"Oh. Well. Yes. My complexion. Is there something wrong?"

"It looks a little tired, that's all."

"It's been a busy week. How's the house coming?"

Donna gave her a brilliant smile. "I'm going nuts. We may be back this weekend, just to get away from the fact the workers aren't showing up. I was so frustrated this morning that I came up to see if you'd like to grab a cup of coffee. Your receptionist dragged out this whacking big chart and said you were going to be tied up most of the day. But I did notice that you were scheduled for this Hundred and Thirty-third meeting and, Dina — is that her name? — said the committees here can use all the help they can get. So I volunteered." She shot a guilty glance in Carol Ann's direction. "I didn't realize you had to be invited," she whispered. "I'm new here, and I'm so screamingly lonesome I can't stand it. But maybe I should leave?"

"Of course you shouldn't leave," Quill said in quick sympathy. "We can always use an extra hand. We don't have a lot of time to get this thing pulled together."

"And what time we've got's being wasted," Marge pointed out. "Come on, Adela. Let's get this show on the road."

If there was one thing at which the citizens of

Hemlock Falls were experienced, it was arranging community events. This was partly because everybody was assigned the same task over and over again. Esther West was always in charge of costumes. Harvey Bozzel was always in charge of publicity. Marge handled the finances, and the various licenses needed to arrange parking and food vendors and tents were just a matter of form. But it was mostly because Adela Henry had a lot in common with Benito Mussolini — if she ran the event (and she ran most of them), the trains ran on time. The inevitable monkey wrench in what should have been the smooth running of this machinery was the agenda.

"And now," Adela said after the various administrative tasks had been sorted out, assigned, and accepted, "we come to the agenda itself." Adela wore a bright orange tunic, wide-legged orange pants, and an amber starburst medallion that hung right in the center of her chest. Adela's outfits always caught the eye; once caught, her gimlet expression and authoritative voice made it hard to look away. "I have spoken with Major Hackmeyer. He has agreed that the reenactment of the Battle of Hemlock Falls will come after the talent show and before the speeches. We will begin the parade —"

"There's a parade?" Quill said.

"Of course there's a parade," Adela returned majestically. "I have already arranged it. The high school band will play a medley of Civil War songs. The Fourteenth Regiment will march behind the band. The Rebel renegades will march behind the Regiment. There will be a float."

"A float?" Quill said.

"The new McDonald's out on Route 15 has volunteered a float."

"They didn't have McDonald's in Civil War times, did they?" Donna Olafson asked.

Adela paused. Then she looked at Donna, who subsided in some confusion. Then she said, "Ronald McDonald will be in Civil War garb. That should be sufficiently historic. The parade will end at Quill's meadow . . . I am assuming, Quill, that you and Meg will agree to this use of your property?"

Quill nodded.

"And the Battle of Hemlock Falls will be re-enacted."

There was a respectful silence.

"The victory parade will take us all back to . . . is there something wrong, Quill?"

Quill looked back at Adela, feeling like a rabbit caught in the headlights of an oncoming semi. "Ah. Um. Victory parade?" She darted a hasty glance at Marge, who was grinning.

"Yes. I am considering whether or not we should have the Rebel renegades in chains. Considering, merely. Miriam, could you check on whether or not this was standard practice in Civil War times? We want to be as authentic as possible, while still maintaining the appropriate level of drama, of course."

"I'm not much of an historian," Miriam said. "Not any kind of an historian, in fact. But I'm pretty certain that neither army put prisoners in chains."

"Perhaps Major Hackmeyer will know. As I was saying, the victory parade will lead us all back to Peterson Park, where His Honor the Mayor will make a speech and present the Award of Merit."

"The Award of Merit?" Donna said. "How nice. Who gets it?"

"As the sole remaining kin of General C. C. Hemlock," Adela said, "that would be me."

Donna said, "I see," in a very flattering way.

Adela nodded gravely, adjusting the medallion more precisely in the center of her chest. "Now, Harvey. I believe I requested that you recruit the cast for the variety show. Would you care to make a report?"

Harvey Bozzel — Hemlock's best (and only) advertising executive — ran one hand over his smoothly styled blond hair and assumed an expression more suitable for announcing the imminent arrival of a band of locusts than the roster of a variety show. One of the hairstylists at the Hemlock Hall of Beauty had told him he looked like Stone Phillips, and he'd dropped his Armani-like black suits and white dress shirts for denim button-downs and charcoal tweed jackets. He didn't, Quill thought in some bemusement, really have the bulk to carry off the sophisticated rough guy look. His neck was too scrawny. "I'm sorry to say," he said in a deeper voice than was usual, "that we seem to have a bit of a problem."

Adela nodded gravely. "Do go on."

"There's no one to be in the show."

"That's ridiculous," Adela said.

"Not anyone?" Miriam said skeptically. "Goodness, I can think of five or six very talented contributors that we could ask right off the bat, Harvey. There's the high school band, the high school chorus, the church choir, the Ladies Auxiliary Sweet Adelines Chorus, the —"

Harvey held his hand up. "Perhaps I didn't make myself clear. I am making arrangements to have this important" — he nodded to Adela — "may I say this very important, occasion in the life of our community filmed." He waited an impressive moment then added, "I've just come from taking a long meeting with the directors."

Quill, who had been doodling a regular-guy Harvey dressed in chinos and a T-shirt, stopped her pencil cold, then added a fishtail at Harvey's feet and drew a bucket over his head.

"Then they can film the high school band, the Sweet Adelines, and the church choir," Miriam said recklessly. "What in the world do you mean, 'film'? Is channel 18 coming out with its nerdy fat boy and a Steadicam?"

"Miriam," Adela said sternly.

"Well, honestly, Adela. From the way Harvey delivered the news, you'd think Steven Spielberg was dragging a production team out here to Hemlock Falls. Come on, Harvey, don't be so annoyingly . . . annoyingly . . ."

Fatheaded? Quill wrote at the top of her sketch.

"Sententious," Miriam finished triumphantly.

Quill looked at her watch. Four-thirty. It'd taken a little longer than usual for the meeting to derail into squabbling. Of course, they'd gotten off to a late start.

Harvey looked hurt. "This is an independent film company, very well known. As a matter of fact, they're having a small, discreet convention right here at the Inn. Aren't they, Quill?"

"Well, if you know anything about these people, Quill, it must be all right," Esther volunteered. "Quill's a very famous artist," she said to Donna Olafson, in response to her quizzical look. "She's written up in the *New York Times* every week, practically."

"You didn't tell me about the film people, Quill," Adela said reprovingly. "Are they indeed interested in a feature set in Hemlock Falls?" She straightened her medallion and squared her shoulders. "Should the Hundred and Thirty-third Committee, I believe the expression is 'take a meeting' with them?"

"They are dealing with me," Harvey said firmly. "No offense, Quill, but famous as though you may be in some areas, you are not prepared to handle this. Am I right?"

Quill gave him a grateful smile, which clearly puzzled him. "Quite right."

"Well," Adela said. "Well. I suppose they are interested in the entire event, Harvey. The parade. The battle. And of course, the presentation of the Award of Merit?"

"I don't have quite all the details," Harvey said a little nervously. "But let's assume they are. They were very interested, I must say, in the possibilities around the variety show."

"Really?" Quill said.

"They have some suggestions and I think this committee —"

"Please hold it right there, Harvey." Adela sat down slowly and put her fist on her forehead in an attitude of profound thought. Then she said, "I have made a decision. This subcommittee requires a subcommittee. Harvey? I will chair it . . ."

"Azalea and Ralph will only deal through me," Harvey said hastily.

"Rape?" Marge interjected. "What the hell kind of a name is Rape?"

"*Rafe!*" Harvey said loudly. "It's how you pronounce Ralph. And Adela, with all due respect, I think that . . ."

"That you will be chair." Adela smiled agreeably. "And I will be the liaison."

"And who else?" Harvey said sulkily. "That pimply nephew of yours that keeps hounding me for auditions to do commercials? That granddaughter who's a Britney Spears wannabe? Or maybe it's ol' Fudd himself . . ."

"That's enough," Adela said, not too kindly.

"The smaller the subcommittee, the more effective it is. The two of us will be sufficient." She scanned the room. "I can promise you all that Harvey and I will put every effort into delivering the most effective, filmable variety show Hemlock Falls can deliver. Thank you for coming."

"That was the worst of it," Quill said to John Raintree a few hours later. "Well, except that Donna Olafson collared me right after the meeting and talked me into coming over to her house for a cosmetics party on Sunday. Marge almost had a fit."

"They're going to try to sell you insurance," John guessed. "I thought Brian was retired."

"Not at a cosmetics party, surely," Quill sighed. "But yes, I'm afraid that's part of the reason behind her desire to be my new best friend. She did let drop that Brian likes to keep his hand in the game, is how she expressed it."

They were sitting in the dining room, near the kitchen doors, at the table traditionally reserved for staff when the other tables weren't full. Quill shoved her entrée around her plate with her fork. It didn't deserve that treatment — it was Dover sole trucked in live from New York that morning, and it was exceptional. Meg had been on a fish kick lately.

John swallowed the last of his risotto and cocked one eyebrow encouragingly. He was looking wonderful these days. His relationship with a young professor at Ithaca College was doing him a lot of good. He'd filled out a little, and Trish had obviously talked him into a new barber; his thick black hair was shorter than it had been, making his cheekbones seem less angular. "So what's up?"

"How's business with you?" Quill asked evasively.

"I didn't think that the world needed another business consultant," John said with a certain amount of ruefulness. "But it seems that it does. Of course, I couldn't have done it without my first and most important client."

"We will always be your client. But you're going to be working with a lot bigger businesses than ours, John. You were getting a little bored with the nonchallenges posed by the Inn."

"I wouldn't say bored."

"You've been gone a lot, too," Quill said. "I hope you're not thinking about moving out of the apartment."

"Not a chance," he said easily. "It's the best deal in the county. Wood-burning fireplace, parquet floors, brick kitchen —"

"It is over the garage. I hope Trish doesn't mind that."

"Nope. Of course, you can't beat the rent."

Quill knew perfectly well that at this point in his career, John could afford to buy any three houses in Hemlock Falls, much less afford the nominal rent they all paid for their living quarters at the Inn. "I hope you're making hundred of thousands of dollars," Quill said with fierce affection.

"We're doing well enough. So. Is there anything wrong, Quill? I'm glad to see you anytime, especially after hours, when it's more relaxed. But is there something specific?"

"You know that Andy lost three patients last week."

John nodded.

"He can't establish a satisfactory cause of death for any of them. I know, I know, there's an obvious explanation for each: Mrs. Nickerson was eighty-six; Mr. Peterson had multiple myeloma; and poor Freddie — well, everyone knew about Freddie's heart.

"But, John, Andy swears they were getting better. Or at least, he'd been able to manage the conditions. He's told me before how far medicine's come in managing diseases that would have killed you like that" — she snapped her fingers — "as little as five years ago."

"Life's pretty random, Quill. And you know that the statistical probabilities that all three of these people died in one week is the same as if they'd died over the span of a year. Which is to say, there's no correlation at all."

"That's not the correlation that bothered him; it's that they all died within a week of one another. It's the fact that none of them were — imminently terminal, I guess you could say — and that all three of them were here overnight at the Inn on the same day."

"Oh?" John's eyes were a true black. When he focused his attention, the effect was unsettling.

Quill shook her head, "Don't give me that . . . that dismayed sort of look. I'm scared to death there's something to this."

"You mean that something at the Inn hastened their deaths."

"Hastened? I'm worried about cause. I mean, I've been having walking nightmares about the Inn being littered with corpses. The more I thought about Andy's concern . . ."

"Quill, there is one thing that these people had in common that is significant. They were all vulnerable physically. So if there is something here . . ."

"It'll just kill the weak and the helpless. Great."

"Just hang on a minute. For one thing, it's a possibility, not a probability. These three people may have died in a year's span of time; the fact that they all died in one week doesn't necessarily mean that there is a common cause. The timing's not statistically relevant. The fact they spent the same three days at the Inn, and then died, may be."

"I just can't believe that people are coming to this Inn and dying, John. Andy's asked me to look into it."

"Oh?"

"Yes. I may be able to pinpoint exactly where everyone was for the whole three days. And do you know how? Did I get a chance to tell you about this new business process I've been trying out? Profit Master?"

John looked down and pushed his fork around his plate, intent, apparently, on scraping off the last of his risotto. "I've heard something about it, yes."

"It's working out really well. Especially the W.A.T.C.H. Sheet. I mean, there's a few glitches, but . . . are you laughing at me?"

"Never," John said.

"It gives the manager an overview of where any employee is at any time. Which reminds me, Kathleen should have cleared these plates by now." Quill turned and scanned the dining room. It was comfortably full, for a Monday night, and there should have been at least three members of the wait staff circulating — or at least standing unobtrusively by the wall where the wine was stored.

"Where in the heck are they?" Quill got up and pushed through the double doors to the kitchen. John picked up the plates and followed. The kitchen looked normally busy. John handed the plates to the dishwasher and settled on the stool by the prep table. The kitchen was one of Quill's favorite spots at the Inn — a period cobblestone fireplace lined the west wall, windows at the south end looked out over the vegetable and herb garden, and dried herbs and Meg's copper pans hung from the old oak beams. The center of the large room was occupied by the prep table and the service area, where her sister was plating asparagus.

"Meg! What are you doing here?"

"Hey, John," she said.

"Hey, Meg."

"Meg! What's going on? I thought you and Andy were going away for a while."

Meg was dressed in shorts, sneakers, and a T-shirt which read: I'VE GOT PMS . . . AND I'M CARRYING A GUN. She placed a fourth plate of asparagus on the service hatch.

Quill looked at the vegetables dubiously. "Shouldn't someone be taking those out to the customers?"

"Yep." Meg leaned back against the sink and folded her arms. "That's what the wait staff is supposed to do, all righty."

"Well, why aren't they? And where are they?"

Meg leaned forward and adjusted a sprig of asparagus to the right. "Out back."

"Out back? What are they doing out back?"

Meg labored under the fixed delusion that she could sing. She couldn't. She thought that everybody else had a problem listening. She broke into song now, and Quill resisted the impulse to stick her fingers in her ears.

"Oh, you can't fire me, / I'm working for the union. / Working for the union. / Working for the union. / Oh, you can't fire me, / I'm working for the union. / 'Till the day I die."

"A fine old Woody Guthrie tune," John said.

"When it's on pitch," Quill snapped. She took

a deep breath, "Okay. What's going on here? Why isn't anyone working the tables?"

"Why not?"

"Why not?! Because there are hungry people out there, that's why not! Because in case you haven't noticed, we run a restaurant!"

"I don't mean why not. I mean the WhyNots. Those stupid little notes that are turning each and every one of our employees into a sneaky spy. They're ratting on each other like crazy. You've should have figured this out ahead of time, Quill. You've got a revolution on your hands."

"Whoa," John said. "Back up a little. Somebody please fill me in."

"This new system she's got . . . Pisser Master . . ."

"Profit Master," Quill said.

"Whatever. If you work here and you see something you don't like . . ."

"If you can see an opportunity for process improvement," Quill corrected.

"Uh-huh. Or if you want to rat on one of your fellow workers . . ."

"If you are uncomfortable with direct confrontation," Quill said. "Jeez!"

"You fill out one of the these things and send it to the boss." Meg dug into the pocket of her shorts and waved a red WhyNot in the air. "You want me to read you this one? Here it is: 'Kathleen Kiddermeister swipes tips. WhyNot fire her?' Unsigned, of course."

"That's to protect the employee who makes the complaint," Quill said. "To reduce the chances of unfair retaliation."

John rubbed his chin and muttered, "Oh, my god."

"Of course, I'm in charge of the wait staff," Meg said. "So someone left this little sucker for me and Kathleen picked it up by mistake, she says, and all holy hell cut loose."

"And they walked out?" Quill said anxiously. "All of them?"

"They got as far as the back parking lot," Meg said. "For all I know, they're out there still, beating each other up."

"I'd better go out there," Quill said, not moving. "Or maybe I better take the asparagus out to the dining room."

"I'll handle the asparagus," John said cheerfully. "Unless you want me out there, too."

"No," Quill said reluctantly. "I started it. I guess I'd better try and fix it."

Outside, the moon was riding high and full in a wine dark sky. A slight summer breeze rustled through the leaves of the tomato plants. The night air was filled with the scent of lavender, mint, coriander, and the sound of squabbling. Quill stopped on the path out to the parking lot for a moment and regarded the clump of angry figures. She didn't paint angry people (or terrified, anguished, grief-stricken people either, for that matter). She worked out less savage emotions and behaviors through her brush: poignancy; irony; a quiet sort of satire. But there was a certain tension between the stiff-legged bodies and the peace of the summer night that might make a very interesting painting.

"Are you going to talk to them or not?"

Quill jumped. "Meg! Don't you sneak up on me."

"I'm not sneaking up on you. I came out to see if you were going to boot it."

"I am not going to boot it."

In the parking lot, Kathleen grabbed Peter Hairston by the collar and tried to shake him back and forth. She was little and he was big and she wasn't getting very far.

"Well, I would," Meg said frankly. "I mean, look at Kathleen. Now she's got his hair. Go on. I'm right behind you."

"You rat fink!" Kathleen shrieked.

"I'm going. I'm going. I just stopped because I thought it might make an interesting charcoal sketch for my exhibit."

"Right. You don't want to take it in the ear and dump that stupid program. Everybody makes a mistake once in a while, Quill. Of course, you tend to more of them than I do, but —"

"I can't dump the program. Not now."

The light from the kitchen was behind Meg, so Quill couldn't see her expression, but she stiffened in surprise. "Why not?"

"Never mind why not. And speaking of that, why aren't you on the road to Syracuse with Andy?"

"We weren't speaking of that at all. You know what? I'm going to make you a T-shirt that says I DIGRESS. Because you do. Why you can't stick to the point is beyond me."

"And I'm not coming back!" Kathleen yelled. A car door slammed.

"Oh, dear," Quill said. "They're leaving."

"They can't leave," Meg said. "We have a dining room filled with customers."

Quill sprinted to the parking lot. Kathleen backed up her Ford Escort, pulled a U-turn, and roared down the driveway. Peter Hairston and Devora MacIntyre stood looking after her. Quill skidded to a halt at Peter's side.

Nobody said anything for a moment.

"Um," Quill said. "Everything okay out here?"

Devora, one of the more competent students at the Cornell School of Hotel Management, stood on one foot, then the other. Peter Hairston, like Dina, a graduate student, rubbed the back of his neck thoughtfully.

"She tried to snatch him bald," Devora said.

"Oh, dear?" Quill looked around for Meg. Her sister had beaten a prudent retreat, presumably back to the kitchen. Quill tried to recall the basic tenets of the course she'd taken called Managing the Irate Employee. "I guess she was pretty angry, huh?"

"She had a right to be," Peter said. He was what Quill's grandmother would have called a presentable young man, tall, with dark blond curly hair and a fresh complexion. His voice was clear and precise. "I don't think she was stealing tips. And I have no idea who'd say that. Or rather, write that. Anyhow, it wasn't me."

"And it wasn't me," Devora said indignantly. "Jeez! You should have heard what she said, Quill. She called me a snotty college kid. And a lot more besides."

"She was upset," Peter said kindly. "And she has a career here, Dee. The two of us are going on to other things, but this pitiful little job is all Kathleen's got. I tried to make her understand that we understand that and we'd never try to take it away from her, but it just seemed to make her madder."

"And you have no idea who wrote the WhyNot?" Quill asked.

"Not a clue," Peter said cheerfully. "Not that one or the other ones, either."

"Other ones? What other ones?" Quill found herself tugging at her hair.

Devora turned to Peter, a question in the set of her shoulders. "I think we should tell her," Peter said. "I've thought we should tell her all along."

"None of us wanted to get fired," Devora said.

"What in the world are you talking about?" Quill reached out and touched Peter gently. "And why would we fire either one of you? You're great at waiting tables, both of you."

"Somebody — maybe more than one person

— has been leaving these WhyNots all over the place," Peter said. "One accused Devora of stealing from a customer's purse . . ."

"And one said Peter was selling off the wine and putting the missing bottles down to breakage. And we did check the wine cellar and there were bottles missing, but Peter didn't do it."

"I wasn't aware of any of this." Quill paused, then said, "I'm sorry. And I don't believe that you were stealing, Devora, or that you've been selling wine, Peter. I promise you I'll find out what's been going on. Okay?"

"Okay," Peter said. "Should we go back to work now?"

"Please. I'd appreciate it very much. And if you find any more of these . . . messages, please bring them to me. I'll call a staff meeting for tomorrow and talk to everyone. Okay? In the meantime, if we can get on with business as usual, I'd appreciate it."

She watched the two of them walk back to the Inn. "I am *not* being paranoid," she muttered aloud. "I'm not."

But somebody, somewhere, was out to make trouble for the Inn.

CHAPTER 4

"What does Myles think?" Andy's voice over the phone was as composed as ever.

It was seven o'clock, Tuesday morning, and the sunshine flooding the French doors in Quill's suite at the Inn was a direct antithesis to her mood. Max prowled around the room, underfoot and smelling like dog. She hadn't slept well. She missed Myles. And she was not looking forward to talking poor Kathleen into coming back to work. "I didn't bother him with much of it. We had an overseas connection and he didn't have much time to talk."

"How long will he be gone this time?"

Quill tucked the phone receiver between her ear and her shoulder and tugged her chinos over her hips. Max grabbed one cuff and tried to tug them off. She had called a general staff meeting for ten o'clock this morning and she'd dithered over what to wear. A suit was too power-mongerish. Her usual long skirt and sleeveless top were too drifty. She'd decided on no-nonsense chinos and a striped cotton shirt. Efficient, but not distancing.

"Quill?"

"Sorry, Andy. I don't know how long Myles will be gone. He volunteered for the anti-terrorism unit at Global and they sent him to England for a few weeks. He feels as John does — there isn't much chance of a correlation between the deaths and the time these people spent at the Inn. But he agreed that it wouldn't hurt to take a look at where the three of them went and what they ate while they were here. And the problem you feel you have with requesting more complete autopsies? He suggested that Davey Kiddermeister order them. If the police request it, the budget point becomes moot. And it takes the burden of the decision off you. The best part is, we won't have county inspectors racing around here unless the autopsies do show some kind of weird food poisoning."

"A police investigation?"

Quill tucked her top into her chinos with one hand. "He suggested it, that's all. There'll be a certain amount of gossip, Andy, but there is now anyway. What do you think?"

"Do it." Andy's voice was incisive. "Shall you call Davey or shall I?"

"I'll talk to him. He's a pretty good deputy sheriff, Andy, and he knows enough not to make a big deal of it. And really, it's a matter of being thorough, that's all."

"And it helps that his sister works for you," Andy said. "Although that wouldn't influence him, I know."

"Um," Quill said. Max sat down and looked at her quizzically. She added cheerfully, "I have a couple of employee problems to straighten out this morning, but I'll try to reach Davey right now, okay? I just wanted to let you know that we're making progress. And you? What's your schedule for the day?"

"My schedule?" he said, startled. "Do you want to get together later?"

"No, no, not right now. I just wondered if you and Meg had talked yesterday."

"She has some idea about couples counseling." The reserve in his voice was clear.

"There are some very good therapists in Syracuse," Quill said. "And Buffalo, too."

His silence was pointed. Then he said, "Something's come up here with one of my patients. I'm not going to be able to spend a lot of time away from the clinic this week."

"Well, never mind. Sorry if I sounded intrusive." She replaced the phone in the cradle. "Max, I feel as if I'm trying to shove five pounds of spaghetti into a one-pound sack."

Max cocked his head to one side.

"I've always wondered why anyone would want to put five pounds of cooked spaghetti into a one-pound sack. Why not get a bigger sack?"

Max cocked his head to the other side. Then he sat up, ears pricked forward, and stared out the French doors to the balcony.

"Would you just go somewhere, please? Down

117

to the Gorge. Take a bath in the river. You smell horrible."

Max barked and clawed at the doors. Quill had closed them against the chill of the night air — although the days were warm this June, the nights were cool — and she said "No!" very firmly, as the instructions in the *Guide to Training Your Dog* had told her to. Max ignored this, as he ignored all the instructions from that manual, and clawed again at the doors.

"You know what? I'll walk with you. It's a good two miles down to the sheriff's office and we can both use the exercise."

Max whined, rolled onto his back, and looked at her upside down.

"You think I should stay here and get to work, don't you. It's gorgeous out there, Max. And I'm going to have a horrible day. I have to find out if something in this Inn hastened — John's word, and a good one — hastened the deaths of three people I liked very much. And I can't tell Meg about it or she'll go ballistic. I really hate lying to my sister. Not to mention I have to tackle a crowd of highly grouchy employees at ten clock."

Max yawned.

"Fine. So you don't give a darn." She ran a brush through her hair, pinned it to the top of her head, and peered in the mirror. She could swear there were gray hairs among the red strands. "Great. The whole staff is mad at me. They are going to rise up in a body and put my head on a pike. Meg is going to go postal when she finds out that we're looking into those deaths.

"Myles is off fighting terrorists. John thinks I'm an idiot, and there's nobody on my side! Come on, let's go downstairs."

Max pattered down the winding staircase to the foyer with more than his usual animation. (Which wasn't saying a great deal. Max was notable chiefly for his extreme ugliness and his laid-back attitude, which had made his antics upstairs all the more annoying.) Halfway down the stairs, Quill became aware of a rhythmic pounding. The reenactors weren't due to set up camp for another three days, but it sounded a lot like tent pegs being pounded into the ground. Max increased his speed from a lollop to a lope. Quill descended less rapidly behind him. When she arrived in the foyer, Max was pawing eagerly at the oak entrance door.

It was an old door — dating back to the early days of the Inn, when it had been a stopping place for the fur trappers headed up north to Canada — and Quill said warningly, "Max," and opened it up to let him outside.

She hadn't heard the sound of tent pegs being pounded into the ground; she'd heard the sound of poles slamming against asphalt. Attached to the poles were signs that read INN PRACTICES UNFAIR TO WORKERS! And WHYNOT? WHY US!? And WORKERS UNITE! Kathleen Kiddermeister carried two of the signs, one in each hand. Dina carried the other. Watching them both with a superior, smug, snaky smile was Carol Ann Spinoza dressed in a jogging suit. Max raced around them in a wide circle, barking his head off. As soon as Dina saw Quill at the door, she began to shout: "WhyNot! Why us! WhyNot! Why us!" and Kathleen (reluctantly) joined in.

It was a beautiful day. The sky was cloudless. The Queen Elizabeth roses surrounding the fishpond were in glorious pink bloom. Mike the groundskeeper had planted gentians around the borders early in the spring and the vivid blue was a startling contrast to the gray rock. The gentle sound of the falls and the splashing of the small fountain provided an aural background to what should have been a peaceful scene.

"Stop that right now," Quill said coldly. "Not you, Max. You, Dina. And you too, Kathleen. I'd like to see both of you inside." Dina, at least, had the grace to look abashed. Quill stepped aside to let both women into the foyer, then said, "And, Carol Ann, can I help you?"

"Just jogging by," Carol Ann said. She smiled sweetly. "I can't help but notice that you're having labor problems."

"I hardly think that two longtime employees of this Inn getting some morning exercise constitutes labor problems."

"Maybe. Maybe not. But I would like to remind you that interference with the formation of any legitimate workers' organization constitutes a felony under New York State —"

Quill slammed the door shut, leaned forward, and then whacked her forehead against the oak several times.

"Wow," Dina said. "I don't think I would have done that to Carol Ann. You know, Quill, she got the town tax assessor job back. You don't have to be all that nice to her. Just maybe suck up a little."

Quill whirled. "What is the matter with you two?"

"Anything interesting going on here?" Azalea Cummings picked her way delicately down the stairs, a video camera in one hand. Her fingernail polish was green this morning. She'd replaced the stud in her nose with a fake emerald. Quill presumed it was a fake emerald. Maybe Azalea was really the head of a Colombian drug ring and she got a supply of real gems for free.

"I love those black leather jeans," Dina said. "They are incredibly, totally hot."

"You'll excuse us, Azalea. You two. In my office. Now."

Quill swept them inside and pointed firmly at the couch. Kathleen sat defiantly in one corner, Dina perched at the other. "I do *not*," Quill said between clenched teeth, "deserve this."

Kathleen started to cry. Dina's own eyes filled in sympathy. Quill pulled her desk drawer open in search of the Kleenex and realized that Meg had used them all up. She sat behind her desk and put her head in her hands. "I give up."

"Huh?" Dina blinked back her tears and sniffed a little.

"I do. I give up. You win. No more W.A.T.C.H. Report. No more time sheets. No more anything."

"I do *not* steal other people's tips!" Kathleen said. Her sobs subsided. She was a short, compact woman with dark hair, three kids, and a husband who was periodically laid off. Unlike her younger fair-haired, pink-cheeked brother Davey (who was acting sheriff when Myles McHale was called out of town), she had glossy brunette hair and an olive complexion that never blotched, even when, as now, she'd been crying hard. She ran the back of her hand under her eyes and Quill said, "Sorry. I'm out of tissues."

"S'all right."

"Kathleen, why didn't you guys come to me? I thought . . ." Quill waved her hands helplessly in the air. "I guess I thought we really didn't have bosses here. And even if I am a boss, that I didn't act like a boss —"

"That's for sure," Dina muttered.

"I mean, the kind of uncaring, mean, rotten boss that created the need for unions in the first place. The kind that would lead you to believe I would ever, ever think of firing you. Or that I would ever, ever believe you would steal tips from your friends. I thought we all had the same goal here."

"Workers and managers never have the same

goals," Dina said. "It's a con job to think that's true. Look at Enron."

"I am sick of hearing about Enron," Quill said.

"The Constitution guarantees . . ." Dina began.

"And I know all about the Constitution. My god, I can't believe I said that. Anyway, it's the Bill of Rights that gives us free speech." Quill knew she was looking haggard. She felt haggard. "Dina, is your not-so-subtle plan in this life to drive me completely and utterly crazy? Because I have to tell you — it's working."

"I was just supporting my fellow workers."

"Well, that's admirable. Up to a point. But wouldn't it be better to talk about this? In a reasonable way? As friends?"

There was an insistent rap at the door. Quill ignored it. The rap was followed by a volley of barks. Max. Who wouldn't stop barking until she let him in or he got run over by a truck. Quill got up and opened the door. Max bounced in. So did Azalea Cummings. "I was thinking maybe a documentary," Azalea began.

Quill shoved her out the door and shut it again.

"You guys come and talk to me when you're finished with that . . . witch!" The shout was muffled by the inch-thick mahogany, but it registered with both Kathleen and Dina.

"Fine. Talk to her. Go on prime time TV and tell the whole flipping universe how you've been abused!" Quill shouted.

"Are we fired?" Kathleen asked timidly.

"No, you're not fired."

"Are we negotiating?" Dina said.

"Nego— Yes. Okay. Whatever. We're negotiating."

"You said you'd ditch the W.A.T.C.H. Report. And those sneaky rotten stupid unsigned complaints. And the WhyNots."

"I hate those WhyNots," Kathleen said. "I hate them."

"Look, guys," Quill began. Then she stopped. Last night's conversation with Myles hadn't been long enough to go into the problem of the Inn saboteur. If there was a saboteur. It'd be easier to catch the saboteur if the Profit Master Program continued. On the other hand, if she stopped the program, she'd have a good excuse to investigate the activities of Mrs. Nickerson, Mr. Peterson, and poor Freddie Bellini without seeming to investigate at all. She'd just tell everybody she was trying to discover where she'd gone wrong. And of course, if she halted Profit Master, she'd have people to talk to if everyone hadn't quit already. She could catch the saboteur. Heck, she'd caught murderers before. A saboteur was nothing. "Just good old detective work," she said aloud.

"Oh, no!" Dina said. "Davey said that if you and Meg ever started investigating anything ever again, he'd quit and move to Des Moines."

"Might not be the worst thing," Kathleen murmured.

"Look, Kath. I know you and your parents aren't all that thrilled about my dating your brother. I have just two words for you. Get over it."

"That's three words," Quill pointed out. "Let's not digress here, okay?"

"You're telling *us* not to digress?" Dina said. "Jeez-Louise."

"Profit Master's history," Quill said with a generous wave of her hand. "It's done. Toast. Gone. But I'd like to find out who's been writing those bogus WhyNots. And there've been some complaints that are a little suspect, too, so . . ."

"Doreen did whack that little kid with the mop," Kathleen said apologetically, "but it would have taken a genuine, unreconstructed saint not to. That kid . . ."

"So," Quill said loudly, "to get to the main point of the discussion here, I just want to let everyone know that I'm going to be verifying the information in the reports." Both Dina and Kathleen sat up in protest. "Not to try to hang anybody. Believe me. I just want to find out" — she stopped and took a deep breath — "where I went wrong."

"So you admit it!" Dina said triumphantly.

"I admit it, okay? It was a bad idea. But I'd sure appreciate it if you help me when I come around asking questions."

"Because you were wrong," Kathleen repeated in a pleased way.

"Yes!" Quill shouted. "Wrong! Wrong! Wrong! *Mea culpa!* Okay?"

"O-*kay.*" Dina grinned. "Want us to tell everybody?"

"Yes. Go ahead. Make me look like a total bozo. I don't care," Quill said recklessly.

"And we can cancel this morning's staff meeting?" Dina said. "I mean, I got here at seven-thirty this morning, which is an hour and a half before I'm supposed to, and if I could bug out for a little while, it'd be cool."

Quill gritted her teeth and said very quietly, "You came in to stage a protest."

"And it worked!" Dina said sunnily. "It is so amazing. Anyhow, can I leave?"

"No."

"Are you . . ." Even Dina appeared to have a rudimentary survival instinct. She took a good look at the expression on Quill's face and said, "Never mind. I can see that it ticks you off a little bit. Maybe Kath and I can get back to work."

"What a good idea."

Quill sat behind her desk after they were gone and seriously considered the advantages of running away from home. She could gain twenty pounds, dye her hair black, and get blue contact lenses. Then she could move back to Soho in New York and paint. Under the name of Saunders. And people would talk about how derivative her style was. "So that won't work," she told herself aloud.

Max thumped his tail on the floor.

"Do you still want to go for that walk? We can stop and talk to Davey Kiddermeister and ask him about those autopsies."

Max did.

She really ought to drive. The entire trip would take half an hour, at most. And then she could come back here and start sorting through all the W.A.T.C.H. Sheets and make a chart showing the whereabouts of Mrs. Nickerson, Mr. Peterson, and Freddie Bellini on what she was coming to think of as the Fatal Day. The one lesson she'd learned from her visits to the therapist those months she had been totally confused about the direction her life was taking was that you should take time for your Self. Even if you felt you were being irresponsible. Or selfish. So she'd take a walk and the heck with it.

Dina was on the phone as Quill and Max left the office. "Here she is!" she said into the receiver. She put it on hold with a rather guilty expression.

"I'm taking Max for a walk, Dina, I'll be back in about an hour and a half."

"I've been canceling the employee meeting," she said.

"Good."

"That gave you an extra hour in your schedule today. That Mrs. Olafson called and asked you to lunch. So I said you were free."

"Oh, Dina! All she wants to do is sell me insurance. I don't want any more insurance, John says we don't need any more insurance. No. No. No. Call her back and tell her I'm dead."

"She's on the phone right now." Dina punched the hold button again and held it out. Quill sighed, put it to her ear, and assumed a hearty cheer she was far from feeling. "Donna? This is Quill. Hello? Hello? Dina, what's wrong with the phone?"

"Oh. Ooops!" Dina punched the hold button a third time. "Sorry. Guess it wasn't on hold after all."

Quill closed her eyes. What had she said? No. No. No, she'd rather be dead. Something along those lines. She'd already banged her head against the wall once this morning; if she did it again, she'd give herself a major concussion. "Donna," she said warmly. "How are you?"

She hung up after a few minutes of reassurance that yes, she'd absolutely love to see Donna and her husband at noon, and had they tried lunch at the Croh Bar? Noontime would be wonderful. Just wonderful.

Quill gave the phone back to Dina and looked at Max, who, in his intuitive doggy way, knew immediately there was to be no walk. "I need all the W.A.T.C.H. Sheets, Dina. And the complaint forms. And while you're at it, I'd like you to ask everyone at the Inn for those bogus WhyNots. I want to take a look at them."

"Everybody? That's, like, fifty people. Can't I use the network system?"

The network system was an easy way to get in

touch with every employee at the Inn within a short period of time. Dina called five employees, who in turn called three employees, who called three others and within a space of half an hour or so, everyone had been contacted. Norm Pasquale had suggested it, since it had been used successfully at the high school for years.

"No. I want you to see everyone personally. And I want you to walk off with the WhyNots in your hot little hand. Okay?"

"No need to be sarcastic."

"Sorry. Devora can cover the phones here for you. And I'd like those W.A.T.C.H. Sheets right away."

The amount of paperwork that the Profit Master system generated was horrible. And Quill had been using the system for just three weeks. The program had seemed brilliantly simple in the well-ordered environment of the Cornell School for Hotel Management. And Professor Wojowski had the evangelical zeal of the true convert. He had been utterly convincing. The goal of all successful companies was a perfect product. The Inn's product was service. The service was twenty-four seven for guests. The professor had helped Quill create a tracking system that showed where every guest and every employee was at every moment of their time at the Inn. If customers were unhappy with the product, the aware manager could pinpoint the area where the defect in the service occurred and do something to fix it.

By the time Quill had plowed through the first week of the reports, she was ready to fix Professor Wojowski, in the same way that Doreen had been encouraging her to fix Max for the last two years. It was impossible. It was nuts. She had a headache right down to her toes. And Dina was right — the system was a total invasion of privacy. She'd discovered that Kathleen and Mike the groundskeeper had been spending a lot of time in the tool shed. Together. That Bjarne, Meg's second in command in the kitchen, took an average of three hours to accept the meat and fish deliveries, which was ridiculous and meant he was up to something else. And she hoped like heck that there wasn't going to be any trouble with the way the food was stored. That was the first thing that food inspectors looked for.

She went on. Doreen had taken a lot of time off lately, which was highly unusual and made Quill think that it was time she had a quiet talk with her irascible though much-loved housekeeper. Doreen was in her mid-seventies now, fiercely independent, and the work might be getting too much for her.

Quill rubbed her eyes and sat back in her chair. She knew too much. Ugh.

Furiously, she riffled through the remaining reports and selected the twelfth of June, the day when Andy's three patients had all been at the Inn at the same time. She bundled the rest of the reports up and stuffed them into her credenza. She tore the sheets containing the notes she'd made on the Inn employees off the notepad and threw them into the wastebasket. She'd take the June twelfth report out to the gazebo by the side of the Falls.

The clock on her desk chimed the half hour: eleven-thirty. She'd drive to the village, see Davey, and have lunch with the Olafsons. After that, she had another meeting of the 133rd Committee, then the reenactors, and then she had to be back at the Inn for the reception for the Short Film Festival people at five. She'd have to save the twelfth of June report for the evening, when she had planned to paint.

She drove her Honda down to the village feeling wistful. Another summer was speeding by. Maybe she should take her own advice to Meg and take a vacation. It'd been five years since she'd left the Inn for more than a weekend at a time. When Myles got back from London, the two of them could pack Max up and just drive somewhere. Maybe those gray hairs she'd seen in the mirror this morning weren't stress. Maybe she was getting old. The average Englishman was dead by thirty-seven in 1663. "Although," she said to a startled Davey Kiddermeister when she walked into the sheriff's office ten minutes later, "to be fair, they mostly died of disease, and not old age."

"Who, ma'am?" Davey sat at what Quill always thought of as Myles's desk. He'd grown into his job the last year or so; he didn't turn pink when he met people anymore and someone, Dina most likely, had talked him into a mustache. It was thick, luxuriant, and darker than his pale blond hair.

"People who lived in the midseventeenth century." Quill sat down in the uncomfortable straight-backed chair that faced Myles's desk. "But I have come to see you about death from disease, Davey, so it isn't as much of a non sequitur as it sounds."

"It doesn't sound like anything to me," he said honestly. "Is Kathleen okay?"

"She's fine. Oh, she told you about the umm . . . protest. Yes, that's all resolved, and I'm sorry, Davey, I didn't realize how that stupid program of mine was going to affect people. I should have known better."

"She wanted me to come and protest with her. Or at least, that Carol Ann Spinoza did. Thing is, Carol Ann wants something, there's usually something fishy about it. And besides, how would it look? Because of my position. Know what I mean? Anyway, I told Kath she should talk to you first." He shook his head. "Kath's not too good at standing up for herself."

"She stood up for herself just fine this morning," Quill said. "And I'm glad you're not too upset about it, Davey."

"Sheriff always says to wait until the facts get in before you act," Davey said. "He's usually right about things like that."

Quill felt a glow of (regrettably) proprietorial pride.

"Any idea when he's coming back?" he asked.

"No. He thought a few weeks, perhaps more."

"Huh. Not any sooner than that?" Behind the mustache, Davey looked a little anxious.

"August, at least," Quill said. "Is there something you wanted to talk to him about? Could I help?"

Davey looked wary. "Not really, ma'am. Especially seeing as how they're right there at the Inn."

"Who's right there at the Inn?"

"All those reenactors. They're coming into town by the busload."

"It's hardly busloads, Davey. And they're harmless, surely."

"The guns aren't. And here's the mayor wanting to fire off the cannon."

"But they don't use real rifles, do they?"

"Sure they do. I mean, they're loaded with blanks, but they're real rifles. I've got to make sure that each and every one of them has a legal permit, and Mr. Murchison thinks we need a liability policy in case someone gets shot accidentally, and I called Albany about the permit for the cannon and they thought I was crazy."

"It can't be any worse than hunting season," Quill soothed.

"Maybe. But I know pretty much every guy that hunts around here. Heck, I hunt with them myself. I don't know any of these people."

"I'll tell you what I think Myles would do. He'd come up to the Inn and introduce himself to Mr. Hackmeyer and his men. They're just ordinary sorts of people as far as I can tell, Davey. I mean, Mr. Hackmeyer owns a huge insurance company and I think the captain of the brigade or whatever it is sells Toyotas and it's people like that. It's a hobby."

"You don't think I should run checks on them?"

"Of course not! Why in the world should you do that?" She wanted to add that this wasn't a police state, and that people had a right to privacy, but she didn't.

Davey hesitated a long moment, then got up and went to the gray metal filing cabinet. He rummaged in it for a moment and withdrew a plastic baggie.

"That's a WhyNot," Quill said.

"A what?"

"May I see it?"

"Sure. I had it dusted for prints. There aren't any. Except mine. Which is suspicious, of course, since I sure as heck didn't send it to myself." He smiled uneasily.

Quill shook the red sheet out of the bag. There was an envelope as well, addressed to Sheriff's Department, 224 Elm, Hemlock Falls, New York.

"Mailed from Syracuse," Davey pointed out. "Whoever it was got it at the Inn. I asked Kath about it."

Quill read the message with dismay.

Who will die at the Battle of Hemlock Falls?
WhyNot wait and see?

"Good heavens," Quill said. She thought a moment. "Maybe no one will, Davey. I mean, more than likely it's a stupid joke." She frowned. "It's not exactly a threat, is it?"

"Sounds like a threat to me."

"We're all a little sensitive to threats these days," she said calmly. "I mean, our sense of security has changed a lot in the few past years."

"I can't just ignore it."

"No. I don't suppose you can."

"That's one of those darn things that got Kath in trouble, isn't it?"

"Yes. And I stopped the program this morning. The thing is, who, Davey? I mean, someone's been creating trouble at the Inn with these things. You saw that with Kathleen. But at most, I thought it was one of the staff that was angry about it, although I've been thinking and thinking about who it could be, and I just can't believe it's anyone who works for us. But this — this kind of widens the scope." She tossed it back on the desk. "I just can't believe it's anything more than a sick joke."

"We got a file for that," Davey said. "But like I said, I don't want to take the chance. And I think I should run checks on those reenactors.

And to do that," he said firmly, "I need a list. Of who's going to be there."

"Wait a second." Quill ran her fingers through her hair. "You want that list from me?"

"Yeah. And I'd prefer that you not mention it to this Major Warrender Hackmeyer."

"Wow. Oh, my. Oh, dear."

"What? What's the problem? It's not like the Inn has a customer confidentiality thing going. I already checked with Mr. Murchison."

"What did Howie say? Don't tell me. He's a Republican. He said it'd be fine." Quill rose and walked up and down the peeling linoleum floor.

"I don't see what being a Republican has to do with it. And if you want to know the truth, he wasn't all that happy about it. Gave me a lot of sh— a lot of stuff about personal freedoms."

"It's not a lot of stuff. It's important."

"Someone getting shot is maybe more important."

Quill sat down again. "What if you take this note to Major Hackmeyer?"

"What if he sent the note?"

Quill bit her lip. "I can't do it, Davey. That list isn't mine to give you. Ask Major Hackmeyer for it. See what he says."

"I don't want to tip anybody off."

"That," Quill said indignantly, "is just sneaky."

"So you refuse to help the police in their inquiries?"

Quill couldn't believe that she was about to

lose her temper twice in one morning. She took a deep breath and smiled as winningly as she knew how. "Of course I don't refuse. As a matter of fact, you and Myles get pretty upset when I do help the police with their inquiries. As an even larger matter of fact, helping the police with their inquiries is one of the reasons I dropped by here today."

Davey chewed one end of his mustache. He set the WhyNot aside reluctantly. "Oh?"

"It's those three patients of Andy's. You know, Mrs. Nickerson, Mrs. Peterson . . ."

"And poor Mr. Bellini. What about 'em?"

"Andy's a little concerned about the causes of death. He'd like to do more tests on them, but the Coroner's Office has all those budget restrictions and it'd help a lot if the request for further inquiry came from here. Just . . ." Quill waved one hand vaguely in the air. "You know. Procedure."

"There's a form to fill out." Davey turned to the filing cabinet again.

"I know," Quill said hastily, "but Myles said that the form's used when there's a suspicion of homicide or some other kind of wrongful death and that really isn't the case here. I mean, you know Andy. How thorough he is. He's concerned, Davey, no more than that. And there's the stupid state regulations about the funds, of course."

"I don't see the difference between this office filling out a form and the Coroner's Office filling out a form. I'll have to open a case file and the whole bit."

"And I'm sure the case will be closed as soon as the forensics results come back." Quill looked at her watch. "Oh, gosh. I have to meet the Olafsons for lunch, Davey. I've really got to run. What do you think? Can you do it? Ask for the autopsies, I mean?" She played her trump card. "Myles thought it would be a good idea."

"Yeah? Okay. I'll make a deal with you. You talk to Myles about this, whatd'yacallit, WhyNot and see if he says you should give me that list of reenactors. You do that, I'll order those autopsies."

"I'll ask him," Quill said. "But I have to tell you up front, Davey, whatever he says won't change my mind. And if you ask me, you're engaging in some not-too-subtle blackmail, and I don't like it."

"Maybe you're right," he said uncomfortably.

Quill gathered up her purse and backed out the door. "I'm headed out to the Croh Bar," she said chattily. "I thought the Olafsons would enjoy Betty Hall's cooking. And I wanted to speak to Betty and Marge anyway. I'm trying to get Meg to take a short vacation and Betty'd be great at handling the food for the reenactors while she's gone. Sorry, didn't mean to babble."

Davey got up and followed her to the door. "You're taking those two new insurance guys to Marge's place?" he asked. He grinned. "Marge has been hauling every person in this town into

138

that new office of hers to sell them insurance, too. And she never misses lunch at the Croh Bar, seeing as how it's her very own restaurant. Think the four of you will get along okay?" He grinned. "Good luck, Quill."

CHAPTER 5

Quill trudged the three blocks to the Croh Bar with the conviction that her day was going to get worse.

The serenity of the cobblestone buildings lining Main Street always helped put events into perspective, and she slowed down a little as she walked around the corner from Maple onto Main. Hemlock Falls was a beautiful village; it was why she and Meg had decided to move here more than ten years ago. It was looking its best in the warm June sunshine. The black iron flower boxes under the lampposts overflowed with scarlet and pink geraniums. Hanging pots filled with fuchsia and begonias swung from the store signs.

Quill dawdled past the cut stone building that had housed the Palate, the restaurant she and Meg had owned briefly the one year that they had sold the Inn to Marge. Marge had swapped the Inn back to them (although she had insisted on a considerable amount of cash in addition to the Palate building) and turned the Palate into her offices. A newly painted sign hung out front: ALL-NEEDS INSURANCE *Casualty and*

Surety. A second sign, below it, read: HEMLOCK FALLS REAL ESTATE, *Marge Schmidt, Prop.*

Quill glanced inside the large front window. Marge's secretary was on the phone; Marge herself was nowhere in evidence. Of course not. It was just after twelve and almost everyone in Hemlock Falls was at lunch. Probably at the Croh Bar, where Marge ate every day. Quill stopped and pulled at her lower lip. She would totally avoid any talk of insurance at all at lunch. Or cosmetics. She'd talk about their new house. Their grandchildren. The 133rd Committee. Pets. The Olafsons had a little bichon frise named . . . what was it? Sweetie. Nasty little thing that bit. And if Marge barged in and started thumping away, well, she'd handled a lot worse at the Inn over the years. She could cope. She was strong. "I am not doomed," Quill said aloud. Marge's receptionist waved cheerily at her, then held up one hand in a "wait" gesture. Quill waved back and moved on. She wouldn't even think the word "insurance."

Behind her, the door to Marge's office bounced open, then closed.

"Wait up, Quill."

"Hi, Marge." Quill paused. "You're looking well."

"Can't complain."

Quill thought about "can't complain" as the universal Hemlock Falls response to questions about well-being. Even Derwent Peterson, whose myeloma had caused him significant amounts of pain, would say "can't complain" when he of all people had a right.

"I said, Quill!"

Quill jumped. "Sorry, Marge. I went off on a tangent."

Marge shook her head. She stumped along, her head barely reaching Quill's shoulder. "I was saying how the insurance business is in the toilet."

"You were?"

"And as how you and Meg should take a good hard look at your premiums and your coverage."

"I'll talk to John about it," Quill promised. "But we have all our coverage with you, Marge. Do we need more?"

"You'll be getting a letter from the company soon," she said darkly. "About this Hackmeyer."

"Now there's a man who wouldn't bother with a small amount of coverage like ours," Quill said hastily. "And I can assure you, Marge, that we're not about to switch coverage. To anybody."

"What'n the heck are you going on about?" Marge stopped in midstump. "I was talking about the reenactment on Saturday."

"What about it?"

"Well." Marge scratched her neck vigorously. "Harland's asked me to drop by with him."

"To the celebration? I think that's won—" Quill stopped herself. Marge would bridle at any intimation that the town approved of the incipient match between her and the dairy farmer.

"I think that's probably very wise. I mean, the town should definitely show some solidarity in front of people like Hackmeyer. So the more of us that turn out, the better."

"You don't like him much, either?"

Now it was Quill's turn to stop on the sidewalk. "No," she said in some surprise. "I don't."

"I didn't walk along with you to get your opinion of Warrender Hackmeyer," Marge said reprovingly. "I wanted to know how you think I'd look in this." She set her suitcase down on the sidewalk, rummaged in it, and withdrew a Polaroid photograph.

"It's a midnineteenth-century ball gown," Quill said. It looked magnificent; the dress was white satin. The skirt was long, with a train dotted with rosebuds. A garland of rosebuds was pinned to the gown's shoulder, obviously ready to be placed on the wearer's head.

"What d'ya think?" Marge asked anxiously.

Quill took a little more time than necessary to look at the photograph. She held it up. "Do they have it in a darker color? You look wonderful in browns, Marge. You're a woman that cries out for strong colors."

"It's from that rental place up in Ithaca," Marge said. "The only other thing they have in my size is this." She took a second photo from her briefcase.

"A tailored riding habit in brown velvet," Quill said. "With the most adorable beaver hat I've ever seen. I think that's perfect for you."

"I don't ride, you know."

"I don't think it matters."

"You're sure."

"I'm positive." Quill took a wild guess at what was really troubling Marge. "There's something very feminine about brown velvet. It's soft. Touchable. I've always loved it, myself." Quill managed a blush. "And Myles does, too, I think."

"Huh," Marge said contemptuously. "Here's the Croh Bar. You coming in?"

The Croh Bar was crowded, as it always was. But any faint hope Quill had that there wouldn't be enough room for the Olafsons and that they could go somewhere else for lunch died when she saw them both sitting at a small round table in the front.

Marge gave her a steely look. "I thought you said you had enough insurance."

Quill slid into the empty chair and apologized for being late.

"It's only five past the hour," Brian Olafson assured her. "We came a little early and stopped at the Inn first, to see if we could pick you up. We've heard how popular this place is."

"If there weren't any tables, we figured we could always go back up to the Inn," Donna said. "There always seems to be enough room there."

"It's always good to have backup insurance," Quill agreed. "I mean, a backup plan."

"Not that you aren't popular, too," Brian said. "We wouldn't want her to think that, would we, Mother?" He smiled warmly at Quill. "The menu at the Inn is wonderful. Now, what would you suggest we try here?"

"It's all good," Quill said honestly. "Betty Hall specializes in American diner cooking. Meg has an enormous respect for her. You're always insured a good meal here."

"She and Marge Schmidt are full partners, aren't they?" Brian asked.

"In the restaurant business," Quill said. "But Marge is pretty independent otherwise. Her insurance business is all her own. But you both would know about that."

"Why, there's Marge," Donna said. "Let's ask her what she'd recommend. And, dear" — she laid one hand over Quill's — "let's not talk business, shall we? We just want to have a nice, quiet lunch with you."

"I couldn't shut up!" Quill said to Meg an hour and a half later. "Every other word out of my mouth was 'insurance.' I used that word in ways Webster never dreamed of. I used it as an adverb, as an adjective, as a gerund, as a verb, as a —"

"You could shut up now," Meg offered. "Not to be rude or anything, but I want to take a look at these period recipes Miriam dropped by for me." She settled more firmly onto the stool at the prep table and tapped the folder in front of her. She shared a perfectly good office with Doreen, just off the kitchen, but she never used it.

"And I promised to go to her house for a makeup consultation on top of it all. Darn it! I know what's happening," Quill said glumly. "I'm displacing. I'm keeping important information from you and I shouldn't be, so I'm spilling all the unimportant things on my mind in inappropriate places. Not to mention agreeing to go to one of those darn home parties. I hate home parties. You always buy stuff you don't use because you feel obligated. I . . ." She put her hand over her mouth, removed it, and said, "And I'm doing it again. Displacing. You're my sister, for heaven's sake. You have a right to know what's going on."

"What about haricot of oxtails for the Civil War banquet?" Meg, who had been totally ignoring Quill's diatribe, made a face. "Too bad. We're fresh out of ox. Or a ragout of mutton. I could probably get a deal on very, very old ewes if I called up Harland Peterson and asked him to scout some of his sheep-herding pals. Ugh." She tossed the folder aside. "I'll tell you one thing home-based cooks from the last century must have been, and that was bored stiff. Not to mention the fact that their taste buds had to have been permanently numbed. And as far as the Union Army goes — *phuut!* Do you know what those lunatic reenactors eat?"

"No," Quill said absently. "What?" She sat in

the rocker by the cobblestone fireplace. In the summer, the grate was filled with flowers from the back gardens. Mike the groundskeeper had cut the first coreopsis of the season, and they straggled over the bronze cache pot in a very untidy way. She kicked at it irritably.

"Boiled beef. That's what our brave boys in blue and gray went to war on. Not stewed with vegetables, which would be a haricot, or a ragout, since there doesn't seem to be much difference between the two. Just boiled. In a pot with water from whatever water source was available. Like the horse trough. And they mash up flour with a little water and fry that in a cast-iron pan. And they eat it!" She tossed the folder aside. "Okay. What's on your mind?"

Quill jumped guiltily. "It's obvious?"

"It's obvious to both Andy and me that you're trying to get us out of here. I mean, Buffalo, Quill? Ithaca's filled with therapists. It's a major university center, for Pete's sake, and all academics are in therapy. We don't have to drive three hours one way to see a couples therapist."

"Are you going to see one?"

Meg fidgeted on the stool. "Maybe. I don't know. Andy's caught up in some stuff at the hospital right now. Anyhow, what's going on?"

Quill glanced around the kitchen. It was well after two o'clock. Two members of the cleanup crew were scrubbing down the sinks. The underchefs would begin to prep for dinner

147

around three. It was just too public. "Let's go into my office."

"Is this going to be a long discussion? I thought you had meetings this afternoon."

"I do. It's not that it'll take all that long . . ." Quill hesitated.

Meg's face sobered. "There isn't anything really wrong, is there?"

"I don't think so. I hope not."

She'd tricked Meg into going to the dentist when she was sixteen and Meg was twelve and their parents had been away on an overseas trip. She led Meg through the dining room to her office with the same sense of guilt she'd had then. And Meg had bitten the dentist when she discovered where Quill was really taking her.

Meg settled on the couch. Quill sat behind her desk, and she told her.

"Well," Meg said soberly. "Let's get this straight. There are two things common to these deaths. All three were getting better. And they all spent the same day here at the Inn. And you and Andy have kept this from me because . . ."

"We didn't want to upset you."

"I see," Meg said mildly. "Of course I'm upset. But I'm more upset about your need to keep me from helping figure this out than anything else."

"I'm sorry," Quill said contritely. "I really am."

"And I can't believe that Andy came to you first instead of me."

"He was trying to protect you, too, Meg."

"I think it's a lot better if we all act like adults here."

"You are absolutely right."

"It's not as if his idea is totally off the wall. I mean, look at Legionnaires' disease. Wasn't that a virus that lived in the air-conditioning system?"

"Yes. But it was an old air-conditioning system and ours is barely a year old."

"And all that fungus that lives in the walls of houses in California." Meg shuddered. "Ugh."

"It's a possibility," Quill said. "But Andy doesn't think fungus flourishes in upstate New York. Half the year is so cold. We pretty nearly covered all the bases."

"It's so *X-files*," Meg said. "And those cruise ships, the ones that they keep disinfecting and disinfecting and people still get sick. Of course, if you ask me, the likeliest cause there is the fo—" She stopped. Her eyes widened. Her face went red. She leaped off the couch and screamed, *"You think it's my food?"*

Quill had once watched Myles interrogate a maddened murderer. As the man became angrier and angrier, Myles became calmer and calmer. Quill folded her hands on top of her desk and said quietly, "It's a possibility. Fish, for example, is a frequent —"

"WHAT?"

Quill became even calmer. "I said, it's a possibil—"

149

"Why the hell are you whispering? *What's* a possibility!? That my reputation as the finest chef in the northeastern United States is blackened beyond repair?! That I'll never be able to cook in this town again? That my life is utterly, absolutely, and positively ruined? How dare anybody accuse me of tainted food?!" Meg grabbed a pillow off the couch, threw it on the floor, jumped on it, and yelled, *"Damn it!"*

"Meg. Sit down. Nobody's accused anybody of anything. And you know how much Andy loves you. You know how much I love you. This is a crisis. Please, I need your help."

"I need a drink." Meg sat down abruptly.

"It's a quarter to three in the afternoon!"

"Okay then, I want a cigarette."

"But you only smoke when —"

"I'm upset. Well, I'm upset."

Quill sighed. "Fine. Where are they this time?" Meg was actually pretty good about smoking. A pack could last her as long as six months. She'd stash the pack in various inconvenient places around the Inn, to give herself time to think it over before she grabbed one.

"I put them in your credenza. Second shelf. In the back."

Quill rolled her desk chair around and opened the credenza doors. "Oh, no!"

"What now?"

"The W.A.T.C.H. Reports are gone."

"Good. Everyone's delighted that you've come to your senses about that crazy program."

"It's not good. It's not good at all. I was counting on them to help find the saboteur."

"The who?"

Quill began pulling items out of the credenza and piling them on the floor. Sketch pads. A stack of receipts that she was supposed to keep in the tax file. Photographs of Max. A handkerchief belonging to Myles. A pack of Marlboros, which she tossed to Meg. But no W.A.T.C.H. Reports. No complaint forms.

Meg got off the couch and sat on the floor beside her. "Did you say saboteur?"

"Yes. That WhyNot that sent Kathleen round the bend? There've been more of them, apparently. Not legitimate ones, troublemaking ones. I put the W.A.T.C.H. Reports in here so I could go over them tonight. I was hoping they'd contain a clue." Quill pulled the last of the detritus out of the cupboard. Nothing. "Darn it."

"Maybe the cleaning crew threw them out?"

Quill looked at her wastebasket. It was still full. "They haven't gotten here yet. And Doreen wouldn't let anyone mess with my credenza anyway. Someone took them, Meg."

Meg sat back on her heels. "I can't say I'm surprised, can you? Everybody really hated that program, Quill. And it was set up to encourage sociopaths, if you ask me. I'd hoped that we didn't have any sociopaths working at the Inn, but you never know."

"If the saboteur took them, why not these complaint forms, too?" Quill reached in the wastebasket and pulled them out. "I threw them out. Along with all the legitimate WhyNots I had. And the notes I made on the employees. Did you know Kathleen and Mike were in the toolshed at the same time on four different occasions for an hour each?"

"No!" Meg said with a great deal of interest. "Mike the groundskeeper? And Kathleen?"

"Forget about it. I'm going to. Anyway, if the saboteur wanted to destroy any evidence of mischief making, he or she would have gone straight to the wastebasket. And those WhyNots are bright red. Hard to miss. No, somebody else took those reports." Quill scrambled to her feet. "Maybe Dina knows what happened to them. She certainly should know who came into my office."

"Hang on a minute."

Quill paused on her way out the door to the reception desk.

"It makes sense that the W.A.T.C.H. Report was going to give us some clues about the deaths of Andy's patients."

"Right."

"Maybe we're dealing with something far more serious than accidental death here, Quill. If someone took those reports, maybe it's because there was a clue to the reason those three people died. Maybe the reports point straight at the murderer."

Quill shook her head. "That doesn't make any sense at all."

"Thank you very much!"

"No! It does make sense, on the face of it. And I've thought about it. But what are the three conditions for establishing a trail to a murderer? Means, motive, and —"

Meg curled up on the couch again. "Yeah, yeah, yeah, opportunity."

"The W.A.T.C.H. Report would certainly give us opportunity, if the murders — if they *are* murders, which we don't know yet — originated, so to speak, at the Inn. I mean, all of them died in the hospital, so if some long-acting poison were administered here, we could pinpoint the opportunity with some precision. But that's a big if. We could probably get a handle on the means, too. But motive, Meg. Why would anyone want to kill three completely unrelated people? And why here?"

"The 'here's' pretty obvious. They're all in one place. And why do we have to worry about motive anyway? The police don't."

"They don't when they have a clear-cut murder case," Quill said tartly. "The police only come in when there's been an identifiable crime. And we haven't got one. Yet."

"Yes, we do," Meg said. "One that excludes food poisoning as a cause of death."

Quill ignored this unsubtle attempt at subordination. "I'll tell you what. We need a plan." She pulled out a fresh sketch pad and smoothed down the first sheet with a pleasant sense of anticipation. "The first thing we have to do is interview the families of the deceased. We can reconstruct the twelfth of June, Meg. We don't need the W.A.T.C.H. Report. Besides, there's no substitution for good old gumshoe work."

The in-house buzzer on her phone rang. She ignored it. It rang again insistently. Meg lit up a cigarette, inhaled once, coughed, and put it out. She picked up the phone.

"I'm not here!" Quill whispered.

"Yes, she's here." Meg handed her the receiver. Quill glared at her, picked the phone up, and said, "Hello? Oh! Elmer! Yes. No, no, I haven't forgotten the meeting. Well, yes, I did forget the Hundred and Thirty-third meeting, but I haven't forgotten yours. Tell the major I'll be right there." She dropped the receiver into the cradle and muttered, "Phooey."

"Too bad," Meg said cheerfully. "But the guests come first!"

"Come up to my room after dinner. We'll start the investigation then."

Meg bit her lip, ruffled her short dark hair, and looked at the ceiling. Quill's office had been part of the old kitchen in the midnineteenth century, and Meg had been very curious about it when they had purchased the Inn years ago. Meg now examined the tin ceiling as if she had never seen it before.

"What?" Quill demanded suspiciously.

"Andy's pretty sure that we've got a problem?"

"Andy's not at all sure we have a problem. We're just ruling things out."

"So we've gone from maybe having a problem to three victims of homicide?"

"*You* were the person who brought up homicide, Meg. Not me! You were the one who wigged out at the mere thought that we were going to" — Quill floundered a moment, searching for the least inflammatory word — "take a glance at the food as being a possible source of the problem. The one we don't know we have yet," she added hastily.

"Maybe we can just forget it?" Meg made a face. "Sorry. Sorry. I just — it's our whole lives, Quill. Not just my reputation, but yours, too. But we can't let it go, can we?"

"No." She turned and looked at the empty credenza. "But we could have missed it. We probably would have missed it. But dammit, somebody stole those reports." She looked wildly at the clock on her desk. "Darn it. I've got to get to that meeting."

"I wish," Elmer whispered as he stood up to pull out Quill's chair, "that you would give these meetings the attention they deserve, Quill. These people are guests at the Inn. And they're important guys."

Quill smiled in apology and patted Elmer's arm.

This gathering of the 14th Regiment was informal, so she had arranged to have a quiet corner in the Tavern Bar set aside for the major and his men. She settled herself in her chair and looked at the group. Elmer was looking harried. Major Hackmeyer was looking impatient. The five other men at the table were so clearly Civil War reenactors that they could have been wearing signs: I LIVE IN THE NINETEENTH CENTURY. Even the ones without mutton-chop whiskers or chest-length beards looked odd, and it took Quill a moment to figure out why. They didn't use shampoo. They used soap to wash their hair. And pomade to keep it under control. The air was heavy with the scent of bay rum and coconut oil. The clean-shaven ones had the slight nicks and cuts that meant they'd used a straight razor. Major Hackmeyer introduced his captain, the man who was going to play the leader of the Rebel army, his gunnery sergeant, his stores sergeant, and the cavalry officer. They all looked incredibly fit, as if they'd worked out in gyms for years.

"Horses?" Quill said intelligently when she was introduced to the Cavalry captain. "You're going to ride?"

"Nimrod Company didn't get up this far north on foot," Major Hackmeyer said.

"As a matter of fact, I didn't know that the War had gotten this far north," Quill said. "I don't recall a lot of Civil War history, but I thought that the northern action was pretty much limited to Pennsylvania. And how in the world did the Southerners get up here?"

Sergeant Fetterman, the supply man, launched into an enthusiastic lecture on the fate of a small company of deserters from the Battle at Gettysburg, who'd been trying to reach Canada and leave the War Between the States behind them permanently. The skirmish was accidental; all of the men from Nimrod Company had been recruited from Tompkins County, and they'd been home on leave when reports of the Rebel band reached them.

"They spotted the Rebel deserters near the Gorge," Fetterman said. "Just south of that gazebo you had built there, Quill. The men of Nimrod Company were down by the train station, ready to ship out to Camp Curtis in Pennsylvania. Rufus Stottle, that's your wife's great great-whatever cousin, Mayor, was the one that sounded the alarm."

"And where was General C. C. Hemlock in all of this?" Quill asked.

"That old fart," the stores sergeant said. "He got off his backside long enough to hornswoggle Secretary of War Stanton into getting him a commission, and that was about it. Far as we can tell, old Hemmy spent all four years of the war holed up right here at the Inn at Hemlock Falls. That was when it was his house, ma'am, as you may remember."

"Well, yes, I do. I mean, from the history of the Inn that our librarian researched for us."

"But he wasn't even here at the time of the skirmish. He was off in Saratoga Springs, taking the cure." Fetterman snorted derisively. "Cure for booze, from all accounts."

Elmer shook out his handkerchief and wiped his forehead unhappily. Quill patted his hand reassuringly. "Gentlemen," she said in her most diplomatic tones, "there's no need at all to go into the, um, background of poor General Hemlock, is there? You know that some of his descendants," Elmer coughed heavily, "still live here, and we wouldn't want to bring up any history irrelevant to the cause."

"The Fourteenth is committed to authentic reenactments," Captain Coolidge — at least Quill supposed she would have to call him captain, since everybody else did — said heavily. "The old coot wasn't there and we're not going to pretend he was."

Elmer's lugubrious expression lightened considerably.

"Wonderful," Quill said sincerely. "Now, what can we at the Inn do for you?"

"I'd like the entire staff dressed in period costume," Major Hackmeyer said. It was a clear command, not a request.

"Yes?" Quill said, not sure she'd heard him properly.

"The mayor here pointed out that the time's a bit short to get the outfits made for your employees, so I'm having some things shipped up for you tomorrow."

Elmer's gaze was pleading.

"You mean *my* staff?" Quill realized after a moment that her mouth was open. So she shut it.

"Of course, your staff. Who else did you think

I meant?" Major Hackmeyer sank his chin to his chest and looked annoyed and stern. Quill felt like a subaltern caught sleeping at his post. Why had she thought this man had a certain raffish charm? She looked around the table; all five of his men were sitting relaxed, but alert, as if ready to spring to their feet at a shout of "Ten-hut!" It was like a cult. Elmer, on the other hand, looked his normal self; his round pink face was earnestly cheerful and his forehead glistened slightly with sweat.

"We'll have at least thirty employees here, Major Hackmeyer, between the wait staff and the kitchen and the housekeeping . . . that's a lot of costumes."

"I'll need a list of sizes, of course," Major Hackmeyer said. "See that you hand that to Sergeant Wilson. He's in charge of uniforms."

"Ma'am." Sergeant Wilson touched his finger to his forehead in a semi-salute.

"Now, at the time of the skirmish," Fetterman said smoothly, "Mrs. Hemlock was at home in the big house. She was quite a brave woman . . ."

"Unlike that old horse thief Hemmy," Wilson said.

"And she raced out of the house with her husband's musket. She fired onto the troops . . ."

"And hit Major Nimrod, unfortunately," Wilson added. "But it was only a flesh wound . . ."

"In a misguided attempt to support our brave boys in blue." This was Coolidge's contribution.

It was as if these men were a single organism. Quill wondered what Dina would say about men who behaved like copepods. Wilson added, "After the skirmish — it lasted a matter of twenty minutes or so — the Rebels escaped by dashing down to Hemlock Gorge, boarding a flat-bottomed boat that was kept there by the big house . . ."

"That's your place, Miss Quilliam," Fetterman said helpfully.

"And disappeared, never to be seen again. The boat was never recovered." Wilson sat back.

"My goodness," Quill said.

"If you would," Sergeant Wilson said winningly, "we'd like you to play the part of Mrs. Hemlock."

"Never mind bending a bit of history when there's a beautiful woman involved," Captain Coolidge said with a smile.

"Bending?"

"Mrs. Hemlock was sixty-five and weighed in at well over two hundred pounds," Sergeant Fetterman said. "I don't know, Wilson. Miss Quilliam's a good-looking woman, and that's a fact, but historical events are historical events. Maybe we should just assign her the part of the madam . . ."

"The madam?" Quill said.

"In a town the size of Hemlock Falls, there wasn't a lot for Bessie Forrester to do except on Saturday nights," Wilson said. "She acted as

Mrs. Hemlock's housekeeper the other six days of the week. And she was a looker, too."

"I'll tell you what I think," Quill said firmly. "I think I'll have a great deal to do without either waving a musket or . . . whatever. And I think it would be a genuinely chivalrous gesture if you would invite Mrs. Henry to take the part of Mrs. Hemmy, I mean Hemlock. She is, after all, a direct descendant of C.C."

"True enough, sir," Fetterman said to Hackmeyer. "Do we have your permission to proceed?"

"Yuh," Hackmeyer said, making Quill think of John Wayne in *The Searchers*. "And, Mayor, do you think the little woman will agree?"

"I do, sir," Elmer said. "She'll be pleased as . . . well, she'll be pleased."

"You're kidding me," Meg said. "No, you're not kidding me. Costumes?"

Quill held her hand up, as if to take the oath. They were curled comfortably on her couch. The night was warm — a good omen for the week to come — and the French doors were open to the air. "I didn't tell you about the horses, either."

"The horses?"

"Hackmeyer's bringing in twenty horses by train. He said it wasn't any more of a hassle than shipping a team of polo ponies around the country."

"Horses? Where is he going to keep them?"

Quill leaned her head back against the couch. "I have no idea. Somebody mentioned the football field. Hackmeyer brings his own portable fencing, so all he needs is a big field."

"Maybe he'll want to buy this Inn after this is all over," Meg said gloomily. "It sounds as if he's got money to throw around."

"Elmer's absolutely beside himself, wanting to impress him, poor old sweetie. He's called another Chamber of Commerce meeting tomorrow." Quill slumped against the back of the couch. "I'm going to go mad."

"Another meeting? Poor Quill."

"It's to keep everyone current."

"No, it's not. It's so that somebody else will tell Adela our brave boys in blue lost the Battle of Hemlock Falls."

"Somebody's bound to," Quill said. "My money's on Carol Ann Spinoza. She's certainly mean enough."

"Maybe you should tell Adela, Quill."

"No. I'm officially investigating our new case. I think you should tell."

"I would," Meg said with every appearance of frankness, "but I'm really really busy tomorrow. I have that reception for the filmmakers and I'm sitting down with Arlo Fetterman, to go over the menu for the banquet. Actually, you're busy tomorrow, too. How are we going to find the time to track the movements of Andy's patients?" Abruptly, Meg got up and moved restlessly about the room. Max, who had been lying belly-up on Quill's Berber carpeting, got up and followed her. "I don't have a good feeling about any of this."

"We're going to come out of this just fine, Meg."

She stopped, her back to Quill. "How do you know that?"

"I don't know that, of course. But we'll find out." Quill propped her feet onto the old oak chest she used as a coffee table. "I'm going to talk to Nadine Nickerson's family first thing tomorrow, then I'm going to make a call on Mrs. Bellini, which I should have done by now anyway, and then I'm going over to see Harland Peterson. Derwent was his brother. I should be back before lunch."

"It certainly would be easier if we knew who stole those reports. You asked Dina who was around the foyer today?"

"I asked Devora. She just said, 'Practically everybody.' Dina would have reeled off names and times. She's good at that kind of thing."

"Then why wasn't she on the job?"

"She wasn't there a lot of the time. She spent most of the day collecting the saboteur's WhyNots. Oh, hell, Meg! The WhyNots!" Quill clutched her hair. "Oh, darn it. I completely forgot about the saboteur."

"Now that you've ditched that program, maybe the saboteur will forget about sabotaging. We can certainly forget it, can't we?" Meg, frowning, turned to face her. "We don't have enough time to do any of this before the weekend, Quill. The WhyNots will keep, won't they?"

Quill shook her head. "No. We absolutely have to find out who's sending them before the rest of the battalion shows up on Friday. I didn't tell you about my conversation with Davey Kiddermeister. I told Dina to leave them on my desk. I'd better go get them and then we can talk about it." She got to her feet and was halfway out the door before an idea hit her. "Do you know what? We can turn that whole sabotage thing over to Doreen. She'll get to the bottom of it."

Meg's frown lightened. "There's a good idea. Shall I give her a call?"

"Yes. I wanted to talk with her about another matter, too. Ask her if she can get in early to-morrow morning."

"Tomorrow's Wednesday. Wednesday is her day off."

"I thought today was her day off. I haven't seen her at all." Quill paused, her hand on the doorknob. "Not since Saturday morning, as a matter of fact."

"Wednesdays," Meg said patiently. "She had Tuesdays off for ten years until last year and now it's Wednesdays."

It was Quill's turn to frown. "Maybe I'll drop over to her house tomorrow morning, then." She closed the door behind her and walked down the hall to the staircase. Her suite was on the third floor at the north end of the building. There was only one guest up here at the moment, and the corridor was quiet. The wall sconces were always lit at night, and their soft glow intensified the night's hush.

Quill took the steps rapidly. Halfway down, she stopped in midstride.

She had set the June twelfth W.A.T.C.H. Report aside. It had not been with the others. Where had she stuffed it? she thought furiously. She'd shoved it in her top drawer, the one with all her charcoal pencils.

Relieved, she continued down the stairs.

It was later than she'd thought. The foyer lighting had been turned down and the big entrance door was closed. The dining room was totally dark, except for the dim glow of the exit sign over the kitchen doors. In a sudden reaction to the silence, Quill turned the foyer lights on full. The Inn was never completely silent; it was an old building, with thick plaster and lathe walls, so that even if guests had the televisions on in their rooms full blast, the noise never penetrated farther than the room itself, but the building's joints groaned and settled, and there was always at least the whisper of the various pieces of equipment that kept the Inn alive and running. But the lack of people noise, the hum of conversation, the thud of footsteps left a spooky sort of void. The mahogany reception desk, more than waist-high, seemed to leer at her.

Quill unlocked her office door and flipped the lights on. The stack of red WhyNots was on her desk. The June twelfth report was in her upper drawer. She took two strides toward them and dropped like a stone into water.

CHAPTER 6

She came to full consciousness in a hospital bed. She knew it was a hospital bed because she was propped up, the walls were a revolting celery green, and the whole place smelled like Betadine and something much less pleasant. Somebody was talking. After a fuddled moment, Quill realized she was talking. After a second fuddled moment, she knew she had no idea what she was saying, but she recognized the people she was talking to. Meg, Doreen, Andy, and Davey Kiddermeister in full sheriff's uniform, including his hat.

"Hi," Quill said. And tried to sit up.

The pain in the back of her skull was incredible. It shot up from the nape of her neck and rushed to the top of her head. The room dimmed, turned red, and she fell back against the pillow.

"Ugh," she said. The pain subsided into a dull pounding. It made her teeth hurt.

"Look at that," Doreen said proudly. "She's smilin'."

Quill blinked hard and brought Doreen into focus. Her beady black eyes were anxious. Her gray hair sprang out in a wild halo around her wrinkled face. There was something different about her. She couldn't quite pin it down. Doreen took Quill's hand gently and patted it. "You're all right, then, missy."

"Looks more like a grimace of pain to me," Meg said cheerily. "Is that a smile or a grimace, Quill?" Meg was pale, but steady. She smoothed Quill's hair back with a hand that was cold and trembled slightly. "You shouldn't try to sit up, sweetie. And don't try to talk anymore. Davey can wait to get the rest of it."

If she kept her head very still, it hardly hurt at all. Quill stared straight ahead, at a really gruesome photograph of a clown with a fistful of multicolored balloons. She swallowed hard.

"She's gonna barf," Doreen announced loudly. "Get the pan there, Meg."

"I'm fine," Quill said. "Really." She turned her head slowly. "What happened?"

"You were telling us what happened." Davey edged in between Meg and Doreen. Doreen jabbed him with her elbow and he stepped back. He peered over Doreen's frizzy head and added, "You thought someone might have been hiding beneath the reception desk."

Gingerly, Quill felt the back of her head. She shrieked, "No!"

"Oh, Quill!" Tears began to run down Meg's cheeks. "Don't make her remember any more, Davey. What happened was horrible. Leave her alone!"

"It's your hair, is that right?" Andy hooked the clipboard he'd been holding to the foot of the bed. "We only shaved a small patch, Quill."

Quill ran her hand slowly up the back of her neck.

"When you wear it down, you won't even notice." He smiled at her.

Quill glared at him. "I thought you had to have a person's permission to do that."

"You're worried about your hair?" Meg shouted. "Oh. Fine. Someone whacks you on the back of the head, you're unconscious forever, and you're worried about your hair?"

Quill winced.

"Loud noises are going to bother you for a while." Andy rubbed Meg's shoulder affectionately. "But you're going to live, Quill. No doubt about that."

Breathing hurt her head, too, but she was damned if she was going to let everyone know. "So what happened?"

"You were telling us what happened," Doreen said. "Said you barged on into your office about eleven o'clock last night and that there was something funny about the place. Said you thought someone'd been hiding in that big old desk and jumped out and whacked you over the head. You were just about to tell us who you thought it might be when all of a sudden you said 'Hi' like you just woke up and then you started hollering about your hair."

"Anybody would be hollering about their hair

169

if they'd been shaved bald," Quill said reasonably. "And I did just wake up."

"You been talking right along," Doreen said stubbornly.

"Not right along," Meg corrected her. "She didn't come to until she was in the ambulance. She wasn't saying a word when I came down and found her on the office floor. She looked like she was dead."

"I did? I came here in an ambulance?"

"You don't recall?"

Quill tried to sit up again. If pain were like hurricanes, she'd rate it as a Category 3. "I'd like to get up, please."

Meg turned to Andy. "Is it okay? Is it okay if she gets up?"

Andy put his cool fingers on her wrist. "I think so. You must have a howler of a headache, though."

Quill didn't dignify this with an answer. Andy should know precisely how she felt; he was her doctor. Doreen pressed the buttons on the bedrails and the top half of the bed rose to a vertical position, taking Quill with it. The room tipped a bit, but settled down after a moment. She wished the same were true of her stomach.

"If you're nauseated, we can give you something for that." Andy reached out to a chrome cart near the foot of the bed and selected a small white paper cup and a water bottle with a straw in it.

170

Quill swallowed the pill he handed her and asked, "Could I have an aspirin, as well?"

"Nothing for the pain. Not for twenty-four hours. I'm sorry, Quill. Coumadin, to make sure we aren't going to get any clots, and the antinausea meds. That's about it."

She swung her legs over the side of the bed and looked at her feet in surprise. She was in a hospital gown. "Wow. What happened to my clothes?"

"Took 'em off," Doreen said with relish. "On account of all the blood. That nice linen shirt's never goin' to be the same again, I'll tell you that. Think I can get it out of the chinos, though."

"Well, I can't leave here in a hospital gown," Quill said reasonably. "I'm going to need some clothes."

"You can't leave here at all," Meg said with asperity. "Not for twenty-four hours at least. Isn't that right, Andy?"

"We wouldn't advise it."

"Then I guess I'll have to walk down Main Street in this thing," Quill said irritably. She stood all the way up. The walls tilted. She sat down again. "I want to go home." She swung her legs back onto the bed. "In a bit."

Doreen covered her legs with the light hospital sheet. Quill stared at the clown until the walls stopped rotating. "Does anyone know what happened?"

"This is very alarming," Meg announced.

171

"Andy, what's going on? I mean she was making perfect sense by the time we got to the hospital."

"She wasn't really conscious then, Meg. This is a form of retrograde amnesia. And she's received a moderately severe blow to the head. Have you ever come out of an anesthetic, aware that you'd been talking?"

"You did when you had your wisdom teeth out," Quill said without turning to look at either one of them. "You were chattering away like a Malaysian parrot. And then you bit the orthodontist."

"I have no recollection of biting the orthodontist. And I was twelve."

"There you are," Quill said smugly. "I have no recollection of telling you anything about my office or the reception desk."

"What's the last thing you do remember, Quill?" Davey removed his hat. He held it awkwardly in his left hand, then set it on Quill's feet and took his notebook from his shirt pocket.

Quill made a determined effort to capture her last clear memory. "Max."

"Max? Oh. Your dog." Davey's face closed. Almost everyone in town knew Max, and a fair number of people found him an annoyance.

"Max was following Meg around my room. Then I remembered that Dina had collected those WhyNots and left them on my desk. So I went downstairs to get them. The Exit sign," she added vaguely, "I remember the Exit sign."

"Nothing about seeing anyone behind the receptionist desk?"

Quill shook her head and was immediately sorry.

Davey closed his notebook and slipped it back into his pocket. "What d'ya think, Doc? She was remembering right along before she came to."

Andy shrugged. "It depends. Full memory comes back in about fifty percent of the cases."

Davey looked at Meg. "You find those WhyNots in the office? Did you bring them with you?"

"I was a little too busy trying to save my sister."

Davey retrieved his hat. "Dina says she put a whole stack of 'em on Quill's desk. Guess I'd better get on up to the Inn and check them out. You don't mind, do you, Quill?"

Quill didn't try to shake her head. "No. But I'll tell you what I will mind, Davey. And that's if you try and talk Dina into giving you the list of the reenactors."

"You remember that right enough." Davey smiled a little. "Already tried that."

Quill closed her eyes. She felt very cross.

"Wouldn't give it to me, either!"

When she opened her eyes again, she was aware some time had passed. The light coming in the window was at a high-noon slant and Betty Peterson was shaking her shoulder. "Yes!" Quill said. "What is it?"

"Do you always wake up like that?" Betty, dressed in her hospital whites, stuck a thermometer in her ear and wrapped a blood pressure cuff over her right arm. "Sorry to get you up, but we have to wake you every few hours and get your vitals."

Quill was aware of feeling better. She pushed herself up. "Wake up like what?"

"You're pretty alert. About half of our patients sleep very heavily and you have to set a bomb off in their ear to get them up and you never know if they're in a coma or if it's just a normal sleeping pattern. They're the owls. They take forever to wind down, and when they do, they crash. It's easier with patients like you. Larks. They fall asleep early and wake up early." She held the thermometer up to the light, looked at the blood pressure gauge, and said, "Good. All you slender people have low blood pressure and no body temperature at all." She patted her own ample hip with a sigh.

"Which was your great-uncle? An owl or a lark?"

"Derwent? The poor soul that just passed?"

"Yes."

"Lark. But almost all our elderly are light sleepers. Part of the aging process."

"I'm sorry he, um, passed."

"Well, he had a good full life," Betty said cheerily. "Although I have to say we didn't expect it to be his heart."

"Did Dr. Bishop speak to the family at all?"

"Oh, Quill! You're such a tactful person. Yes, Andy spoke to the family. Said that he wasn't happy with the recoding of Uncle Derwent's death as a heart attack even though the EEG showed a garden-variety infarct. But that's Andy."

"What do you mean, 'that's Andy'?"

"He's just the most thorough doctor this town's ever had, that's all." Betty scribbled on the chart clipped to the foot of the bed. "Now you just go right back to sleep, Quill. We're going to take you down for another CAT scan later in the afternoon. But until then you just snooze away."

"I had a CAT scan?"

"Early this morning. Just as soon as he got you shaved and stitched up."

Quill put her hand at the back of her neck and closed her eyes to better assess her baldness.

When she woke up again, Myles was seated in the chair next to her bed, long legs stretched out in front of him.

"Hey!" she said.

He just looked at her for a long moment, smiling faintly. Then he leaned over and stroked her cheek with one finger. She wound her arms around his neck and kissed him hard. He tasted of coffee and toothpaste. His cheek was rough under her hand. She sank back onto the pillows, holding his hand tightly in her own. "I'm so glad to see you. But . . ."

"I'm not back for long. And no, I didn't come rushing in to save you. I have to go to DC for a few days. Besides, you'd hate that."

"I would," she agreed. "I don't need saving." She tightened her grip. "But I'm very very glad you're here. Did Meg call you?"

"Yes."

"Then you're dissimulating. You swapped assignments with somebody, I'll bet."

He shrugged a little. "I was spending most of my time in an office poring over satellite pictures. And it didn't look as if a field assignment was coming along before September. So Davey said someone hit you over the head."

Quill felt the back of her neck. She was vaguely aware of having felt the back of her neck before. The shaved part was smooth and there was a fat gauze bandage in the middle. "I guess somebody did. I don't remember a thing. It's the weirdest sensation, Myles. As if a huge black curtain dropped right over my head." She looked up at him. "Can you get me out of here? I want to go home."

"Tomorrow. You were hit on the head before, and Andy just wants to be thorough."

"That was years ago. I feel fine now. As a matter of fact, I don't think I can stand being in this stupid bed another minute."

Myles put his arm around her and she eased to her feet. The room was steady. The floor was solid. Her hospital gown, on the other hand, was drafty and she clutched it with an exclamation of annoyance. "I'd appreciate it if I could have some clothes. Do you think somebody could bring me some? Just jeans and a T-shirt. Perhaps Doreen . . ." There was something different about Doreen. Quill shook her head to clear it, which was a mistake. "You know what?" she said crossly. "Half the Zen of being a patient is having to wear hospital gowns. It makes you feel as if you ought to feel ill." She pushed Myles's arm gently away and began to walk around the room. It felt odd, as if she'd just removed a pair of roller skates. "Oh, dear," she said, and was suddenly very sick. Myles grabbed the bedpan, patted her back, and then brought her a cold washcloth.

· She got back into bed with a sigh. "Okay then, tomorrow."

Quill woke with a jerk that made her head throb. The room was dark, except for the glow of lights from the hall. Someone had been there, leaning over her bed. Myles? Meg? She glanced at the chair next to her bed. Someone had placed a stack of clothes on it, neatly folded. The clock on the wall said two in the morning. Had the night nurse been in to take her vital signs? No; when she'd been wheeled down to the x-ray room for the CAT scan, they'd told her that her blood pressure and temperature had been normal the last three times they'd checked and enough was enough. Whoever it was, was gone.

If there had been anyone there at all.

And there was something else. Just before she'd been hit. The smell of garlic. And there was the smell of garlic now.

She was starving to death; that was half the problem.

She lay back with a sigh. She felt fine, except for the headache, which (in hurricane terms) was reduced to a Category 1. And if it was two o'clock in the morning, which meant more than twenty-four hours had passed since she'd been whacked on the head, she could have aspirin. She also needed the bathroom.

Quill snapped on the light and blinked in the sudden glare. She walked to the bathroom, feeling fine. She returned from the bathroom, feeling fine. She picked up her clothes, set them on the bed, and sat there, wide awake.

Quill couldn't think of one single person in her life who would welcome a phone call at two in the morning. She poked at the television clicker. A sign appeared on the screen offering the service of HospHem cable TV, for a mere three dollars and seventy-five cents a day. That slogan had Harvey Bozzel written all over it. ("Sounds a lot like a cough, Harvey." "It's good, huh? I mean, what do most patients do anyhow? Cough, right? I'd like to think this is one of my better campaigns.") She pulled aside the vertical blinds at the window and looked out: a fine summer's night; the bright moon was half-full, and a slight summer breeze stirred the poplars around the

178

high school athletic field. And the field was full of . . . horses. Warrender had made good on his promise. Quill watched the horses with a great deal of interest. She knew more about cows than she wanted to, after the visit of the Texas Longhorn Association to the Inn several years ago, but she knew nothing about horses.

They seemed to have an even more boring life than cows. Portable round pens were spaced at twenty-foot intervals around the field and each pen contained two or three. Most stood with their heads down, dozing. One ambled over to a bucket and seemed to drink. Another one nosed a pile of hay.

She let the blinds fall back into place. She picked up the stack of her clothes: a worn pair of size 6 Ralph Lauren jeans, an old T-shirt that she slept in when Myles wasn't around, a pair of sneakers, and bright yellow socks. Quill didn't own any socks except for two pairs of white athletic socks she'd bought when she'd vowed to get fit at the local gym. So Meg had brought her clothes. And the bright yellow meant Meg, at least, was feeling cheerful.

Her purse was there, too. Quill pulled out her hairbrush and some lip gloss. If there was soap in the shower, she was all set.

Twenty minutes later, she sat on the edge of her bed, bathed, dressed, hair (awkwardly) brushed, and more wide awake than ever. Absently, she folded the hospital gown and placed it on the pillow.

That was what had been odd about Doreen. She'd been wearing a hospital gown.

Quill froze.

She dove into her purse and found her cell phone. She keyed Andy's number and waited impatiently through three rings.

Then, "Dr. Bishop."

"Hi, Andy. It's me, Quill."

He paused. "Well, Quill. You're awake."

Quill heard a brief scuffle, and then her sister's voice, hazy with sleep, "Quill? Are you all right?"

"I'm fine. I'm calling about Doreen."

"You're fine? You're not unconscious or anything?"

Quill bit back exasperation. Betty Peterson would have pegged her sister as an owl. It took her forever to wake up. "If I were unconscious, I wouldn't be on the cell phone, would I?"

"You're at the hospital?"

"Of course I'm at the hospital. Give the phone to Andy, would you? I want to ask him about Doreen."

Meg put her hand over the receiver. When she came back on the line, she said reasonably, "It's two-thirty in the morning."

"I'm calling about Doreen. Meg, she was in a hospital gown. Just tell me why she was in a hospital gown and I'll hang up and let you go back to sleep."

"Andy says —"

"Andy won't talk to me if Doreen's his patient. He can't stop you from talking to me, though. All of this extra concern about his elderly patients is suddenly making sense to me. His refusal to go out of town because 'something's come up' makes sense to me, too. I want to know what's going on, Meg."

"We were going to tell you tomorrow."

"That's not an answer."

"I just *hate* it when you get like this. You're like Max with a bone."

Quill didn't say anything. Meg sighed heavily. "I didn't know, either. She didn't want anybody to know. Well, Stoke knows, because he's her husband, and he's the one that found it."

Quill's stomach knotted. "Found what?"

"A lump in her breast. This was about two weeks ago, I guess. What? Andy says yes, it was two weeks ago. They went to some dork in Syracuse — well, he is a dork, Andy, and you saw what he did to her! Who slammed her into the hospital and performed a lumpectomy."

"Why Syracuse?" Quill said. She found, to her surprise, that she was crying. "It doesn't matter. I know why. That generation says the word 'cancer' in a whisper. It's still something to be ashamed of. Oh, my. Oh, my, Meg."

"I know." Meg, too, was crying. She blew her nose. Quill pulled the receiver away from her ear. Andy was right about loud noises.

"So what's the prognosis?"

"Andy says it's very good, depending. She had a three-centimeter Stage Two invasive ductile carcinoma."

"I have no idea what any of that means," Quill said. "Depending on what?"

"The lumpectomy didn't get it all. Andy wants her to have the breast removed. She's thinking about it."

"Well, she's not going to think about it very long," Quill said indignantly. "Of course she should have the breast off. What can she be thinking of? Where is she? Is she still here, in the hospital?"

"She was discharged yesterday afternoon. Andy had her in for a biopsy and a complete physical."

"I want to see her."

"If she knows you know, she won't be at the hospital to visit you. I tried to talk to her about it and she practically took my head off. She is one pissed-off person, Quill. Andy says that's normal in a cancer patient, and it's a lot better than depression. She's planning on coming in to work tomorrow."

"You're kidding. No. You're not kidding. Shoot."

"Andy says don't worry."

Quill was getting very tired of 'Andy says.' Of course, it was a lot better than the weeks of 'Andy's an idiot.' Meg just didn't seem to be able to find a middle path.

"Quill?"

"I'm still here."

"It's now three o'clock in the morning. I'm going back to bed."

"Okay."

182

"I'll be up first thing tomorrow to see you. Right after breakfast. Andy thinks you might be able to go home in the afternoon."

"I'm ready to go home now," Quill said truthfully.

"Very funny. I'll see you in the morning."

Quill put the cell phone back into her purse, made the bed, and wondered whether she should leave the nurses a thank-you note. She was pretty sure that patients didn't tip nurses, although with the amount of money they made, they would probably appreciate it. But it wouldn't do just to walk out. There was a notepad and a ballpoint pen by the phone. She drew a smiling Quill waving goodbye, scribbled "Thanks!" underneath it, and scrawled "Quilliam" at the bottom. Then she picked up her purse and pushed the door to the corridor farther open.

CHAPTER 7

"You can't just walk out of the hospital!" Meg shrieked. She flung cooked spinach into the colander in the sink and turned the water on full blast. Friday mornings Eggs Florentine was on the menu.

"I don't see why not . . . Ow, Doreen. That hurts!" Quill wriggled away from her housekeeper's fingers in her hair. She sat in the rocker near the fireplace. Mike the groundskeeper had replaced the straggly coreopsis with equally messy Michaelmas daisies.

"There's dried blood all over you. And you can't wash it for another two days when the stitches come outa your skull." Doreen gave her hair a final tug. "That's most of it."

"Thanks," Quill said dubiously. She felt the nape of her neck. There was an almighty bruise under the bandage. She turned and squinted up at Doreen. "I suppose you'd know all about stitches."

Doreen's birdlike eye was evasive. "What'd you do? Walk home last night in the dark?"

"It was a beautiful night. I stopped and watched the horses." Quill reached out and folded Doreen's skinny hand into her own. "Can we go into your office for a minute?"

"I got work to do!"

"It's only seven o'clock in the morning. There's time."

Doreen worked her lips. "You're the boss," she said angrily.

Quill led the way to the small room off the kitchen where Doreen kept her linen count and the maids' time cards. She sat Doreen down in front of her desk, and then leaned against the wall opposite.

Quill had never thought of Doreen as elderly. Her spirit was too vital, her energy level too high. Even now, after what must have been a harrowing experience, her back was straight, her gaze fiercely proud. But she'd lost weight. And in the oddest way, she seemed to occupy less space.

"I suppose you're going to fire me," she said. Her lip stuck out at a belligerent angle.

Quill could have wept. Instead she said cheerfully, "Do you remember when you came to work at the Inn, ten years ago?"

She tilted her head suspiciously. "Hm."

"You showed up at the back door in blue pedal pushers, a red checked gingham shirt, and a bandanna tied around your head. You were carrying a black plastic leather purse. You'd cut holes in the sides of your tennis shoes because of your corns."

"I don't have that purse anymore," Doreen

said. "Handle tore off and I couldn't fix it with my glue gun. Tennis shoes just wore out." She grinned. "Still got the corns."

"You said, 'My name's Doreen Muxworthy and I hear you got a job for a maid. Well, I'm it.' "

"And you said you couldn't pay me much." Doreen thought about this for a moment. "You were right."

"Meg was the greatest chef on the Eastern Seaboard. But I knew nothing about running an Inn."

"Didn't stop you, though," Doreen said grudgingly. "You would have learned a lot faster without those darn courses you're always taking."

"I can't count the number of times we would have gone toes up if it hadn't been for you. I can't count the times you've . . ." Quill searched desperately for exactly the right thing to say. ". . . put things into order. You're a genius at it, Doreen. Housekeeping. Not just keeping the rooms clean and the towels counted and the damn toilets scrubbed. Any halfway energetic person can do that. You sort of keep the universe in order."

Doreen looked slightly alarmed. Quill leaned over and put her arms around her. "You're just like those hero majors in war movies. While the brass back at HQ dither about what to do, you just go on in and take the hill. And what would I or Meg or John do without you?"

Doreen sniffed in a pleased way.

"Now. About this lump."

Doreen rubbed her left breast, and then dropped her hand to her lap. "Fella in Syracuse took it out," she said.

"I wish I'd been there with you."

She shrugged. "You wouldn't believe how easy they take it these days. Stoke and I went in, they put me out, they took that sucker out, and I went on home. Slept a bit the next day but I was back on the job by Saturday. Piece of cake."

"And now what?"

"I was supposed to go get radiated. Like a chicken." She snorted. "Then the fella that took it out called back and said I had to go back and have more of it taken out." She scowled. "But I didn't like the job he did, and neither did Stoke. It's all crooked."

"May I see?"

Doreen unbuttoned the top half of her blouse and pulled it open. Half her left breast was gone. A long, ugly wound spiraled up the remaining half of her breast. The tissue itself was pulled together like a badly stitched pillow.

Quill pinched her hip hard, to hold back sudden tears. "Well, that's a hell of a note," she said. "Where did this guy learn to cut? At the butcher shop?" She dropped a kiss on Doreen's head.

Doreen peered down at the wound. "I'm seventy-three," she said. "I suppose it doesn't matter."

"Of course it matters." Quill buttoned Doreen's shirt up. "Did you talk to Andy about a mastectomy?"

Doreen's eyes were bright with unshed tears. She blinked rapidly two or three times. "There," she said. "We're both cryin'. Happy now?"

"What's going to make us all happier — because I'm perfectly happy, except for this bruise on my head — is for you to go back and have another little surgery. I've seen the scars from mastectomies, Doreen, and honestly, if it's done properly, and we'll make sure it is this time, it's a nice neat little line that gets fainter and fainter. And if you want another lumpectomy, we can make sure that your breast doesn't look so awful."

"It is awful, isn't it?"

"It's horrible," Quill said promptly. "No wonder you feel as if you've been sideswiped and suckered. It is a gruesome, miserable scar but it can be fixed. I promise."

"I thought so," Doreen said. "I could have done a better job with my Exacto knife."

Doreen was perfectly capable of removing a lump from any part of her body with an Exacto knife. Quill shuddered. "So. What do you think?"

"I don't think I want to get radiated. But if I don't get radiated, I got to have this whole thing off. Or it might come back." For a brief, terrifying moment, her face changed with fear.

"You have lots of sick leave," Quill said. "More than two months. So you can get radiation treatments if you like. On the other hand, if you have a mastectomy, Andy says you'll be back to work in a week." Andy's actual words had been "I won't be able to keep her down for more than week," but she figured that was moot. "What does Stoke think?"

Doreen's face softened. "That old fool. Says I can have both of 'em off and he'll take me to Florida and buy me a bikini with fake boobs in the top. Says if I get radiated, he'll let me beat him at gin rummy while they're zapping me. *He* doesn't give a darn either way."

"You haven't asked me what I think. I think that I need you back here as soon as possible. So I'd vote for the mastectomy."

"Well." Doreen gave a gusty, martyred sigh. "Seein' as how you're hard put to get along without me here, I guess I get the dumb thing off."

"Thank god. I mean, whatever you like. When do you think you'd go in?"

"Andy says the sooner the better. Doctors!" she snorted. "They're just after your money, you know. Faster you get some poor soul in, the faster they get paid."

"Yes," Quill said, wondering how virulent the remaining tumor was. She drew a shaky breath. "Monday, then. That gives us two days. I hope you're up to it."

Doreen eyed her in much the same way a buzzard would eye a dead rodent. "I'd like to see the thing I'm not up to, missy. What is it?"

"It's not pretty," Quill admitted. "I'm going to need to give you a little background first."

"So. We got another case. It's about that whack on your head."

"I don't think this problem has to do with whomever hit me on the head. The WhyNots were still in the office when Davey went to look."

Doreen scratched her jaw.

"Sorry, I'm starting in the middle. You know that somebody's been leaving fake WhyNots around the Inn."

"Yeah. As a matter of fact, there was a fake one about me! I swear to goodness I never whacked that little kid. Now I got to say, if I hadn't thought twice about it, I would have whacked that kid but —"

"Just a minute, Doreen. I asked Dina to collect all of them she could find. There were six altogether, I guess. Some of the staff threw the nastier ones out, so we don't have a lot of hard evidence. But we need to find out who's behind them."

"Gotcha." Doreen ruminated a bit. "Any idea how to go about it? I mean, I got a few ideas, but I'd better hear yours first."

"First, go down to the sheriff's office and take a look at all of them. One was sent to the sheriff's office, so you'll want to ask Davey for that one as well. See if there's any similarity in handwriting. And then — somehow, Doreen, you'll need to get samples of everyone's handwriting to compare them to the originals. That's almost fifty people, if you exclude you, me, Meg, and John. If I went around asking for people's handwriting, the person behind this —"

"The perp," Doreen said in a professional way. "That's the guilty party."

"Yes. It'd be as easy as anything to disguise one's handwriting. If you could come up with one of your inventive ideas to get everyone to write something down — a contest perhaps? I don't know." Quill rubbed her head a little pathetically. "Anyway, we'll have a reasonable sort of evidence."

"Got it." Doreen got to her feet. "You want progress reports and that?"

"Sure." Quill smiled at her. "But watch yourself. It might be dangerous."

CHAPTER 8

"As soon as I said it, I realized it could be true. What if it is dangerous?" Quill bit her thumb in distress. Myles rubbed his jaw. He'd shown up at the Inn minutes after Meg had called him to tell him not to bother to go to the hospital; Quill had staged an escape. She'd drawn him outside to the gazebo in case he was going to raise his voice. "I couldn't stand it if anything happened to Doreen."

Myles looked at the Falls and Quill followed his glance. The sound of the rushing water always calmed her, as it calmed her now. She gazed up at the sky. The sun was pale today, veiled by a light skein of gray. It would rain later. Quill hoped that the five-acre meadow wouldn't get too muddy for the reenactors. The rest of them were coming in today. If they were rained out, there wouldn't be enough room at the Inn for them all. She'd have to give the Marriott a call to see what backup space could be provided. "Oh, for Pete's sake. I don't have time for any of this."

Myles sat up and narrowed his eyes. "Do you know who that is? There are two of them. Down in the Gorge. They're carrying cameras."

Quill squinted into the sunlight. "I don't have time for them, either. It's Azalea and Ralph. The film people."

Myles pulled his cell phone from his pocket, hesitated, and put it back again.

"What? What is it? You can't be suspicious of Azalea and Ralph."

"You're right, Quill. I'm sorry." He propped his feet against the railing. "Let's take a look at your problem here."

"No. Let's take a look at your problem." Quill got up from her chair and positioned herself to face him. "We weren't going to do this, this time around. Remember? You were going to talk about what's on your mind. I was going to ask what was on your mind. This is so we don't drift apart again. Because both of us are keeping silent." She bit her lip. "You're not worried about our relationship, are you?"

"No." He touched her cheek, as he had in the hospital. "No. If you want to marry, we'll marry. If you don't, we won't. I love you, Quill. I will always love you."

"Is it this job you have with Global?"

He was quiet for so long she was afraid she'd lost him. She did love him. But love didn't flourish in silence, at least not for her. Love was a lot harder when you never talked.

"I've been a cop all my life," he said finally. "I don't know how to be anything else but a cop."

"And you're a brilliant one."

He smiled at that. Then the smile faded as his face saddened.

Quill stifled an exclamation. "What is it, Myles? Tell me."

"To do the job right, I have to leave. For a year. Maybe longer. I'm torn about whether or not I should go."

"A year!" Quill felt as if the breath had been punched out of her. "A year!" she repeated.

"I was able to come back this time. When you were hurt. But I won't be able to come back again. Not if I accept this assignment."

"Can you tell me what it is?"

"Middle East."

"That's a pretty broad geographic area," she said wryly. "Can you be a little more specific?"

He was more specific. Quill felt herself pale. Then she said, "I see."

"What do you think about it?"

"What do I think about it?" Quill looked at him wildly. "What do you think I think? I think it's the most dangerous thing I've ever heard of."

"I doubt that," he said, his tone dry. "If you want me to turn it down, Quill, I will."

Don't go! She gripped her hands so tightly together that her fingers were numb. Aloud, she said lightly, "Let me ask you something. You haven't said a word about my walking out of the hospital last night."

"It's your choice, Quill. I'll be here to pick up the pieces, whatever you decide to do. But I'm not about to tell you what decisions to make."

"Well, there you are. That's the perfect answer. 'I'll be here . . . But I'm not about to tell you —' "

He reached over, picked her up, and swung her into his lap.

"Do you have any idea what those characters are doing in that big field next to you?" Azalea Cummings gave Quill a sharp poke in the back.

Quill jumped off Myles's lap and banged into one of the gazebo's sturdy posts. He grasped her elbow and steadied her.

"I want to get some footage." Azalea's fingernails were back to black. She stood in the sweet peas that edged the gazebo, her chin resting on the railing. Her eyes were bright with malice. Ralph stood behind her, a small grin on his face. He made a kissing noise at Quill and gave Myles a wink. "I want to get some footage," Azalea repeated, "and the asshole in charge said the land was private property and tried to throw us out. It's not private property, is it? The land belongs to you, doesn't it? It's part of the Inn, right? And if it's part of the Inn and I'm a guest here, we do have rights to access. True?"

"True," Myles said, amiably enough.

"Good." Azalea turned abruptly and crashed through the budding sweet pea buds, her camera slung over her shoulder.

"You do know who's out there, however." Myles didn't raise his voice, but something in his tone stopped Azalea's progress. She turned back.

"I don't give a rat's ass who's out there," she said indifferently. "For all I care, it's W himself and the grunts sweating with those tents are Secret Service agents. I'm an independent filmmaker . . . what was your name again?"

"McHale."

"Fine, McHale. I can go where I like and shoot what I like. There's a little thing called the Bill of Rights which you — folks, Ralph? Don't they call themselves folks out here in the sticks? — yeah, folks — seem to forget about. Anyway, you can't stop me." She smirked.

"It's Warrender Hackmeyer," Myles said.

"Who the hell is Warrender Hackmeyer?"

Ralph, suddenly poker-faced, bent over and whispered in her ear.

"So? As if I care?" Azalea switched her camera to her other shoulder. "Anyway, I've changed my mind. I want to get some shots of the dump site on Route 15 anyway." She stared angrily at Quill. "The brochure says there's a van available for the use of guests. Where is it?"

"Dina will be at the reception desk around nine," Quill said. "You can make arrangements through her. There's an hourly charge."

"Put it on the bill." She whirled on Ralph. "I thought you were going to get me some food. Come on."

Quill watched them walk up the slope to the flagstone terrace off the Tavern Bar. "Who *is* Warrender Hackmeyer? I thought he owned an insurance brokerage."

"He does. He's also on the Board of Governors of their university."

"Oh." She bit her lip. "How do you know that? Myles, I haven't had a chance to tell you that Davey's been demanding the reenactors guest list from the Inn. He wants to run background checks on them. It all started because I tried out this new management program and part of it are these little . . ."

"The WhyNots. Yes. Dave and I have talked about it."

"Talked about it? Just talked?" Quill stamped down the steps of the gazebo to the lawn, rigid with indignation. "Or have you just gone ahead and started running background checks? You can't just violate people's privacy like that, Myles. It's not fair. It's not right. And that stupid WhyNot isn't even a real threat." Then she added reluctantly, "Not a direct one, anyway."

"Let's get back to how dangerous it might be for Doreen to spearhead the investigation into who is behind the WhyNots." He followed her onto the lawn, then began to walk back to the Inn. He stopped and said over his shoulder, "Coming?"

Quill, standing still out of sheer consternation, wasn't sure what to say first. "Just hang on a minute. And please don't walk off until we talk about this. Okay?"

"You see my point?"

"I see that you're being obscure. I have no idea why."

"What if I told you that yes, I think Doreen may be risking some physical harm if she tries to find out who is sending those messages."

"I have to find her and stop her," Quill said. "How could I have been — ?"

"Hang on, Quill. Furthermore, what if I suggested that Hackmeyer might be the threat. How would you feel about doing a background check on him then?"

"His address and credit card numbers are in the registry," she said promptly. "I'll get them for you."

"So he's lost his right to privacy? Even though I have only a suspicion and no hard evidence?"

Quill scowled. Then she fanned her face with her hand. "Is it hot out here? Or is it my concussion? Maybe I should sit down again."

He came up, folded his arms around her, and said into her hair, "It's different when it's someone you love, isn't it. It changes the level of the threat."

"I'm feeling faint," Quill said crossly. "Let go of me."

"I'm holding you. You won't fall."

Quill pushed him away. "Tell me what you want to tell me, Myles. Should I give you the list?"

"Do you think you should give me the list?"

"No. I don't." She rubbed the back of her neck. She didn't feel faint, but her head was beginning to throb. "Yes. No. I don't know."

"Good answer," he said. "The Supreme Court struggles with these issues all the time. Yes, the reenactors do have a right to be free of government interference, except under extraordinary circumstances. You're an honorable woman, Quill, and you have a great deal of integrity. Your instincts are good ones. But there are no hard-and-fast answers."

"Especially these days," Quill said glumly.

"It's not just these days," Myles said easily. "Tests of the Bill of Rights have been coming up for the past two hundred and thirty years. You're on the side of the angels, Quill."

"So how did you know Major Hackmeyer was on the Board of Governors of Ithaca University?"

"I ran a background check on him."

"Myles!"

"I didn't say *I* was on the side of the angels. I'm a cop, Quill."

Quill looked around for something to throw at him. Mike the groundskeeper kept the lawn in immaculate shape, and there wasn't a thing on the velvety surface except grass.

"I think I'd like some breakfast," Myles said.

"Marge serves breakfast at the Croh Bar."

"I thought about Meg's brioche all the way back from Gatwick." He raised one eyebrow. "I can be pathetic, too. I just need a little practice. But I haven't eaten since I came back."

"You haven't eaten since you came back? Oh, for heaven's sake. Of course I'll feed you. You are the second most annoying man I've ever met."

They began to walk back to the Inn, side by side. "Oh? Who's the first?"

"I don't know. But it's a big world out there. There has to be someone more exasperating than you. In Tibet, maybe." Or Iraq, she thought, and held his hand tightly.

"So did you really check on him?" They sat at the table overlooking the Falls. The dining room was full — Friday mornings during the summer always were. There was the usual contingent of tourists on their way through the Fingerlakes, a few people from town, including the Olafsons, and at least twenty fit, muscular, hairy re-enactors. Some of them were already in costume, or rather uniform — Quill wasn't quite sure where the distinction lay. They wore blue breeches with gold stripes up the sides, leather suspenders, and long wool undershirts. Hackmeyer had a blue coat with gold buttons slung over the back of his chair, and his boots were well worn, but beautifully cared for. He ate with concentration; the men around him maintained a respectful silence that Quill found very irritating. "Myles? Did you?"

Myles finished the last of his eggs and began on his steak. "I checked what was on public record."

"You know, I don't like him."

"You don't?" Myles put his fork down.

"That's very interesting. You normally have a very good reason for not liking someone. You're a professional host. Do you know why you don't like him?"

Quill was still trying to work through the professional host comment. Did he mean professional host like the infamous Bessie Forrester, who had run the Hemlock Falls bawdy house in the 1860s? Or a professional host like Charlie Rose, who was charming, erudite, discriminating, and intellectually curious?

"Quill?" Myles asked patiently.

"I don't know, exactly. I mean, he's so John Wayne it's ludicrous, but I don't have any particular animus toward John Wayne. I'd drop dead before I married John Wayne, of course, or even invited him to dinner — do you know he contributed money to the Ku Klux Klan in the fifties? — but he'd certainly be welcome at the Inn. Which means I'm more like Bessie than Charlie, I suppose."

"Quill," Myles said, not so patiently.

"There's something ominous about Warrender Hackmeyer." Glad that she'd identified that, she began to eat the rest of her Eggs Florentine.

"You're right."

"I'm right?" Quill looked at him, bemused.

"Hackmeyer's Fourteenth Regiment is the front for a private militia."

Quill gasped and choked on her spinach. Myles patted her kindly on the back. "I wish we could parse your intuition and put it into a training program for Global. Do you think you can break down the reasons why you think he's ominous? Here, take a sip of water."

Quill pounded her chest a few times. "I'm fine." She drew a deep, unimpeded breath. "You didn't find that out by going to the library," she whispered fiercely.

"I said that Hackmeyer's position on the Board of Governors is a matter of public record, and it is. But no, Quill. The, er, other matter was brought to my attention by a friend of mine. After you were hit on the head, I did make a few phone calls," he said almost apologetically.

Quill felt the back of her neck. She'd actually looked at the wound when she'd gotten back to the Inn last night. It was much smaller than it felt. "Do you think he hit me over the head?"

"I can't imagine why he'd want to, unless he wanted to carry you off, and for that, I can't blame him. And after all, you're right here with me, and he didn't carry you off at all."

"Very funny," Quill said sourly. "What am I supposed to do about it?"

"About what, Hackmeyer? Not a thing."

"But what if he's here to . . ." Quill spread her hands helplessly. "I don't know. Practice."

"You stay out of it." Myles wasn't being funny now. "He is a dangerous man, Quill. And I mean it. You leave this to me. Understand?"

Quill eyed the men in her dining room. She wanted to throw them all out. "What sort of private militia? Is it a cult? Isn't it illegal? Can't we arrest them?"

"Do you have a mouse in your pocket?"

She blushed. "I mean, you and Davey?"

"They haven't done anything illegal. As far as we know, they aren't engaging in a plot to overthrow the United States government."

"But you have to do something."

"What would you like me to do? The same freedoms that you want to protect allow men like Hackmeyer to set up private militias." He touched her hair. "I'm not making light of this, Quill. You know there aren't any simple answers. I have three concerns right now. Whoever sent the message about the reenactment to the sheriff's office might know more about the militia activities than is safe. And I want to be sure there aren't any deaths."

"That's two concerns."

He smiled at her.

Quill found herself smiling back. "Hackmeyer couldn't have anything to do with the WhyNots, could he?"

"Disaffected employee is my best guess."

"Mine, too," Quill sighed. She hated to think it was anyone who worked for them. "Then who did hit me over the head? It couldn't have been the disaffected employee, because the WhyNots were still there."

Myles's eyes were shrewd. "All of them? And how do you know they were the originals?"

Quill caught herself before she choked on her

spinach again. "Do you know something you're not telling me?"

"I'm telling you now. I took a look at the WhyNots Dave took from your office. We compared them to the one sent to the sheriff's department. The handwriting's different."

"But the person that's been leaving them around the Inn might not be the same person who sent the one to the sheriff's office."

"We checked with Dina. She's a bright girl, Quill. Not only did she confirm that the WhyNots Dave found weren't the same ones she'd collected yesterday, she was reasonably certain that the handwriting on the originals matched the one in our files. And no one had access to that except Dave and me."

"You were busy yesterday," Quill said ruefully.

He took her hand. "You fell asleep every time I came in to see you. It was pick up the strands of this case, or take Carol Ann Spinoza up on her invitation to go to the Croh Bar for dinner."

"Oh, ugh!"

"May I take that, Quill?" Kathleen nodded at Quill's empty plate.

"Yes, thanks."

Kathleen gathered the dishes and nodded to Myles, "Hi, Sheriff. Davey's sure glad you're back. Me, too."

"Thank you."

"Quill? Are you and the sheriff going to be much longer?"

"A bit. Can I do something for you?"

"A couple of us in back would like a word."

"Are you carrying signs?"

"Signs? Oh! No!" She laughed lightly. "Not at the moment. Anyway, we'd like to see you if we could."

Myles rose to his full height. "I'll see you later then, Quill."

"Just a minute, Myles. Please. Kath, tell everyone I'll be there in five minutes. I promise."

"Okay. Five minutes?"

Quill nodded and waited until Kathleen was out of earshot. "Davey told you he ordered the autopsy on Freddie Bellini?"

"Yes."

"And for Nadine Nickerson and Derwent Peterson? And have you spoken to Andy?"

"I have."

"Did he tell you he hired me to investigate? Unofficially?"

"Yes. And officially, Quill, you are off the case."

"What do you mean, 'off the case'! You can't interfere like this!"

"And Andy can't hire a private citizen to do the county's work."

"He hasn't hired me, precisely."

"He's asked you to turn over any information about the activities of those three on the day they were all at the Inn. As a conscientious, honorable citizen, that's what you should do. But that's it, Quill. You aren't investigating anything. It's officially an inquiry now, and Davey will be along to interview you when you've gathered the relevant information. It's out of your hands. I hope you understand me. Focus on helping Doreen track down who sent those WhyNots."

Quill glared at him. Myles shook his head. "I'll see you later tonight?"

Quill, who had dealt with Myles's resistance to her detective activities for years, switched gears abruptly and said warmly, "Yes. If you stay with me, there's food available. Not to mention a better-quality mattress."

He laughed at that. Quill watched him cross the room. He was big, but he moved easily among the crowded tables. She saw him nod expressionlessly to Hackmeyer. And then he was gone.

Sergeant Fetterman had been watching Myles, too. He caught Quill's eye and signaled to her. Quill looked at her watch. It had been more than five minutes, since she promised Kathleen she'd meet her, but the guests, even revolutionaries disguised as reenactors, came first.

Sergeant Fetterman rose politely as she approached his table. "We just wanted you to know that the costumes will be arriving this afternoon."

"The costumes? Oh!" Quill ran her hands through her hair. "Oh, my. I'd forgotten all about them. Oh, dear. We don't have to rehearse or anything, do we?"

"It's all been taken care of. We'll be starting the reenactment at two o'clock sharp, and all of you are welcome to come out and watch, unless you have duties with the town activities."

"We don't have a thing to do for the celebration," Quill said thankfully. "I mean, not that we wouldn't if we'd been asked. Most of the staff will come out and watch the parade, and of course everyone's welcome to go to the award ceremony. But thank you for sending the costumes. We'll do our best to look Civil War–ish." Quill nodded to the rest of the table and turned to go.

Hackmeyer, who'd been sitting in MacArthur-like silence, raised one hand. "Miss Quilliam?"

"Yes. Good morning, Major."

"My aides tell me there was an unfortunate incident the night before last. You're looking remarkably well this morning. Considering."

"Yes, well, all part of the job," Quill said lamely.

Sergeant Fetterman said smoothly, "What the major would like you to know is this. You find out who did it . . . just a word in his ear. Or mine. Leave the rest up to us."

"I don't quite understand," Quill said frankly.

"Cowardly thing, attacking a woman," Hackmeyer said. He seemed truly angry. "We don't stand for that, Miss Quilliam." There was a murmur of agreement from the rest of the men at the table. Quill had a sudden vision of Hackmeyer on top of one of the sleepy horses in the football field, chasing an unidentified Inn employee, saber in hand. She shuddered. "Yes, well. Is there anything else at the moment?"

Hackmeyer shook his head. "The important thing is the banquet tonight. That you're all in costume for that."

"Yes," Quill said, and escaped to the kitchen. She could swear the next word on his lips was going to be "dismissed."

CHAPTER 9

The kitchen was almost empty. Just Meg and
the part-time dishwasher. Quill skidded to a
halt. "Where is everyone?"

Meg poked at a large unappealing lump of
meat. "Outside," she said briefly.

Quill went to the large windows that overlooked the herb and vegetable garden. She
could see part of the employee parking lot from
the window, and all of the five-acre meadow.
The meadow was filled with half-erected tents
and big flatbed trailers. The parking lot seemed
filled with employees. "Is that Doreen? Standing on a crate?"

Meg abandoned the meat and came to peer
over Quill's shoulder. "Yep."

"Do you see any signs?"

"Signs?"

"You know: WORKERS UNITE! DOWN
WITH BOSSES!"

"I'll check." Meg pushed the screen door
open and went outside. She came back in a few
seconds. "No signs."

"Can you hear what Doreen is saying?"

"Just mutter-mutter-*shout!* Same as you

hear." Meg trailed back to the prep table and the meat. Quill joined her. "What is that?"

"Mutton."

"What are you going to do with it?"

"I would like," Meg said, "to throw it out. The authentic Army recipe says to boil it. *Boil it!*" she roared suddenly, "with some pitiful little sprigs of celery, bits of carrot, and an onion. One. Onion. It is going to taste like a dog's dinner." She folded her arms and sunk her head on her chest. She looked up suddenly. "Aren't you going out there?"

Quill went back to the window. "I don't know," she said thoughtfully. "Doreen's not going mutter-mutter-*shout!* anymore. She's going yada-yada-yada in what sounds like a reasonable way. I think I'll wait until she's finished." She crossed over to the fireplace and sat down in the rocking chair. Peter Hairston came through the swinging doors from the dining room, untying his apron as he walked. "The last of the breakfast crowd is gone," he said. "Do you mind if I wait to clear? I don't want to miss the meeting."

"Sure," Meg said.

"Thanks."

Quill stopped him as he headed past her. "Can you tell me what the meeting is about?"

"I don't know. Doreen used the what's-it system to get everyone to come in this morning, which was a good thing, because everyone is pretty annoyed."

"Annoyed? About what? Everyone knows the W.A.T.C.H. program is over, done with, kaput, don't they?"

"That? Oh, yeah." Peter shrugged. "Yesterday's news."

"They aren't mad at me, are they?" Quill asked cravenly. "You know I would have met with everyone yesterday, as I promised, but I did get hit on the head."

"That? Oh, yeah," Peter repeated with maddening unoriginality. "Did you get our flowers? We took up a collection."

"They're in her office," Meg said. "The hospital sent them over once they discovered her escape." She turned the slab of meat over with a long fork. "This has to come from the oldest sheep in the state. Maybe the oldest sheep in the nation. Maybe this sheep was born and raised in Minsk and walked all the way here to die. Yuck."

Peter shifted from one foot to the other.

"Just a word about the meeting's topic," Quill said sternly. "It's either that, or I'll demote you to dishwasher."

"Tights."

Quill's eyebrows rose. "Tights?"

"Word is we have to wear costumes tomorrow. And nobody wants to wear tights. I don't mind," he said modestly, since it was perfectly obvious that he would look very good in tights, "but some of the fatter guys aren't too happy about it. Or the fatter women, either."

"Peter," Quill said. "What are you studying again?"

"First-year med student. I switched from creative writing. You can't make a living at creative writing."

"You're going to have to work on your bedside manner. Trust me."

"Well, Doreen said the meeting was an open employee discussion and that's what we wanted to discuss. Are we going to wear tights tomorrow?"

"We are going to participate in the re-enactment of the Battle of Hemlock Falls. And yes, our guests have requested that we all dress in the period."

"Tights, then."

"Not tights!" Quill shouted. "It's cravats and trousers and tall hats."

"And corsets," Meg said. "I give up on this mutton." She pulled open her spice drawer and began to rummage.

Peter blinked. His eyes were a very clear, innocent blue. "Of course. Sorry. I'll let everyone know, okay?"

"Tell them they are going to look fabulous," Quill said reassuringly.

"And we'll all be in the movie?"

"The movie? Oh. I wouldn't . . ." She caught Meg rolling her eyes. "Yes," Quill said, "everyone is going to look wonderful, and yes, they'll be . . . on film. Or at the very least, videotape. And I'll come out, as soon as you want me to. Just send somebody. I'll be right here."

Peter left with the happy mien of a man with good news to deliver.

"Another day, another crisis." Meg began rubbing various spices onto the mutton. "I soaked this sucker in brine for twenty-four hours. And if I wrap it in cheesecloth when I boil it, it might taste like something. So. Is Myles going to catch the murderer?"

"The murderer?"

"You haven't forgotten poor Mr. Bellini and Derwent Peterson," Meg said. "Not to mention Mrs. Nickerson." She shook her head. "You shouldn't have left the hospital. Remember, we figured it couldn't be my food, or anything else at the Inn because the murderer stole the W.A.T.C.H. Reports." She shot Quill a sharp glance. "You did tell Myles and Davey about the W.A.T.C.H. Reports."

"No," Quill said thoughtfully. "No. I didn't." She pushed the rocker back and forth. "And I don't think I'm going to."

Meg stopped rubbing the mutton. "You aren't?"

"It's the only evidence we have that a person, not an event, is behind these deaths."

"I'm missing something here."

"You know how much I love Myles," Quill began.

Meg rolled her eyes at the ceiling and began to hum. It sounded like the old waltz "Fascination," but Quill couldn't be sure. The words were: *She's headed towards digression, I know. I*

can-hear-it COM-ing from eight miles awa-a-ay./
She-can't-keep-the point/in-this-or-any-other joint.

"But!" Quill said loudly. "He thinks we have no business investigating crime."

"We don't."

"He's a cop."

"True."

"He tries hard, but he can't help this macho, don't bother-the-little-lady's-head-with-facts-ma'am behavior. Very cop-like. I am saving him from it."

"How?"

"Myles dissimulates . . . Will you *stop* that so-called singing, Meg? I *am* answering the question. He thinks he's diverted us from searching for whomever's behind this campaign to hurt the Inn, for example, by encouraging me to help Doreen. And he admits that there's an open file on those deaths, but he's assured me — very unobviously, Meg, I have to admire that — that the sheriff's department's going to have it all under control once the autopsy results are in."

"Maybe the answer does lie with the autopsies," Meg said soberly. "Andy says they should be able to determine what caused the heart attacks."

"Well, what caused these heart attacks?"

Meg looked surprised. "Well, Nadine Nickerson had an embolus. A clot. And Derwent Peterson must have had a clot, too, except that Andy couldn't find anything. And poor Freddie

Bellini's secondary artery just collapsed. Andy thinks it may have been an aneurysm, but he's not sure about that, either. He's not looking at what caused the heart attacks, Quill. He's looking for something that could have stressed their systems so that the attacks were fatal. And when I press him on that, he just goes into long, medical lectures that I barely understand — Derwent's myeloma was in remission, and he was healthy as a horse otherwise; the veins and arteries feeding Nadine's heart should have been able to compensate for the embolus; the artery that killed Freddie was healthy — the poor guy had it tested in Rochester a few weeks ago, and it was the only part of his cardiovascular system that was working properly. I guess aneurysms just don't pop up out of nowhere. He just says he doesn't have enough facts. And it's facts he wants from us."

"Are you okay with that?"

Meg rubbed her eyes. She looked suddenly tired. "Yes," she said in a low voice, "I'm okay with that. But once in a while — which is to say about every five minutes — I just wish he'd *leave it alone*."

"I think it's great that he can't."

"Even if the medical examiner in Syracuse comes up with some vague idea that eating a lot of beans at lunch gave all three of them severe indigestion and *that's* what led to their vulnerable conditions? *Phuut!* We'll be in court for years on that one." She looked at Quill and her eyes were haunted. "I can't believe I'm saying this, Quill. But I hope to heck it's murder."

"Oh, it's murder all right." Quill stopped the rocker with her toe. "I remembered something about going down to my office that night."

"You have?" Meg furrowed her brow anxiously. "You know, we've all been making light of your injury. But you *are* okay, aren't you?"

"I have a slight headache," Quill admitted. "But I'm fine. My memory's coming back in bits and pieces. It's like a camera flash. Halfway down the stairs I remembered the twelfth of June."

"Bastille Day's the fourteenth."

This stopped Quill cold. "Bastille Day? What does Bastille Day have to do with the price of bananas in Brazil?"

"The oppressed masses storming the prison." Meg raised a spice-covered hand. "Like right there."

A crowd of waiters, waitresses, maids, cleaning guys, sous chefs, and dishwashers streamed past the back window. Mike the groundskeeper brought up the rear. The back door slammed open. Doreen trudged in. She didn't look shrunken anymore. She looked larger than life. She was carrying the plastic milk crate she'd been standing on in the parking lot. "You want to come out back for a bit?"

"Why?"

"We got to vote."

"On what?"

216

"If you come out there, you'll find out."

"Does anybody have any rotten fruit? Bananas or tomatoes, for example?"

Doreen snorted.

"Is anyone mad at me?" Quill asked in a practical way.

"Mad at you? Not so you'd notice."

"Okay, then."

Meg wiped her hands on a towel. "Do you want me to come with you?"

"No. They won't attack a wounded woman. I hope." Quill followed Doreen out the door.

The sun had clouded over and the first faint hint of rain was in the air. Seeing all of her employees — or what looked like all of her employees — in one place gave Quill a peculiar feeling. She thought about it for a moment. She was proud, that was it.

Doreen planted the plastic crate on the ground and stood on it. "You all can see me," she said.

"We could see you before," Devora said. "We can see Quill just fine, for example. You don't have to stand on the crate, Doreen."

"She likes the crate," Peter said. "It gives her authority."

"I'm talking," Doreen snapped, which shut everyone up. "Now, listen here, Quill. We decided to forget all about that Profit Master."

"Good."

"Nobody's gonna bring a lawsuit for invasion of privacy . . ."

"For what?" Quill said, alarmed.

"Or workplace harassment or any of that stuff. Right, folks? We figured an apology would be enough." Doreen stepped down from the milk crate and indicated that Quill should step up.

"You want me up there?"

"You said you were sorry to me. You should say you're sorry to the rest of us."

Quill took a deep breath, stepped up onto the milk crate, and said, "I'm sorry."

"And you were wrong," Kathleen Kiddermeister said from somewhere in the depths of the crowd. "I told them, Quill, that you told Dina and me you were wrong!"

"I was wrong," Quill said. "I made a mistake. I apologize most sincerely." She stepped down. Doreen hopped back up. "You folks all heard her admit to her mistakes!" she cried. "So you're gonna drop the complaints to the Labor Board!"

"Right!" they all yelled. Or most of them.

"Good! Now what we did decide is we're gonna have a suggestion contest."

"A suggestion contest?" Quill tugged at her ear. "What kind of suggestions?"

"The Best Way to Make This-Here Inn a Better Place to Work," Doreen announced. "Right, everybody?"

"*Right!*"

"And we thought we'd tell you since we're goin' to all the trouble of *writing these-here sug-*

gestions down" — Doreen's grin was both triumphant and complicit — "that you'll guarantee to take the top suggestion and do it."

Professor Wojowski would approve of this. This was employee participation. This was employee input. This was a step in the right direction toward one hundred percent employee satisfaction, which was a well-known goal of quality programs the world over.

"Okay," Quill said.

"Okay?" Doreen turned to the crowd and shouted, "She says she'll do it!"

A few cheers greeted this. Somebody shouted, "Can we go home now?" and somebody else shouted, "I'm not wearing no tights!" and Quill announced the meeting was over and went inside.

Meg had disappeared, on a quest for more seasoning, or another piece of mutton, and Quill went to her office. She would check her messages, grab her purse, and get to what she'd intended to do all along, which was interview as many relatives of the deceased as she was able to that morning.

Dina sat behind the reception desk, and greeted Quill with a cry of joy. "Hey! You're back! Are you feeling okay? You don't look as if you've been hit over the head one little bit. And I knew that business about being paralyzed for life was a crock."

"Who said I'd been paralyzed for life?"

"Carol Ann Spinoza, down at the Croh Bar."

"Figures. Why weren't you at the meeting?"

Dina's expression was reproving. "With you out sick? Somebody has to be around to run the place. Besides, I don't care if we have to wear tights tomorrow or not."

Quill was touched, "Well, thank you." A sudden shriek sounded outside the big oak door. She jumped. "What the heck was that?"

"That? Better get out of the way."

The door slammed open. Quill jumped behind the reception desk. Adela Henry ran into the lobby. She wore a crimson ball gown with a lace decolletage and a very tight waist. The skirt was huge. "To arms!" she cried. "To arms! The Rebels are attacking! Once more to the beach, my friends! Once more!" She ran out again, slamming the door behind her.

"Wow," Quill said.

"She's rehearsing," Dina observed. "She's been doing that since yesterday. If you ask me, with that tight girdle and in this heat, she's going to fall right down flat on her face if she keeps it up."

The door swung open again, and Adela reappeared. "To arms!" she shouted. She saw Quill and waved. Then she sat down on the cream leather couch and drew an elaborate fan from her reticule. (At least Quill presumed it was a reticule. Whatever. She knew it was a purse.) Adela plied it vigorously. "Well?" she asked with an inquiring tilt of her head.

Dina applauded.

"Very dramatic," Quill said with a warm smile. "That color is magnificent on you, Adela."

She may have blushed with pleasure; it was hard to tell, since she was red from the heat. "Thank you. The gown is precisely what I specified. Say what you may, Esther has a gift. I am not, however, entirely pleased with the speech. Harvey assures me that part of it is Shakespeare . . ."

"Umm," Quill said. "Is it the part about the beach? Because I think it's 'breach,' Adela. *'Once more into the breach, my friends! For God, King Harry! And for England!'* Very stirring. But it's breach."

"I have the script right here in my reticule," Adela said with a great deal of firmness, "and it's says 'beach.' " She thrust a piece of paper at Quill, who read the paragraph. "So it does," she agreed.

"Of course I was right," Adela said with maddening self-satisfaction. "I am going to take a short rest, and then I will resume rehearsal."

Quill got stubborn. She knew she was being stubborn. She always regretted it when she got stubborn. But she'd already had to confess to being wrong to her entire staff and nobody seemed to care that she was recuperating from a concussion, and Myles was leaving for a year to go into terrible danger, so she said loudly, "It's *breach!*"

"Beach."

"The speech is from *Henry the Fifth*, Adela. He's addressing his troops. They're at Agincourt . . ."

Adela seemed taken aback. Then she asked coldly, "And where is Agincourt?"

"In Normandy . . ."

"Ha! Elmer and I went to France last year. We went to Normandy. *And Normandy is on the beach!*"

"*That is so not true!*"

"Quill?" Dina said.

"I suppose you think you know everything there is to know about everything?" Adela asked dangerously.

"Quill!" Dina shouted. "You have a phone call! In your office!"

Quill marched into her office and slammed the door. Outside, in the foyer, she heard the big oak door slam, too. Then Dina tapped on her door and opened it at the same time.

"Thanks," Quill said gloomily.

"Jeez," Dina said.

"Is she gone?"

"Yeah. I heard that big Caddy she drives take off. Are you sure you're okay?"

"Oh. My head? Yes. The only problem with a concussion is something Andy calls *contra coup* . . ."

"The opposite side of the brain whacking against your skull," Dina said. "I know. Brains are so cool, Quill. I took an anatomy course last year and they're just like Jell-O! And if you get whacked on the head, the brain goes 'splat' against the other side and you can die from a blood clot." She tilted her head to one side. "Maybe you'd better take it easy for the rest of the day."

"I had at least three CAT scans and nothing showed up" — Dina snickered — "that was *abnormal*. My brain is just fine. I'm not supposed to lift heavy objects or do any strenuous exercise for a while, but I don't like to do either one of those things anyway."

"So what are you going to do today? The costumes are supposed to come in around three and everybody has to show up to try them on, but I cleared your schedule because Meg said you were going to be in the hospital today. But I can call everyone and tell them you can make the meetings after all."

"No." Quill picked her keys up. "I'm going out."

"Sheriff McHale said to let him know where you were today. Where are you going?"

"Out," Quill said.

"Don't forget your cell phone. Sheriff McHale said . . ."

Quill turned her cell phone off and put it into her purse.

"Will you be back for the costumes?"

"If I'm not in Detroit."

Quill marched out of the Inn and into her car and wondered how long it would take her to drive to Detroit. She'd brought the subject up with the guy Meg called Dr. Whosis during her brief brush with psychotherapy, and all he'd said was that most people's escape fantasies had to do with Tahiti and muscular beach boys, and that she must like her life in Hemlock Falls a lot more than she thought.

It began to rain about ten minutes out of town, a hard rain that wasn't usual to Upstate New York. Quill decided to drop in on Harland Peterson first; he was one of the biggest dairy farmers in Upstate New York, and almost always at home. And his farm was hard to miss, even in rain that was coming down like water out of a Kohler showerhead. The paved driveway up to the big white frame house was a quarter of a mile long, lined with neatly painted three-board fencing. Quill pulled up to the farmhouse and debated her chances of finding him there or in one of the long red dairy barns at nine o'clock in the morning. He would, she decided, be at breakfast after an early milking.

She dashed to the back door and opened it. It'd taken years — and a number of unintentional insults — before Quill had adapted to the country practice of walking into unlocked houses. You went to the back door; then knocked, opened, and hallooed all at the same time. It wasn't polite to walk all the way in; it was equally rude to stand there, knock, and wait for somebody to come and let you in.

She'd been right. Harland was at breakfast. He sat at the big square table with his hired man, T.K. At least a pound of fried bacon, a huge pile of scrambled eggs, and a gallon of milk rested in the center. Quill smelled burned toast, bitter coffee, and a rather pleasing odor of cow manure.

Harlan wiped his mouth and rose. "Get yourself in here, Quill. It's raining pups and kittens out there!" He pulled out a third chair at the table, then took a white ceramic plate from the cupboard, a fork from the drainer by the kitchen sink, and a mug from the stack by the twelve-cup coffeepot. He smacked them in front of the chair.

Quill sat down; accepted coffee, bacon, and eggs; and sipped the coffee.

"Glad to see you're out of the hospital. June'd been here, she'd been right up to see you."

Quill liked Harland a lot. She liked the slow, steady way he moved, his big farmer's frame, even his thinning fringe of white hair. His wife June had died three years ago, a loss that had stricken him silent for more than two. It was only recently, since he'd been squiring Marge Schmidt around the village, that he'd resumed a reasonable amount of conversation. He had never been loquacious.

"Find the guy that whacked you one?"

"Not yet," Quill admitted. "But I'm working on it."

Harland's eyes twinkled. "Sheriff's back in town, I hear."

"Yes. He was in London for a bit. He'll have to be going back for a while, I'm afraid."

"Ought to marry the man, Quill. Get yourself a coupla kids."

Quill knew how to handle this. "You ought to get married again yourself, Harland. Good man like yourself."

"Yeah. Well. Ain't out of the question."

Quill's eyes widened. This was news. "And how does Marge feel about that?"

T.K., who was even bigger than Harland, poked his boss. "Ain't asked her yet, has he? I keep tellin' him. She's willin'." Harland poked him back. The two men roared with laughter. The preliminaries over, Quill began: "I was sorry to hear about Derwent, Harland."

"Yuh. You never know. Tumors all over his body, you know. But I have to say that doctor did his best."

"Your time's your time," T.K. said.

"True enough."

All three lapsed into silence.

"You were with him up at the Inn, the day before he went into the hospital," Quill said. "In the Tavern Bar."

"Yessir. That I was. Damnedest thing. I hadn't seen old Derwent for — let me see now — couldn't have been less than five months. Just before I had that setback with the foundation on my new barn. Yuh. Anyway. He calls me. Says he's treating all of us to the best lunch in town, which'd be your place, he said, although I'm a meat loaf man myself, and then he was going off to Florida."

"Florida?" Quill said. "Derwent was moving to Florida?"

"Yuh. Bought himself a condo down there, and all. Said the doc told him he had a few good years left and he might as well enjoy 'em. Well, poor old soul, turned out to be wrong there. Just goes to show."

"That it does." T.K. offered the egg and bacon platter again to Quill, who refused with a smile. He dumped the remainder on his plate and began to eat in huge, methodical bites.

"That is a shame." Quill pulled thoughtfully at her lower lip. "Did he invite Mrs. Nickerson and Freddie Bellini to the party, too?"

"Fred? A mortician to a going-away party? Hell, no."

"And Mrs. Nickerson? Was she there?"

Harland frowned. "She and that lot of grand-nieces were in the dining room, as I recollect. We were in the Tavern Bar. Derwent says you can scratch your belly there, and no one'll look at you crosswise, the way they might in that fancy dining room."

"What did you have to eat?"

Harland chewed a piece of bacon as ruminatively as one of his own cows. "What'd we have to eat?" He glanced at her briefly, and Quill was reminded why he was one of the most successful agribusinessmen in the county. "Steak. I had steak. Derwent had steak. T.K. here, he had steak. Damn good stuff, too, even if it was itty-bitty."

"The filet mignon," Quill guessed.

"Yuh. That would be it. They say that's the best part of the cow. I wouldn't know."

Quill set her coffee cup down with a thump. "Okay, okay. Yes, I'm investigating again, if that's what you want to know."

Harland jerked his head at T.K. " 'Bout time you checked that manure spreader."

T.K. nodded, took his dishes to the sink, shrugged on a bright yellow slicker, and left.

"So what's up, Quill?"

"Mrs. Nickerson, your cousin Derwent, and Freddie were all at the Inn on the same day, the twelfth of June. Derwent was admitted to the hospital with shortness of breath, a headache, and a general complaint of not feeling very well on the thirteenth. Mrs. Nickerson went into the hospital on the fourteenth, the same day as Freddie Bellini. Same complaint. And you know what happened."

"They were all pretty sick, Quill."

"Was there anything unusual about your time at the Inn? Anything at all?"

Harland thought for a long moment. "Just that Derwent took his wallet out of his pocket for the first time in seventy-five years."

"Did you meet anyone there that you didn't expect to see?"

"Dookie and Mrs. Dookie were sitting with Adela and the mayor. Adela was having tea, she said. Marge dropped by, but that wasn't as much to give Derwent her regards as to make sure those Olafsons weren't selling us insurance. And that fella Hackmeyer passed through."

Quill scribbled the names on her sketch pad, but this wasn't anything she hadn't known. She bit her lip. "Who waited on the table?"

"Nate," he said promptly. "He always does on weekdays."

"Derwent stayed overnight because he became a little dizzy at lunch. How did that happen?"

"I don't know. He had a few beers, got up, went to pee, came back, said he hated garlic, and didn't feel so hot. Wouldn't go to the hospital right away, so we took him . . ."

"Hated garlic?"

"It was them garlic mashed potatoes. Garlic always upset his stomach."

"Garlic," Quill repeated. "Did he say who he met in the bathroom?"

Harland gave her a puzzled look, but said, "Nope."

"And who was next to you when Derwent felt dizzy?"

Harland shrugged. "Just the regulars."

Garlic, again.

CHAPTER 10

Nadine Nickerson had borne three sons, all of whom had gone into the family hardware business. Each of the sons had married and had sons — which argued for the prepotency of the X chromosome. (Quill had always wished that Henry the VIII had known about the Y chromosome; Anne Boleyn might not have lost her head.) The daughters-in-law all took their turns at the store's cash register. After she left Harland's farm, Quill decided to stop at Nickerson's Hardware before going on to the Bellini Funeral Home.

She couldn't find a parking spot on Main close enough to the store to avoid getting drenched. She dashed in, holding her purse over her head, and Alicia Nickerson held a towel out to her without a word. Quill dabbed futilely at her wet hair. "Wetter than a mad hen," Alicia observed. Quill wasn't sure if this was meant for her or the weather outside, but she returned the damp towel with thanks.

"How've you been, Quill? Heard you got an almighty bruise." Alicia came out from behind the cash register and turned Quill's back to her.

"Looks like the bandage's pretty good. You don't want to get it wet, though. Stitches can't come out for a while."

Quill felt the back of her neck. The bandage was dry, but her hair was sopping. She grabbed her hair and twisted it to the top of her head. "All's I got is a rubber band." Alicia rummaged on the counter and offered one up. Quill wound it into place and immediately felt conspicuous.

Alicia folded her arms on the counter. "So. What's doing?"

Alicia was married to the middle Nickerson son, the good-looking charming one. Everybody liked Neil, but nobody really listened to him. (The two other Nickerson boys were irascible but better businessmen, so the town listened to them; anybody that mean with money ought to know plenty.) Alicia, a forthright, sturdy woman, didn't listen to Neil any more than anyone else. And fifteen years of marriage to Neil had increased her sense of her own importance to an interesting degree.

"I was very sorry to hear about Nana's passing," Quill said in the vernacular.

"It was her time," Alicia said. "Had a bad heart for years."

"I'll bet you were glad to have the time with her at the Inn. It must have been one of the last happy times all the women were together."

"First time in her life that woman does something for somebody else and she kicks off,"

Alicia said. "I swear, no good deed goes unpunished. My Colin's off to college this September and do you know what she gave Colin at that party we had at your place? A computer." She shook her head. "A good one. Offered to pay tuition for technical school for Roger Junior, too. That's Roger's oldest. She was a good woman. A good woman."

Since Alicia and her mother-in-law were widely known to be at odds, usually over the old lady's well-known thriftiness, Quill took this with a grain of salt.

"And now" — Alicia's eyes filled with ready tears — "she's lying there in that cold morgue sliced open like a turkey. I can't stand it. She ought to be buried. She and Knox bought plots right next to each other and it's waiting for her. So is he." She dabbed at her eyes with a wad of Kleenex. "Did you come in for something special, Quill? What can I get for you?"

"Kleenex," Quill said. "I'm out."

Nickerson's was the sort of independent hardware stare that provided milk, eggs, butter, laundry soap, and toilet paper along with every known variety of screw, gasket, or bolt required by modern man. Alicia bustled three aisles down and returned with a stack of tissue. "Three-for-one special. Anything else?"

"Umm. Some gauze bandages, I guess. And some adhesive tape."

Alicia pulled Quill around again and peered at her bandage. "Medium size ought to do it."

"I hope you all had a good time at the Inn," Quill said, trailing her down the aisle.

Alicia's tears threatened to overcome her again. "The Last Party." Then she said briskly, "One package or two? Two, I think. That's going to take a while to heal. And you probably want a couple of yards of adhesive."

"Did you enjoy the meal?"

"Oh, yes. We hadn't eaten there before, Quill, except the occasional breakfast. It's really out of our reach, especially now, with the economy so bad." She added an extra box of gauze bandages to the pile in her hand. Quill saw they came fifty to a box. "But it was delicious."

"What did you have?"

"Me? The shrimp. The filet. The Baked Alaska. And some champagne. Nana insisted that we get whatever we want," she added hastily. "And as I say, it was so rare for her to give, if you know what I mean, I wanted to encourage her in every way. What about some Betadine? You'll want to keep that thing clean."

"A gallon's a lot," Quill said.

"Major Hackmeyer didn't think so. Came in and bought three this size. Needs it for the horses. Now that," Alicia said, a reminiscent smile on her face, "is a fine-looking man."

"And Nana," Quill said. "Did she enjoy her lunch as well?"

"Didn't eat much of it. Said it tasted funny, but you know, she was old."

"Tasted funny. Oh, dear. Meg won't like that.

Maybe we should take it off the menu. What was it?" Alicia held the gallon of Betadine up with an inquiring expression. "Fine," Quill said.

"What did Nana eat? Umm. Some fancy thing that we really aren't used to. We have a simple way of life, Quill."

Quill decided that if she didn't say anything at all (or more to the point, dumped the gallon of Betadine over Alicia's head), she might get more information.

"A hamburger, that was it. With that stinky cheese."

"Roquefort."

"Whatever. Now, look. That wound is going to need to be kept nice and moist, so you don't scar. Have you tried Donna Olafson's face cream?"

"Oh, dear. She got you . . . I mean, no, I haven't yet."

"Nana swore by it." She added a large pink jar to the basket in her hand. "Now, what else?"

"Did anyone join you at the party, Alicia? Do you remember seeing anyone unusual? The reason I'm asking," Quill added hastily, "is that new management program I've been trying out. I don't know if you've heard anything about it."

"Oh, I've heard about it, all right. I'm telling you, Quill. We don't have the money to spend on those fancy courses to train employees, but even if we did, I don't think I'd waste my time. Well, let's see. We were in the main dining room and who else was there. It wasn't full, I can tell you that, and with your prices, who can wonder? That Major Hackmeyer ate there, of course. He's got more money than God as far as any of us can tell. But he stopped by the table to say hello to Nana and congratulate her on her birthday. And who else? Some tourists. Oh! And how could I have forgotten? Some weirdo girl with black fingernails. She had some lunch and skipped out."

Quill stared at her.

"What?"

"A weirdo girl? With black fingernails?"

"You're upset, and I can't say that I blame you. You don't want types like that coming into your Inn. Lowers the tone. She paid with a credit card," Alicia added. "Probably stolen, is my guess, but Kathleen took it and didn't say a word."

"Kathleen waited on your table, too?"

"Yes." Alicia piled the contents of the basket onto the counter and started ringing them up. Quill winced at the total, and handed over her credit card.

"Tell me, Alicia," she said in respectful tones, "did Nana have anything to say to the family? You know, a last good word to remember her by?"

"As a matter of fact, she didn't." The Kleenex came out again. Alicia dabbed at her eyes and said, "It would have been so nice, you know? We'd just had this wonderful party, and she was counting out the cash for the bill, and you'd think, wouldn't you, that she'd bless us all, or thank us for being her family, and all she said was . . ." Alicia paused. She was not without a sense of drama. "Too much garlic in that stinky cheese. We should have gone to McDonald's."

Mrs. Freddie Bellini was the saddest widow Quill had ever seen. She was dressed in black from head to toe, her face was swollen with tears, and she looked utterly bewildered. She was tiny, with carefully penned hair and a lightly wrinkled face.

The Bellinis lived in back of their funeral home in an immaculately kept two-bedroom cottage that smelled like sandalwood. Mrs. Bellini was pathetically grateful to see Quill. ("Morticians don't make many friends. They tell you that right off when you go in for training.") She drew her inside her little house, tsked over her wet hair, and suggested hot tea. "Because, my dear, it's the best thing to ward off a cold, you know. You can't be too careful this time of year."

"Thank you," Quill said.

"Now you just sit right here." She gestured toward a green cut-velvet couch with a fleur-delys design. "And I'll put the water on to boil."

She pattered out to the kitchen. Quill looked at the living room with curiosity. There was a lot of Queen Anne furniture, the sort you can buy at the Bombay Company. Prints of English hunts, framed in heavy gilt, were on all the walls. The couch she was sitting on was beautifully kept — but Quill had seen ones just like it at discount furniture stores all over Syracuse. She'd thought, vaguely, that morticians made a lot of money.

A silver-framed photograph sat on a small, freestanding keyboard in the corner. Quill rose to look at it.

"Our son," Mrs. Bellini said. "His high school picture." She placed a tray with a teapot, two cups, and a plate of cookies on the coffee table in front of Quill. She sat in the armchair next to the couch and leaned forward to pour.

Freddie had been in his sixties, and so was his wife. Quill smiled and said, "He looks a lot like you, Mrs. Bellini. Did he go to school here in Hemlock Falls?"

"Walter? No. We were living in Syracuse when he was young. That was years ago."

"Did he follow in the family business?"

"No. I'm afraid Walter lives in California. He's . . . between jobs right now."

Quill felt like a rat. But she had a good idea of where poor Freddie Bellini had spent his money. "I just came to tell you how sorry I was that Freddie is gone."

"Thank you, my dear. We were married forty-two years. It's going to be very hard to go on without him." She didn't seem to notice that tears were streaming down her cheeks. "We were so close. But we knew it was just a matter of time. Would you like sugar with your tea?"

"No, thank you. Just lemon." Quill took the cup and wondered how the hell she was going to find the nerve to pester this poor woman with her investigation. She always forgot the part of amateur detecting that required the detective to be rude, intrusive, and careless of other people's feelings. She set her cup down on the coffee table and said, "Is there anything at all I can do for you? Will you let us know when the service will be?"

"We have friends in the business, you know. As soon as his body's released, I'll have him shipped to Rochester. The embalmer there is a master, Freddie always said so. And he would like to know that Eddie had prepared him."

"So the funeral will be in Rochester?"

"No, California, actually. We were able to send Walter a bit of money recently, just to help out, you know, and he's promised to take care of everything. I'll be selling all this and moving out there permanently. Just as soon as poor Freddie is buried." She burst into sudden, violent tears. Quill's eyes stung and she bit her lip. Mrs. Bellini sobbed. Quill held her hand.

"And I felt like a complete and utter rat." Quill swung her feet up on her couch and stared at the ceiling.

"Oh, dear," Meg said. "So you didn't get a chance to ask her about Freddie's lunch here? Or garlic?"

"No. But we have a list of the morticians who

238

were registered for the convention. And the menu they ordered was, guess what . . ."

"Filet mignon, baked chicken, or pasta," Meg said promptly. "That's what conventioneers want and that's what they get. I've long ago given up trying to convert any of them." She settled behind Quill's desk and put her feet up, too. "Bjarne handles it."

"Was there any garlic in the meal?"

"That's like asking if brine has salt in it. Of course we used garlic. What about it?"

"It's just so . . . odd. I smelled garlic just before I was hit on the head. Derwent ate garlic and his stomach was upset. Mrs. Nickerson said the Roquefort was too garlicky, which is silly, because there isn't any garlic in Roquefort."

"And we don't know if Freddie had an encounter with garlic because Mrs. Bellini's too grief-stricken to talk about it."

"Encounter with garlic?" Quill said. "What kind of language is that?"

"Detective language," Meg said airily. "Shall we call one of the morticians from the convention and ask about garlic?"

"Could there be a dangerous mold on garlic?"

"Would I use it if there were?" Meg's voice was dangerously sweet.

"A mysterious invisible mold on garlic?"

"I doubt it." Meg picked up the phone. "But the Cornell Ag School is only a phone call away. Could I point something out?"

"You're asking permission?"

"Did you have any garlic before you went downstairs to get the WhyNots?"

"Of course not."

"But you smelled garlic?"

"I did."

"Are you sure?"

Quill felt the back of her head. "As sure as I can be. I mean, I was concussed."

"Was it garlic breath?"

"It was garlic breath," Quill said positively. She drew a deep breath. "There was someone behind me. I felt him. And I smelled his breath. I'm sure of it."

"So we table the garlic for the moment."

"We can't table the garlic. It's a clue."

"What other anomalies did you discover?"

"Anomalies," Quill said. "Azalea Cummings had lunch in the dining room on June twelfth. That's an anomaly. She and Ralph didn't check in until Tuesday of this week."

"But she told you that they were wandering around here last week looking for subjects to shoot. And the only reason they were staying here was because she had that grant from their university."

"Some excuse."

"It's a good excuse. We're expensive. They're poor students. What else?"

Quill rubbed her eyes. It was only two o'clock, but she felt as if she'd been up for hours. "I have been up for hours," she said aloud. "I got up at two o'clock this morning and I haven't been back to bed."

"You should go to bed right now," Meg said anxiously. "We can talk about this later."

"When? The reenactment's tomorrow. The banquet's tomorrow night. The reception for the film students is this evening. We're busy."

"It can wait until Sunday."

"Doreen's contest is due Sunday. We'll be going over the evidence to see if any of our employees' handwriting matches the fatal WhyNots. And Sunday night . . ."

"She's checking into the hospital." Meg nodded. "We have to be there for that. Andy says she'll be fine, you know."

"Is he sure?"

"Of course he's sure. He's a doctor."

"You're worried, too."

"Of course I'm worried." Meg swung her feet off the desk and slumped down in the chair. "It's an invasive cancer. She's lucky, Andy said. The sentinel nodes are all clear, and the tissue left in the breast is Stage Zero."

"Which means it's not cancerous now . . ."

"But it could be. Heck, Quill. She's seventy-three. She's not going to die from cancer. She'll outlive us all." She slapped the desk. "Right, then. What other oddnesses cropped up, other than my poisonous garlic?"

"Everybody mentioned seeing Warrender Hackmeyer."

"That's not surprising, is it? He's rich, and

people are fascinated with the rich. And everyone's excited about the reenactment. And what could he possibly have to do with our three nice elderly victims?"

She knew one reason. A reason she couldn't tell Meg. Quill sat up and put her head in her hands, thinking hard.

If Freddie Bellini and Derwent Peterson had been members of the militia, had Hackmeyer killed them? And there wasn't any reason why Nadine Nickerson had to be excluded. From all accounts, she had been a tough old bird, and her husband Knox had been a tough old bird, too. Were they about to betray the militia's secrets? Did the militia have secrets?

"Nothing." Quill yawned. "Actually, something nice. Every one of them chose the Inn to celebrate in, Meg. There were three important occasions — Derwent was going to spend the rest of his life in a nice condo in Florida, Mrs. Nickerson was spending money on her family for the first time, and even Freddie was having a great time. He was out with friends, and Mrs. Bellini said they're in short supply for morticians. So I'll tell you what was good about today. People like coming here. They have a good time when they're here. And I like that a lot about what we do." She got up. "I'm going to take a nap. Make sure I'm up in time for the film party thing. I want to find out why Azalea was here last week. It seems highly suspicious to me.

242

And it's time for a talk with Warrender Hack-meyer."

She went upstairs and curled up in her extremely comfortable bed.

She awoke to a touch on her shoulder, and concern in Myles's face. "Sorry to wake you." He sat next to her on the bed. "How are you feeling?" Max poked his head over Myles's knee and panted heavily. He looked concerned, too.

Quill sat up. The lamp in the corner was on. It was dark outside her bedroom window. She'd slept in her clothes and she felt wrinkled. "What time is it?"

"A little after nine." Myles smoothed the hair away from her face. "Let me see your eyes."

"Nine o'clock at night?" Quill yawned, blinked, and tried to keep her eyes open. Myles took a penlight from his shirt pocket, switched it on, and shone it into her face. "Hey!" She pushed his hand away.

"Just want to make sure that your pupils aren't dilated."

Quill squinted at him.

He switched the penlight off. "You were sleeping pretty heavily. Would you like to get up?"

"I was sleeping hard because I was tired. And yes, I'm going to get up. Is the reception for the film people still going on?"

"They were breaking up when I came in."

"Darn it. I wanted to catch Azalea Cummings after she's had a few glasses of wine."

Myles narrowed his eyes. "Why? You think she had something to do with the WhyNots?"

She'd forgotten about the WhyNots. "Oh? Perhaps."

"Do you think she wanted to cause a crisis at the Inn so she could film it?"

Quill shook her head. "No. There's much more interesting things to shoot than a lot of cranky employees. Of course, up until today, I didn't think the timing could have worked out, but if she was at the Inn on the twelfth . . ." She drew her knees up to her chin and sat there, thinking.

"You are limiting yourself to getting to the bottom of the WhyNots," Myles said. It wasn't a question.

"You've made it pretty clear that it's important," she agreed. She smiled at him.

He sighed. "Just be careful, Quill. Are you going to get up?"

"Yes." She stood up. Max jumped up and put his paws on her chest. She scratched his ears. "And what have you been doing all day, you good boy, you?" She buried her face in the top of his head. "Ugh, Max. What have you been into today? You smell like . . ." She sniffed again. "Horse manure. I'll just bet all those horses in the five-acre field are pretty inter-esting, huh, boy." Max dropped to the floor, ambled across the Berber carpeting to the leather couch, and jumped on it.

"Myles, what do you think Warrender Hackmeyer is doing with his militia?"

"I am going to be very angry if you start poking around with that, Quill."

"It's more a matter of information than anything else. I'm curious." She yawned again. "I'm also starving to death. Have you had anything to eat yet?"

"No. And Meg was pretty sure you hadn't, either. I brought up some food from downstairs. I put it in the kitchen."

Quill wandered into the small kitchen that she'd had installed in her rooms when they'd first remodeled the Inn. It was fully equipped, with a small four-burner gas stove, an under-the-counter refrigerator, a narrow dishwasher, and white Corian countertops. Two covered plates stood on the small breakfast bar that separated the kitchen from the living room. She lifted one cover: boneless pork chops with mango chutney. "I was afraid it was mutton."

Quill set out napkins, cutlery, wineglasses, and a bottle of Pinot Grigio from the fridge. Myles settled beside her at the counter. "So," she said after a moment's contented silence. "About militias. Why aren't they illegal?"

"Because we have the right to keep and bear arms."

Like almost all the law enforcement people she knew, Myles was in favor of gun control. But he was even more in favor of individual rights. Quill was of the opinion that if people didn't kill each other with guns, they would kill each other with clubs, knives, and large rocks, as they had done for the centuries before gunpowder was invented. Laws that made it easier to act on that basic human urge seemed counterproductive to her. She swallowed a delicious portion of chutney.

"What is a militia for?" She frowned. "Or would it be militiae? It's from the Latin, isn't it? So the plural would be militiae."

"What are they for?" Myles repeated, taken aback.

"Yes. When Warrender recruits for his militiae, what does he say? Why do people join?"

Myles laughed. "I suppose he presents it as a hobby."

"Do you suppose or do you know?"

"Are you planning on joining?" There was steel in his voice.

Quill poured him a second glass of wine. "He's a guest here. Professionally, I have a duty to welcome all comers. Personally, I'm trying to decide whether or not I should ask him to leave."

"I thought the first rule of innkeeping was don't insult the guests."

"There's always a first time." She poured herself a second glass of wine. "Of course I'm not going to throw him out. I'm sure it'd be against some law or other."

"There's a small matter of civil rights," Myles said.

"But I do have to deal with him." She glanced over at Max. "Maybe we can talk about horses."

Myles took the wineglass from her hand and set it on the counter. He cupped her cheek in his hands. "Do you still want to go downstairs this evening?"

Quill slid her arms around his neck. "To-morrow. Tomorrow morning will be just fine."

She woke again at two o'clock in the morning, hoping it wasn't going to become a habit. If she were in New York City, there would be places to go; many of her friends in the art world worked at night, so there would be people to see, too. Hemlock Falls closed down at night — curtains drawn, windows shuttered, doors closed.

Myles slept quietly beside her. The moon shone through the bedroom window, casting the strong bones of his jaw in shadow, smoothing out the fine lines at the corners of his eyes. When they had first become lovers, he'd waken when she woke. As time when on, and they'd become accustomed to the feel of each other in bed, he'd dropped his guard with her. She had asked him once if he slept as deeply in other places as he did now with her. He'd laughed, shaken his head, and told her that was one of the reasons he'd come home.

She slipped out of bed and went into the living room, Max padding along beside her. She closed the bedroom door and curled up on her couch. The French doors were open and the scents of a summer night drifted through the air: cut grass, heavy with dew; a faint odor of roses; the smell of damp earth after the morning rains.

She couldn't get Mrs. Bellini out of her mind. Quill cried out of frustration, anger, occasional sadness, and once after a particularly bitter quarrel with Myles, out of a deep and alarming self-pity. But she had never cried with the kind of deep, abandoned grief she'd seen in Mrs. Bellini today. She would hear those primal sobs for the rest of her life.

She drew her legs up and rested her chin on her knees. She admired artists who drew from some terrible well within themselves. But she couldn't, wouldn't put that kind of pain on canvas.

She heard the bedroom door open and Myles's long strides across the floor. He shoved Max aside and settled beside her. "How's your head?"

She felt the nape of her neck. "It's fine. I took the bandage off when I took my bath tonight. The bruise is going away, I think."

"I'll find who did it." His voice was distant and calm.

She glanced at him out of the corner of her eye. "Do you really think it was the saboteur?"

"The . . . ? Oh. It may have been, yes."

"No, you don't." Quill wriggled around to face him. "Have the autopsy results come in yet? The ones on Mr. Peter—"

"I know which autopsies you're referring to, Quill. We'll have them Monday. Until we have them, there's nothing but supposition to go on. We have no facts. Don't spin your wheels over this, please. Let's get our priorities straight."

"I really object to being lectured," Quill said mildly.

She felt him jerk. "Sorry. But if you keep moving the personal into my professional life, what is the fairest way for me to react?"

"If I were you," Quill said honestly, "I would tell me to butt out."

"Good. Then you won't mind if I tell you to butt out. For my sake if not for your own."

"I won't mind, no." She slipped into the circle of his arm. "You said you were going to leave. For as long as a year. When?"

His arm tightened. "Soon. Too soon."

"I saw Mrs. Bellini today. I hadn't had a chance to make a condolence call until now, and there were some other things I wanted to check with. Myles, her grief was horrible. Unimaginable. She'd been married to Freddie for forty-two years. She's going out to California to stay with their son because she doesn't have any friends here . . . Myles, it was so sad." Her own eyes filled with tears.

"First, I have a lively sense of self-preservation." He sounded amused. "Second — and really, it's important for you to realize this — you have a life of your own. Apart from me. You have connections, friends, people who love you. If something should happen to me, Quill, you will go on."

Quill settled against his shoulder. "I will." She

felt utterly sad. "But my painting would change. It would never be the same. And how much of me would be left then, Myles?"

He didn't say anything to that.

No one had an answer to that.

CHAPTER 11

"That dog needs a bath." Doreen scowled horribly and stamped by as Quill and Max came down the stairs Saturday morning. She wore a blue calico gown with a bow at the throat, high button shoes, and a bonnet. The bonnet was of calico, too, and Doreen had added a sequin pin to it, just over her ear. The strings dangled free under her chin. She looked hot.

"He does need a bath. I thought I'd take him down to the Gorge and throw him in the stream for a bit."

"Good idea." Doreen disappeared through the archway and into the dining room.

It was eight o'clock. Myles had gone. Dina wasn't in yet. Quill went into the dining room. The room was alive with excited chatter. Devora was waiting tables this morning, with two of the other members of the wait staff. The men were dressed in coarse linen shirts that buttoned up to the throat, narrow trousers, and thin suspenders. Devora was in a full blue skirt, a white ruffled blouse, and some kind of material wound around her waist that Quill recalled (vaguely) was named a waist. She had a flat straw hat titled prettily over one ear. The reenactors were in full uniform. Sergeant Fetterman wore a forage cap squashed down low on his forehead. Captain Coolidge had a plume on his hat. Major Hackmeyer was not in evidence. The civilians — those guests not dressed like refugees from some addled time machine — gazed around with pleased anticipation.

Quill inhaled. There was the usual scent of breakfast: Meg's fresh breads, strawberries, good coffee, the freesia on the tables, and something else. Something gluey. She passed through the dining room, greeting the regular guests. She smiled encouragingly at Devora. "You look terrific."

Devora took a deep, choking sigh. "This thing is hot," she said. "And the corset you have to wear to get the darn dress to fit around your waist is choking me half to death and these stupid shoes suck." She thrust out her foot. Like Doreen, she wore high button boots. "Did you know that there was no difference between the left shoe and the right shoe in olden times?"

"Yes," Quill said, who had forgotten that she knew.

"I'm supposed to walk around all day in these?" She clumped indignantly off. She turned around and yelled, "And where's your costume?"

"In a minute," Quill said. She stopped at the reenactors' table. "Good morning."

Nobody said anything.

Quill looked at their plates in horror. It was the source of the gluey smell. There was a small bowl of porridge-like stuff and lumps of dough. "What in the name of goodness are you having for breakfast?"

Sergeant Fetterman passed the milk jug to Captain Coolidge, who emptied it into his coffee. Max stuck his nose onto the table, tail wagging eagerly. He whined. "Hush, puppy!" Sergeant Fetterman said, and tossed him a sludgy bit of dough. The table broke into laughter. Max snapped the dough up, mouthed it with a puzzled expression, and dropped it on the floor.

Quill glared at them all, picked up the dough, and stamped into the kitchen. She was beginning to understand Doreen's bad mood.

The kitchen was a little quieter than usual. Sullen, Quill might call it. The air-conditioning was turned way up. The cooks, chefs, and cleanup crew were all dressed like the wait staff. As soon as they realized Quill was in the room, they began to walk with exaggerated limps. Quill said, "Good morning, everyone," and told them how nice they looked. Somebody dropped a pot on the floor with a pointed "clang!"

Meg stood at the fireplace, stirring a large pot suspended over an open fire. She was dressed in baggy shorts, a T-shirt, and tennis shoes. Her socks were red.

"What in the heck are they eating out there?" Quill tossed the dough into the disposal.

Meg turned around. "Barley porridge. Boiled in salt water. For hours. I'm staring at the rest of it right now. They want it for lunch. And that stuff you threw out? That's a hush puppy. Don't even ask how we made that." She dropped the wooden spoon into the pot. "There. That ought to give the sucker some flavor."

"Did they *ask* for this? I mean, I passed through the dining room just now and they won't even speak to me. I think they're mad at us."

"They aren't mad at you. They just won't speak to you unless you're in costume."

Quill looked down at herself. She was dressed as she usually was in the mornings — light challis skirt that fell to her calves, linen blouse, and sandals. "They spoke to Max."

Meg sat at the prep table. "A dog is a dog whatever the century." Max barked. "He needs a bath."

"I was planning on taking care of that this morning." Quill went to the windows at the back of the kitchen and looked out. The tents were up. They were a curious circular shape — not large, but more tepee than tent. The clang of hammers on metal rang through the air. The field itself was filled with men in long woolen shirts, blue trousers with yellow stripes, and horses. "There are a lot of guys out there."

"Vans and trucks started rolling in last night. There are reenactors and their families from all over New York. We even have people from

Hemlock Falls taking part. They love it. They *love* it. The campsite in the park is full and so are all the motels on 15. And we're booked solid for breakfast, lunch, and dinner through tomorrow night." Meg bounced on her toes. "I've called in all the extra staff. And I put the telephone message on that we're not taking any reservations."

"What if we get cancellations before Dina comes in?"

"This is why we're not the Marriott, Quill. I'm looking forward to a few cancellations. Now go away. You must have work to do. And put your costume on."

"I'll put my costume on if you put your costume on."

"I'll get to it," Meg said irritably. "You put yours on first."

"I don't think I have a costume," Quill said. "No one's given me a costume so far."

"You have a costume. It's in your office. You're not going to believe this, but Doreen went and spent a ton of money on mine and yours."

"She did?" Quill was touched. "She shouldn't have done that."

"She sure shouldn't have," Meg said feelingly.

Obediently, Quill went back to her office. There was a large, ominous-looking bag on her couch with a hanger poking out of the top. A big shoe box lay next to it, and a smaller box next to that. Quill opened the large box. High button shoes, size six. She held the shoes up. No left or right sole. She opened the smaller box. There was a body-smoother, stockings, and garters. Quill picked the body-smoother up. It seemed to be made of tire rubber. She dropped it back on the couch.

The message light on the phone answering machine was blinking, but it was the Inn line, not their personal line. Dina would take care of that. As a matter of fact, Dina became very annoyed when Quill took down the messages from the answering machine because Quill would forget where she'd written them down.

She paged through the accounts payable. The bills seemed up to date. She checked the accounts receivable ledger; nothing outstanding. She checked the daily schedule Dina wrote down for her every day: All that was scrawled on it was COSTUME! followed by the events agenda, which Quill knew already. "So I do have a little time for investigating," she said to Max. "Come on. We'll go down to the stream for a bath — by way of the five-acre field."

Yesterday's rain was gone and the sky was a clear, pale blue. It was already hot. The guest parking lot was full. It looked as if the entire village of Hemlock Falls had emptied Nickerson's Hardware of aluminum beach chairs and brought them to the edge of the field. An amazing number of people were in costume. Esther West wore a huge hat, a white muslin gown dotted with green embroideries, a wide green sash, and an off-the-shoulder ruffle. Marge Schmidt was in a no-nonsense brown velvet skirt and jacket with riding boots and a cravat. Betty Hall, like Doreen, was in calico with a wide-brimmed straw hat. The VFW had their hamburger kiosk set up at the edge of the field and dispensed coffee and lemonade.

Adela, in her scarlet ball gown, stood next to a small group of men clustered at the edge of the meadow nearest the pine woods. They wore butternut gray. These, Quill presumed, were the Rebels.

Quill greeted Miriam Doncaster and Howie Murchison. The librarian was dressed in a neatly tailored blue riding outfit, a beaver hat on her gray-blond hair. Howie had opted for a simpler effect — he wore baggy corduroy pants and a flannel shirt. He was sweating in the heat.

"That's not much of a costume, Quill," Miriam said disapprovingly. "And Max needs a bath."

"My costume is in my office. I have to get Max rinsed off a little bit, and I didn't want to ruin it. I'll put it on later."

"How much later?" Miriam said crossly. She tugged at her tie, which appeared to be choking her. "My goodness. Would you look at her! She's gorgeous and I've heard Revlon is interested in acquiring her hand cream. I can't stand it."

Quill looked. Donna Olafson strolled through the crowd, a lacy parasol over her head. Her costume was amber silk, looped at the side with a demibustle. A necklace of square topaz circled her neck. Her auburn hair was piled high, and three creamy ostrich plumes curled over one cheek. She didn't look hot at all. And she walked as if her shoes didn't pinch. Mr. Olafson walked beside her, dressed impeccably in gray wool and top hat.

And there was Carol Ann Spinoza, dressed in a starched shirtwaist in red and white checks. Quill fought the desire to duck behind the nearest tree. And what the heck was she handing out to people? Quill craned her neck and squinted. It looked like the Inn brochures, which made no sense at all. Carol Ann usually made a great deal of sense, in a sneaky kind of way.

Quill made a management decision not to tackle Carol Ann at this particular point. On the other hand, she was perfectly ready to tackle Azalea Cummings and Ralph Austin. They were conspicuous in black jeans and T-shirts. They circled the colorfully dressed crowd, looking contemptuous.

"Hi," Quill said as she walked up to them. "Enjoying the day?"

Azalea planted her boots wide apart and glared at her. "You didn't tell us you were Sarah Quilliam."

"I didn't?" Quill blinked. "Who did I tell you I was?"

"The woman who manages this place." Azalea gave the meadow, the Falls, and the Inn itself a comprehensive glance.

"But I do . . . oh! You mean that I paint."

"Paint," Azalea said. "I guess so."

"It's all right, Zale." Ralph gave her arm a little shake. "She's got to earn a living too, you know."

"Do you know what her pieces go for?" Azalea shook her head. "Of all people. You. To sell out."

"You know what, Zale? A place like this takes in a lot of cash."

Azalea narrowed her eyes. "So it does."

"Can't blame her for that," Ralph said. He winked encouragingly at Quill. "Save a bit on the old taxes, huh, Zale?"

"I just wanted to say how sorry I was that I missed you last week," Quill said. "I was away for the day in Syracuse on the twelfth of June. I guess you and Ralph dropped by."

Neither said anything. Nor did they look at each other.

"Doreen thought she saw you in one of the rooms."

"Just checking the place out," Ralph said. He seemed embarrassed, and angry about it. "Our university is a little concerned about the way we spend their money, okay? If it's too lavish, they'll end up making us pay part of the bill. All right?"

"We haven't sold out," Azalea said with a distinct edge to her voice.

"But, Zale." Ralph shook his head admiringly. "It's a gold mine here. Lotta cash in this business. Bet a lot doesn't get reported, right,

Quill?" He gave her another wink, and then smirked.

Quill excused herself and walked on. She took a breath with each stride, and by the time she found Major Hackmeyer, she'd subdued the desire to whack both Ralph and Azalea up the side of the head with a manure fork. And to turn them into the IRS.

She found him in one of the larger tents, with the horses.

Quill didn't know a great deal about the day-to-day routine of the cavalry in the 1860s, but she was willing to bet that Hackmeyer had it right, down to the last detail. A farmer worked over an open forge, banging away at a horseshoe. Saddles were neatly draped over wooden sawhorses. They were styled much differently than the English and stock saddles Quill was familiar with from her girlhood riding days. The cantles were low, there was a modified horn in front, and the skirts were plain, smooth leather. The blankets underneath them were navy blue wool, bordered in yellow. In addition to the horses, the tent was filled with long, flat boxes painted a dull brown.

The horses themselves were lined up at the rear of the tent, separated by ropes tied to stakes driven into the ground. Hackmeyer squatted next to a big black, vigorously rubbing its left foreleg. Ann Brightman, the local vet, stood slightly back from them, her hands on her hips. Max sniffed curiously at them, wrinkled his nose, and snarled.

Hackmeyer looked up, and then rose to his feet. He tipped his hat and said, "Ma'am."

Quill smiled as she approached. "I'm glad you're talking to me at least. I haven't had a chance to get into costume yet."

"Any of my men talk to you?"

"Ah. No."

"Good. They're under orders."

Quill nodded to Ann, who said, "Hello, Quill."

Quill patted the black's neck. "He's beautiful. I hope he's okay."

Hackmeyer bent back to the leg. "Knee's swollen. Been treating it for a couple of days. Looks a bit better right now, though."

"He's a Trakhener," Ann said. "Gorgeous, isn't he? The, um, major calls him Ulysses."

"It's a shame about his knee." Quill bent down next to the major and put her hand on the glossy leg.

"Watch it," Ann said.

Heat spread through Quill's palm and up her arm. Her whole body tingled.

She tasted garlic.

"You all right?" Ann took her elbow and gently pulled her aside. "DMSO's powerful stuff."

"What?" Quill said.

"You're pale. And you've had a concussion recently, right? Here, sit down." She pushed Quill onto a large flat box. "It's dimethyl sulfoxide," she said. "We think it's safe for humans. But we can't be sure." She spoke a little more loudly.

261

"Horse liniment, Quill. It's a vasodilator. Best anti-inflammatory around."

"What?" Quill said again. She stared at Hackmeyer. He straightened up slowly, his eyes narrow.

Ann put her hand on Quill's forehead. "Hey, kiddo," she said. "Take it easy. Do you feel faint?"

"I feel fine," Quill said. "I think. I think I'd better go put my costume on."

"Let me walk up to the Inn with you. Just to be sure."

"Good idea," Hackmeyer said. "You want to get her off that box, Dr. Brightman? I've got the ordnance stored in there." He grinned at Quill, his teeth white in his bearded face. "Sure like to see you in a frilly dress, ma'am."

Quill let Ann put her arm around her waist and lead her out of the tent. Once out of Hackmeyer's hearing, she said, "I'm fine. I just need some information. The stuff I just touched —"

"DMSO, yes."

"How powerful is it?"

"How much is an airline ticket?" Ann smiled. "Sorry, but you need to be more specific."

"Why did I taste garlic?"

Ann shrugged. "You just do. DMSO sweeps through your system within seconds. It's amazing. If you have any arthritis or musculoskeletal aches and pains, it wipes it all away. It's terrific."

"What kind of effect does it have on humans?"

"It's approved for human use in Europe, in

much smaller dosages, of course. But it drops the blood pressure. It can give you a headache, stomach cramps. And I'm not at all happy that you've gotten a dose in your condition. Will you let me give Andy a call?"

"No. I'm fine. Ann, if you had a horse with a — a — heart condition —" She interrupted herself, "Horses do have heart conditions?"

"Oh, sure. Just like people."

"Would you give DMSO to an elderly horse, with a heart condition?"

"Good heavens, that would be risky."

"Would the horse feel quite ill?"

Ann gave Quill a very skeptical look. "An elderly debilitated horse receiving a massive dose of DMSO would probably feel very strange. Woozy. Stomach upset. Headache. Erratic heartbeat, if the horse was on medication for a cardiovascular disorder. I wouldn't recommend mixing anything with DMSO at all. But, Quill, I have to tell you . . ."

"What?"

"My patients don't talk to me about these things."

"A frilly dress," Quill muttered furiously as she tore open the bag containing her costume. "I'll frilly dress him!"

Meg shook her head. "I think you ought to call Myles right now."

"Hackmeyer hit you over the head?" Dina said. "How come? Did he, like, make a pass at you and you rejected him?" Her brown eyes sparkled. "Did he hit you over the head to have his wicked way with you?"

The three of them were in her office. If Quill was going to continue her investigations, she wanted to circulate as unobtrusively as possible, which meant dressing up as though she were in the nineteenth century, since everybody else in Hemlock Falls was, too. She'd grabbed Meg out of the kitchen and Dina from the reception desk. She wasn't going to suffer alone.

"These costumes are going to your head, Dina. You're behaving as if you're in a romance novel." Quill shook her dress free of the wrapping and gasped.

"It's gorgeous!" Dina squealed.

"So's mine." Meg held up a blue velvet walking dress, trimmed in fur. "How in the heck am I going to cook in *this?*"

Quill spread the skirts of her costume with one hand and held it against her body with the other. It was made of copper silk, the same color as her hair. "Oh, my goodness." She leaned forward and punched the intercom on her desk. "Would Doreen come to the Inn office, please? Would Doreen come to the Inn office, please?"

"She shouldn't have," Meg said. "Wow. This must have cost a bundle. Even to rent."

"I like mine," Dina said, a little wistfully. It was white muslin, with a simple round collar. A demure ruffle edged the long skirt.

"Very Emily Dickinson," Quill said. "So. Okay. How do we put it on?"

"Body-smoothers first," Dina said. "I mean, like, you're skinny, Quill, but look at that waist. It's teeny."

Quill shook out the body-smoother. It still felt like it was made out of a tire. Meg shook out hers. Dina looked at the one she carried doubtfully. "It's, like, way too little to get over my hips."

"You don't pull it up," Quill said with authority. "You pull it down. And let's go. I want to get back out there." She tugged the smoother apart and pulled it down over her head.

"I'm stuck," she said after a minute.

"So am I," Meg said. Her voice was muffled. Quill couldn't see her, but she could understand her. "I don't think we should have tried to pull these body-smoothers over our heads. I think you pull it up."

"Well, there weren't any instructions," Quill said crossly. "Dina, you're going to have to give me a hand here. I can't get any leverage." She tugged at the top of the body-smoother with one hand. She couldn't see a thing. Her nose was mashed flat.

"Just a second," Dina said. "Honestly, Quill, why did we listen to you — ouch!" Dina must have tripped over the couch. She fell against Quill. Since both of Quill's arms were stuck up in the air, they both crashed into the desk.

Quill heard the office door open, and Doreen said, "What the heck!"

"Just help me *off* with this thing," Meg yelled.

"Why did you pull 'em over your heads?" Doreen asked.

"Because Quill's an idiot!" Meg's voice wasn't muffled enough, Quill thought. If she could get this thing off her head, she'd muffle Meg, all right.

"Good," Azalea Cummings said in her flat, nasal voice. "Finally, some interesting footage."

"You don't look half-bad," Doreen said, after she'd thrown Azalea out, jerked off the body-smoothers and helped them get dressed. Quill smoothed the bronze silk over her hips. "It's very beautiful."

"The thing is, I don't think I can cook in this, Doreen." Meg spun around. The blue velvet swirled gracefully around her feet.

"I can answer phones in this, for sure." Dina looked extremely pretty in her simple white muslin. "Can I go show it to Davey?"

"Certainly," Quill said. "Just make sure the answering machine's on. And Dina — not a word to him about Major Hackmeyer, okay? I want to talk to Myles first."

"I'm not going to say a word about Major Hackmeyer," Dina said. "I'm going to have him arrest that Azalea Cummings. She taped us stumbling around here with our hands stuck in the air and body-smoothers on our heads. How could you, Doreen?"

Doreen shrugged. "Can't help it if she was

follering me around. And how was I to know you three would . . ." She turned around and coughed heavily into her hand.

"Are you okay, Doreen?" Dina asked anxiously. "I know you don't like to talk about your operation, but do you need to sit down, or anything? Can I get you some water?"

"Not the operation!" Doreen gasped. "Oh, ha-ha!"

"She's fine," Quill said shortly. "She's laughing."

"At us?"

"Evidently."

"I am *not* hanging around for this!" Dina stamped out the door.

"Thing is," Doreen said with a happy sigh, "that Azalea's gonna show her film to the Chamber tomorrow night. There's a meeting called, special, just to — there's a word for it. Seen it?"

"Screen it," Meg said. "Oh, boy. Maybe we can offer her a bribe, Quill. We looked like idiots in those things."

"We don't believe in bribes," Quill said.

"I believe passionately in bribes," Meg said. "Especially if it's a mere matter of money. Do you want the entire town of Hemlock Falls to see us with body-smoothers stuck on our heads?"

"No. I don't."

"Well, then."

Quill gave her body-smoother a kick. She'd

thrown it on the floor. She ignored Azalea's suggestion that she sell it on eBay.

"I'll talk to her. I want to talk to her anyway. But first" — she looked at Doreen — "I want to talk to you."

"I'm going back to the mutton," Meg said. "And Quill — stay out of Hackmeyer's way. Okay? Leave it to Myles."

"Hackmeyer," Doreen said after Meg had shut the door. "What's this about Hackmeyer?"

"I'm pretty sure he's the one who hit me over the head."

"Him?" Doreen looked worried. "I gotta tell you, I don't like that guy. What makes you think it was him? You want I should get the sheriff?"

"Not just yet. You know Myles can't act without facts, Doreen. And I don't have any facts yet. Just supposition. I want you to tell me something."

"Okay."

"Where did you get the money to rent these costumes?" She looked down at her dress. "It's from New York. It has to be. And I know the rental for this kind of quality is really high. Meg's and mine have to cost a thousand dollars a day. At least. Did you go into your savings?"

Like most of her generation, Doreen didn't tolerate open talk about money very well. Quill put her hand on her arm. "I wouldn't ask if it weren't really important."

"Thing is, when I got diagnosed with the cancer, I cashed in my insurance policy."

"Your life insurance policy?"

"Yeah. Figured, what the heck. I haven't got that much ahead of me. Figured Stoke and I could get one good last run before I kicked off."

"Who talked you into this?"

"Nobody talked me into anything! As a matter of fact, I had one heck of a time talking 'em into it."

"I'm sorry, Doreen. I didn't mean that the way it sounded. Who cashed in your policy for you?"

"Marge Schmidt."

"Marge Schmidt! But . . ." Quill sat down on her couch. "It doesn't make sense."

"It's perfectly legal!"

"Wait a minute." Quill put her hands over her face, the better able to concentrate. "Did Marge carry life policies on Derwent Peterson, Mrs. Nickerson, and Freddie?"

"Marge carries policies on everyone in this here town, far as I know."

"This isn't making any sense at all. Look, Doreen. I went out and spoke to the families yesterday."

"Of Derwent and them?"

"Yes. You know that they all spent the day of June twelfth here at the Inn. All three of them were admitted to the hospital with pretty much the same symptoms. And all three of them died."

Doreen went *"Tcha,"* then said, "It was their time."

"If I hear that one more time, I'm going to

scream," Quill said fiercely. "It was *not* their time. They were managing quite well. There were four things these people had in common: They were all at the Inn at the same time, they all were spending money they didn't seem to have before, they were all sick with terminal diseases, and they all ran into Warrender Hackmeyer. And Warrender Hackmeyer somehow dosed them with DMSO. Which he has on hand because it's a horse liniment. And he hit me over the head, Doreen. I know he did. That stuff gives you terrible garlic breath and I smelled it. He had motive and opportunity!"

Doreen patted her hand. "Those concussions are something." Then, "Y'know, they all passed in the hospital."

"I know." Quill pounded the couch in frustration. "He got to them somehow. I know it."

"Sheriff's gonna want facts."

"No kidding."

The intercom on Quill's desk buzzed, and Dina's voice said cheerily, "It's quarter to two! The reenactment's going to start pretty soon."

"We're coming out, Dina," Quill said. "Doreen, I'm going to get those facts."

"Maybe there aren't any to get."

"Why would someone steal the W.A.T.C.H. Reports?"

Doreen shrugged.

"And why would someone hit me over the head?"

"Because someone's a durn fool," she said violently. "The idea!" Her lips worked. "You don't suppose it's the same person that's been planting the fake WhyNots? Some bozo that's just out to make trouble for you? Big jerk. Trying to wreck a great place like this."

Quill was touched at her vigorous defense of the Inn. "The idea you had for the contest? It was brilliant! And I bet we'll discover who wrote those complaints by tomorrow afternoon. And maybe I'm wrong. Maybe the person who hit me *is* the saboteur and those three deaths were coincidental. I don't know — maybe my logic is faulty somewhere — although I just can't see it." Quill shook her head. "I know I'm right about this, Doreen. Those three people were murdered."

A shout came from outside the office door. "Once more to the beach, my friends!"

"What'n the heck was that?"

"Adela. Come on, the Battle of Hemlock Falls has started."

Quill and Doreen emerged from the office in time to see three reenactors spring from position in the foyer and run out after Adela. Doreen, Dina, and Quill followed them out into the circular driveway. Dina, in an excess of spirits, broke into a run after them, her brown hair flying, white skirts whirling.

The five-acre field was alive with activity. Major Hackmeyer stood outside the cavalry tent, arms folded, intently focused on the action. Fetterman and Captain Coolidge stood with him.

The Rebels burst out from the pine trees on horseback. One waved a sword over his head. Several others knelt in the grass and fired blanks into the sunlit air.

The Union troops mounted and wheeled in formation. They charged the Rebels. The Rebels charged back. The citizens of Hemlock Falls cheered and hollered.

Adela reached the field, the three reenactors just behind her. They used their muskets as clubs, taking fake swipes at each other. Several of the soldiers on both sides howled artistically and fell dramatically to the ground. Then, the head Rebel, wearing a colonel's hat and waving his sword, raced his horse to the center of the field. The Confederate flag fluttered bravely from his saddle. He challenged the lead Union soldier with a shout.

"This is where the boys in blue quit," Doreen said. "It was mostly Stottles in that company. Them Stottles never have been any good, and from what I hear, the Johnny Reb just scared the bejesus out of 'em. They laid down like little lambs."

"They're still Stottles around here, after a hundred and thirty-three years?"

"All moved over to Trumansburg," Doreen said. "Well, will you look at that!"

"Oh, my!" Quill said.

Adela, skirts hiked to her hips and her red

plumes blazing like a beacon, thrust to the front of the small Union contingent. Head high, face crimson, she pushed her jaw close to the Rebel commander and yelled, "Surrender or die! For God! The President! And the United States of America!"

The lead Rebel (who, Quill saw now, was that infamous contrarian Roger Nickerson) threw down his sword, lowered the Confederate flag, and surrendered.

"Hooray!" Quill shouted. "We won after all!"

And the crowd went wild.

This threw the Union reenactors into considerable confusion. After an embarrassing couple of minutes (in which the Union soldier offered Old Glory to Roger Nickerson and Roger Nickerson kept giving it back) the Union soldiers raised their voices in a victory cheer, and shoved the Rebels off the field toward the beer tent.

"That Adela," Doreen said with intense admiration. "It just goes to show you." She grinned happily. "Nobody told her we lost."

The crowd surrounded Adela and cheered and cheered again. Somebody shoved Roger Nickerson off his horse, and Harland Peterson, his hired man T.K., and Peter Hairston hoisted her onto its back. The Hemlock Falls High School Marching Band struck up "The Star-Spangled Banner." People started to sing, and the whole crowd moved off toward Peterson Park, with Adela in the lead. Elmer strode beside her horse, beaming like a halogen lamp.

Warrender Hackmeyer spat onto the grass and went back into the tent.

"Why don't you go back and see if Meg needs anything," Quill said to Doreen. "I just want to see if the banquet's still on."

"If you're going to talk to that bozo, I'm coming with you. What if he knocks you on the head again?"

She picked her way across the meadow, Doreen trailing behind, as obstinate as a six-year-old left out of a birthday party.

The Union soldier at the front of the tent was particularly grubby. His face was filthy, and he was chewing tobacco. He grabbed her arm as she started to go in. "The major's not accepting visitors at the moment."

"I'm Sarah Quilliam," she said pleasantly. "I'm just checking on the banquet arrangements for this evening."

"Quill, goddammit. *Get out of the way.*"

The Union soldier was Myles. Quill stared at him, then grabbed Doreen and ran.

What seemed like hundreds of people in black jackets swarmed from the woods. They surrounded the tent, guns drawn. Myles stepped to one side of the opening and called out. "It's over, Hackmeyer. FBI."

CHAPTER 12

" 'The Inn is not friendly to kids,' " Quill read out loud. " 'My suggestion to make the Inn a better place is to put a video game arcade in the Tavern Bar. A good place to buy video games is from my husband.' " She laid the entry next to one of the suspect WhyNots and looked at the handwriting. "No match," she said. As the only professional artist, she'd been elected handwriting expert, a piece of reasoning that seemed logical but probably wasn't.

"That'd be Jerrianne Dubusky," Doreen said. "Her husband got laid off last month from the Paramount Paint Company. Guess he's selling video games now. I looked into it," she added. "It's a scam."

Doreen had made up contest forms using the office printer. A headline ran across the page: MY THREE SUGGESTIONS TO MAKE THE INN A BETTER PLACE. The line below that read: *Prizes for the Best Entry!!!!!* (*No typewritten suggestions accepted.*)

"I still want to know what prizes we're supposed to give out," Meg said. "Why did you tell them we would hand out prizes? Is everybody supposed to get a prize?"

Doreen looked hurt. Quill, dressed in loose jeans and an old white shirt of Myles, swung her bare feet up on the coffee table. It was Sunday afternoon, and the three of them had gathered in Quill's rooms to go over the contest entries and compare handwriting samples.

"I'm surprised we got as many entries as we did." Quill patted the back of her head. The wound was beginning to itch. "Everyone was so excited about the FBI raid on the reenactors that I thought they'd forget all about it."

Meg flipped the final contest entry into the Forget It pile. They'd divided the entries into three sections: Forget It, Maybe, and Great Idea. There were no entries in the Maybe and Great Idea piles. "I'll bet it was these mythical prizes. What kind of prizes did you promise them, Doreen?"

"Will you get off this prize thing?" Doreen heaved herself up from the Eames chair Quill had next to her couch. "You want me to take those stitches out? I got some nail scissors."

"No!"

"Don't be such a baby, Quill. Andy says he wastes a lot of time with stuff like that."

"Stuff like *what?* Taking stitches out of a person with a concussion?"

"Yeah."

"Well . . ." Quill scratched her head again. The wound really was beginning to itch. "Okay."

"Get all that hair out of the way," Doreen demanded. Obediently, Quill pulled her hair onto the top of her head. Doreen stood behind her, nail scissors in hand. "Don't look too bad. Bruise is something else, though. And there's a good bit of your scalp that's nice and bald." Her hands were gentle. "Still think that Hackmeyer busted you one?"

"I know Hackmeyer busted me one," Quill said ruefully. "And here's the FBI hauling him off for the possession of illegal assault weapons. How am I going to prove Hackmeyer did it now? And how am I going to prove those three murders?"

Meg took a long swallow of iced tea. "Did Myles say anything about it?"

"He went down with the FBI team to Rochester. Hackmeyer, Fetterman, and Coolidge are going to be arraigned in federal court. Myles thinks that Fetterman is going to testify. I told him last night I was sure that Hackmeyer was behind these deaths, and even more certain that he was the one who hit me over the head."

"What did he say?"

Quill made a face. "That Hackmeyer had been under surveillance since the reenactors came to Hemlock Falls. He and Fetterman weren't anywhere near the office on Wednesday night. They were up in Suite 312 conspiring to do goodness-knows-what to the federal government."

"*I'd* call that incontrovertible evidence," Meg said. "But what do I know?"

"There." Doreen smoothed the back of Quill's neck and presented the slightly bloody catgut for Quill's inspection. Quill waved the evidence away. "Ugh, Doreen. But thanks. It's not as itchy."

"So what do we do now?"

"My goodness, you're persistent, Meg." Quill got up and roamed restlessly around the room. "I know what I have to do, I just don't want to do it. We need more evidence. Maybe when the autopsy reports come in, we'll know more."

"I asked Andy about the DMSO. He called that in. They're going to check for it."

"Did you ask him what he thought about my idea? That Hackmeyer dosed all three patients with DMSO, it made them feel awful, so they checked into the hospital and that something happened to them there?"

"You know Andy. He said, 'Why?' "

"Why? That's it?"

"It's a reasonable question, Quill. You haven't established any motive."

"I've established one motive. Thanks to Doreen."

Doreen smiled with satisfaction. "What did I do?"

"You told me you cashed in your life insurance policy. And I know how that works: You sell your life insurance policy back to the insurance agent at a discount. They give you cash up front. When you die, they collect the whole amount from the insurer. It's a variation on a re-

278

verse mortgage. It's called a viatical. Hackmeyer's agencies not only sold reverse mortgages, they bought out lottery ticket winners and . . . they sold viaticals. So I called Harland Peterson last night to ask him if he knew whether Derwent had a life insurance policy and if he had cashed it in."

Meg look very interested. "And what did Harland say?"

"Harland said, 'Could be,' " Quill said triumphantly. "Then he said, 'Wouldn't put it past him.' "

"*There's* incontrovertible evidence for you," Meg said dryly. "One thing occurs to me, though. Doreen, how much did you insure your life for?"

Doreen had the expression of a trapped duckling. "Enough," she grumbled.

"I know you aren't comfortable talking about money, but this is important," Meg said. "Was it more than one hundred thousand dollars?"

"A hundred thousand dollars?" Doreen said, affronted. "What would I be doing with that kind of money? It was ten thousand dollars. Enough to bury me on. That's all."

"And how much did Marge pay out?"

"A third. Three thousand three hunnerd."

Meg made a face. "You barely got your premiums back."

"Yeah. But I got the money now, didn't I? No use to Stoke, he said, after I was dead. He's got his Xerox pension and the Social Security."

Quill saw where Meg was going. The elderly citizens of Hemlock Falls would see no need for a large life insurance policy past the age of sixty or so. Most of them didn't even see the need for a life insurance policy at all. She sighed, but persevered. "Would Mrs. Nickerson and Derwent Peterson and Freddie Bellini have large policies, do you think?"

Doreen shrugged. "Nadine wouldn't pay a nickel more'n she had to get herself buried. I don't know about Freddie. You'd think he'd want to leave enough for that wife of his, but you never know."

"My guess is that he did cash his policy in and that he sent it all to his son."

"That miserable kid," Doreen said. "Been no good for years, from what I hear."

"Maybe we're back to the invisibly poisoned garlic," Meg said, depressed. "Which puts the causes of these deaths right back into my kitchen, dammit."

Doreen rubbed her chin vigorously. "But Andy's pretty sure something funny's going on, huh?"

"Actually, he said we should wait until Monday. He's not sure of anything. The guy in Albany promised to fax the reports as soon as they're complete."

Quill went into the kitchen, poured herself a fourth cup of coffee, looked at it, dumped it into the sink, and came back out into the living room again. "I have to talk to Marge, Meg. I know we

280

want to keep this investigation as discreet as possible and not start any more gossip, but Marge will know all about this stuff with the insurance. I can't, won't believe that she had anything to do with any of this. But I have to say I have my doubts about Hackmeyer. He's a very wealthy man. I wouldn't put it past him to kill for profit, but it would have to be a lot more profit than thirty or forty thousand dollars."

"We were the ones who had doubts about Hackmeyer," Meg pointed out. "You were the one who kept insisting that he gave you that concussion. And you based it all on garlic breath. People can have garlic breath from eating — guess what — garlic! And that opens the investigation up to roughly one hundred percent of the residents of Hemlock Falls, since practically everybody eats pizza."

Quill circled restlessly around the room, eyeing the pile of contest entries. "I'm discouraged," she said frankly. "Even the search for the Inn saboteur's been a bust. None of the handwriting in the contest entries matched the bogus WhyNots at all."

"It would have to be a pretty stupid saboteur to hand over a nice, fresh, incriminating handwriting sample," Meg said.

Quill stood in the middle of the living room, her chin up. "I'm not finished with this."

"I am." Meg sprang up from the couch. "I vote we wait for the autopsy report and go from here. Myles was right all along. And since we're through here, I am actually going to take some time off. Andy and I are going for a drive."

"You can't yet," Doreen said. "We have to pick a winner."

"A winner?" Meg shrieked indignantly. "From those ideas? We received three suggestions to put in a water park, one with a slide down Hemlock Falls to the Hemlock River that would disable any healthy person in two minutes flat. Annie Fassbinder thinks we should put God into our hearts and Bible verses on the menus, which would be violating somebody's civil rights, even if we wanted to, which we don't. What about that one from the French sous chef who offers to run off for the weekend with me or with Quill? We get to pick."

"Quill promised to execute the best one," Doreen said stubbornly. "And you'd be undermining your authority with the buggers if you backed off on your promise. Not to mention," she added thoughtfully, "undermining my own authority. So pick."

"Fine. I'll pick." Meg leaned forward, grabbed the top item from the Forget It stack, and said, "Here. This one."

"It's from Dina," said Quill, who recognized *that* handwriting. "It's the one that says we should be able to vote to kick out obnoxious guests. We can't do that."

Meg smiled. "Why can't we throw out unwelcome guests? Just tell me why not?"

"I don't ever want to hear those two words again," Quill said. "And who are we going to throw out? We didn't even throw out Hackmeyer and his lethal buddies."

Meg's smile became bigger. "Why don't we kick out Azalea and Ralph?"

"We can't kick out Azalea and Ralph," Quill said. "The only time we ever kick anybody out is when we discover that their credit cards were stolen. And even then, we don't kick them out. Mike just politely packs up their things and escorts them off the property."

"Maybe it's time to start a new policy."

"We'll be the ones who'll be kicked out! Right out of the Innkeepers' Association of America. Plus, we could get sued." Quill appealed to Doreen, "This is dumb."

Doreen shrugged. "We got to pick something. If we don't, my authority with . . ."

"Stop," Quill said.

Meg leaned forward and said quietly, "If we kick them out now, they won't be able to show the film that shows us with the body-smoothers on our heads at the Chamber dinner tonight."

"Oh." Quill tugged at her lower lip. "They've run up quite a bill, Meg. What if they refuse to pay?"

"It's the university that's supposed to pay. It's not even their money."

"And just how are we supposed to kick them out?"

"I don't know. Make up something."

"Me? I'm supposed to do this?"

"Well, sure."

"You're the manager," Doreen added. She packed her nail scissors into her purse and said, "I'm off, too. Stoke's waiting."

"You didn't drink your coffee," Quill said.

"Gotta keep off the caffeine today, Andy says."

Quill gave Meg a quick glance. "We thought we'd drop by this evening, after you check in to the hospital. We could play gin rummy."

"Keep your mind off the fact you can't eat a thing after eight o'clock," Meg added. "And we'll be right there in the morning, Doreen, before you go into surgery."

"Stoke said you didn't want too many people around." Quill put her hand lightly on Doreen's arm. "And if you don't want us there, just say so."

"You two won't make a fuss," Doreen said pragmatically. "My daughters would just make a fuss, not to mention my grandkids. But you two want to waste your time dropping by, you just do that." She stamped out the door and slammed it behind her.

"She *is* going to be okay, Meg, isn't she? I honestly don't know what we'd do without her."

"Andy didn't seem too worried. But then, he has this whole distancing thing when it comes to his patients."

The phone in the kitchen rang.

" 'Distancing,' " Quill said. "That's a fine old psychological phrase. Have you decided to see a couples therapist after all?"

"I have decided that it's none of your business," Meg said crossly. "Are you going to get that? If it's Andy, tell him I'm on my way. Our drive is scheduled for three o'clock."

Quill picked up the phone, said "Hello," then "If you'll excuse me just a moment . . ." She held the phone to her chest and waved to Meg. "I'll see you at the banquet tonight."

"Sure. This is me, leaving." She, too, stamped across the living room floor and slammed the door behind her.

"Our drive is scheduled for three o'clock?" Quill muttered to Max, who'd finally emerged from his afternoon nap on the kitchen floor. "My left foot. Ha." She put the phone to her ear. "Hi. This is Quill. I'm sorry for the delay. Oh, dear, Donna. How are you? Was the party scheduled for today? No, no, of course I hadn't forgotten. Yes, it was terrible, wasn't it? But at least Hackmeyer's gone off to prison."

Quill drove her Honda east down Route 15 and practiced saying "no" to all the cosmetics Donna was going to try to sell her. She didn't use many cosmetics, just lip gloss and mascara, and she'd wasted way too much money on miracle skin care products she didn't use. One of the many advantages of living in Hemlock Falls was that she had to drive an hour to get to a department store with its seductive displays of elegant bottles, jars, and boxes.

"No, thank you," she said earnestly to the rearview mirror. "I buy all my skin care products from my handicapped niece, who is putting herself through college selling Avon." She tried an earnest expression: nope. A sincere expression: better. A rueful, regretful expression: best. That should work. A truck horn blared and she swerved to the right, skidded a little, and threw a sheepish, apologetic glance out her window at Carol Ann Spinoza, who had been driving west on Route 15 toward town.

Carol Ann pulled a U-turn and came after her.

Quill's first impulse was to passionately regret the sale of her beloved Oldsmobile Delta 88. That fine old vehicle could go from zero to sixty in less than ten seconds and had a top speed of 120 on the flat. Her second was to affect complete, supreme indifference to the Chevy Blazer on her tail. The third was to remember something Howie Murchison had told her about citizen arrest, which had to do with your average, vigilante-oriented citizen seeing a crime being committed and legally being able to arrest the poor soul who was committing it.

Quill slowed to a legal thirty-five miles an hour, then pulled over to the shoulder and stopped. Carol Ann pulled over, too. She got out of her Blazer. She was wearing her usual spotless tennis shoes, spotless sweatshirt, and painfully ironed jeans. Her blond hair bounced in a perky ponytail on the top of her head. And she was wearing mirrored sunglasses, just like the more predatory Georgia State Troopers Quill had seen in the movies.

"Hey, Quill."

"Hey, Carol Ann."

"Not paying too much attention to our driving, were we?"

"We seemed to have pulled a U-turn in the middle of a state road," Quill said pleasantly.

"I just wanted to drop this by for you." Carol Ann held out a sheet of paper. It was a sheet titled, I THINK THE INN AT HEMLOCK FALLS COULD BE IMPROVED BY:

"Our contest is just for employees," Quill said suspiciously. "Sorry but I can't take this." She handed it to Carol Ann. Carol Ann handed it back.

"I am an employee," Carol Ann said. "I asked the mayor about it. Remember? I volunteered to be an employee of the Inn for the reenactment. I handed out your brochures. The mayor said that would qualify me under the contest rules. I wouldn't have bothered, of course, but I heard about the five-hundred-dollar prize and I figured I have very good ideas about how to improve the Inn. Anyhow, the ideas are supposed to be in today, so here it is."

"The five-hundred-dollar what?"

"Prize," Carol Ann said clearly and precisely. "And I just wanted to remind you, Quill, that the county is going to go through a reassessment process later in the year. Not that that is connected to the prize or anything. But I had these two messages for you: the contest entry and the 'heads-up' on the reassessment, so that's why I stopped you." Carol Ann sounded as if she were practicing testimony in defense of a bribery charge. Which was probably one of the many reasons she hadn't been nailed so far. Quill tossed the entry onto the front seat and grabbed the Honda's steering wheel hard so that she wouldn't scream.

"Thank you, Carol Ann."

"Thank *you*."

Carol Ann minced back to the Blazer, pulled another U-turn, and drove off west toward town.

Quill was so annoyed at Carol Ann that she drove past the turnoff for the Olafsons' house and had to back up on the road, to the discomfiture of the driver of an oncoming tour bus.

Donna and Brian had purchased five acres from Schmidt Realty Company. They'd hired an architect out of Syracuse to design it and a builder from nearby Trumansburg to put it up. The house was almost finished, although there was still a lot of dug-up dirt in the back. A bulldozer and a concrete mixer were parked next to a site for a second, smaller building at the back of the property. Quill pulled up the long, newly asphalted driveway and sat looking at Donna's new house. She was already in a bad mood, and the house made it worse. It was a small house, actually, although the oversized columns in the front (Greek Revival) made it look large. The forward-slanting roof (Salt Box) warred with the wrought-iron railings surmounting the upper windows (Mediterranean). Elaborate trim had been mounted under the porch roof (Carpenter Gothic). So this was Donna's passion. Quill sighed and prepared to perjure her soul.

"This was the one time I just went nuts and got everything I wanted," Donna said as she greeted Quill at the front door. She was, as usual, beautifully dressed. She wore carefully tailored sharkskin pants and jacket and a deep blue silk shell top. A heavy gold necklace circled her neck and drop diamonds hung at her ears. "It all had to be perfect. And it is!"

"You look perfect," Quill said, which was true. "Am I the first one?"

"The very first. Come in and let me show you around." Quill followed her across the marble foyer. She slipped a little on the highly polished surface. The house opened up past the foyer; a large open dining room flowed to the left and the living room was off to the right. The ceilings were at least nine feet high. Sunlight poured into the rooms from a huge rectangular palladium-style window in the living area, and an arched window at the south end of the dining room. The living room had wall-to-wall white carpet. The chairs and couches were upholstered in shades of muted green: celery, sage, lettuce, and apple. An elaborate glass coffee table in front of a large sectional couch was piled with boxes of pink cosmetics. Quill groaned to herself.

"And the kitchen's back here."

Quill followed the sound of Donna's voice. The kitchen was large, open, and incredibly white. White granite countertops, white Smallbone cabinets, white appliances.

"A white kitchen is so elegant, don't you think?" Donna sank gracefully into a chair at the kitchen table. The top was covered with invoices, bills, and a calculator.

"You certainly know when it's clean," Quill said in her most enthusiastic tones. The appliances were all top-of-the-line residential. A Sub-Zero refrigerator, with a custom paneled door; a Dutch dishwasher; and a huge Wolf range. The granite countertops were a speckled white that Quill knew was very hard to come by. "That's a beautiful view out these windows, Donna. You picked the perfect spot for your house."

"Marge Schmidt certainly knew its value to us," Donna said tartly. "You'd think after we purchased her insurance business from her, that she'd be willing to give us a break. But that woman's a . . ." She compressed her lips into a tight, hard line. "Well, I won't say it. You must have had run-ins with her, too. She's so bossy. But I'm sure I know what you're thinking."

Quill hoped Donna didn't have a clue what she was thinking. She was thinking that all Marge's complaints about the insurance business being risky in these economic times were clever ploys to stave off the competition, but the actual truth was a lot different. Marge had sold her insurance business, because it was too risky for her. And if Marge had sold her insurance business, the assets would go with it. Assets such as the payouts from the viaticals. And Donna's cosmetics: the hand cream, the miracle face cream, and Derwent's eczema and Freddie's hands, vulnerable from years of wearing rubber gloves to do his . . . She'd walked into the house of a murderer or . . . "May I sit down?" Quill sat at the table, her legs rubbery. "That structure out there. Is that a horse barn?" Quill was careful to keep her voice level.

"It will be. We hit some foundation problems, so the construction's been delayed. Can you believe? There's an underground stream that runs right across the property back there. We had to put in a half-basement. In a barn!"

"I didn't know you had horses."

"Oh, yes. My boys are all stabled up in Syracuse at the moment, but I'll have them trucked down as soon as we get the barn up. The concrete people are supposed to be back a week from tomorrow morning. It shouldn't take them long. The barn's twenty-four by forty-eight. A perfect size for four stalls."

"Do you take care of them yourself? The horses?" Quill was starting to feel like the nightgown-clad heroines in the more lurid type of Gothic novel. The kind that always walked into the basement when it was perfectly obvious the murderer was lurking beneath the stairs. "I mean, it's an expensive hobby. And they always seem to have one problem or another. Sore backs, sore legs, sore feet."

"Oh, I take care of them myself. And you'd be surprised how my nursing training helps. I can stitch up any wounds, give injections, and massage their bruises. Whatever's needed." She smiled. Her lips seemed very large to Quill. "I even mix up my own special medicines for them."

"I didn't know you were a nurse," Quill said hollowly.

"Oh yes. I've been working part-time at the hospital for the past few weeks. I even dropped in to see you when you were there for your concussion. But you were so nicely asleep, I didn't want to wake you up." She looked around her all-white kitchen with a fanatic sort of pride. "Well, what do you think of the house? I so wanted you to see it. Everyone talks about your wonderful taste, Quill. But people haven't seen this yet." Something malicious gleamed in her eyes.

"It's an interesting house," Quill said. There

seemed to be something stuck in her throat. She cleared it and said, "Did you say Marge was going to be here? Or can we get at those lovely cosmetics I saw set up in the living room right away?"

"You are a nosey little bitch, aren't you?" Donna said conversationally. "Why couldn't you let well enough alone?"

"I have no idea what you're talking about." Quill didn't back up, and she didn't look away. One of the chapters in *Happy Dog, Happy Owner* had been full of advice on angry dogs. Quill was glad she'd read it. "Look. Maybe this is a bad time for the cosmetics party, Donna."

"Oh, it's a bad time, all right," she said bitterly. She sprang from the chair and began to circle the kitchen. She touched the countertops, the stove, and the cupboard doors. She moved in a restless, frantic spiral. "Brian's whined that song once too often for me. 'Bad time to buy anything right now, Donna. We're a little short this month.' 'New house? We're not in that league, Donna.' I'll tell you this, you nosey little creep: I'm tired of *not being in that league!*" She stopped in front of Quill, hissing with effort.

"It's hard, isn't it?" Quill said sympathetically. "I know just how you feel. Here." She picked up Donna's purse from the kitchen chair and pulled the chair away from the table. "Why don't you sit down? I could use a cup of coffee." She rose and moved toward the

293

coffeemaker. "I'll make some for the both of us. And I can tell you something about missing out. Sometimes I feel as if everyone but me gets the breaks."

"Everyone but me!" Donna struck her chest with her fist. "Everyone but me! *Do* you know what I could have been? Do you know what I looked like when I was young?"

"You're very beautiful," Quill said. She turned away from those frantic eyes and set Donna's purse on the counter next to the coffeemaker. Her cell phone was in the side pocket. Quill slipped it into her skirt pocket. "Maybe a glass of wine would be better than coffee, Donna. What do you think?"

"I think that it's time you got out of my way." Donna stood up slowly. "I've got a little more money to collect." She smiled in a scary way. It didn't reach her eyes, which were mad. All the smile did was expose her shiny white teeth. "The bill for the countertop's due. It's a little over three thousand dollars. And that son-of-a-bitch Brian says he doesn't have another dime."

So you're cashing in another customer, Quill thought to herself. Somebody else was going to die. Someone scheduled to go into the clinic for surgery, perhaps.

Quill could feel her face pale. "Doreen?" she shouted. "You're after Doreen!"

This time she saw very clearly who hit her over the head.

294

★ ★ ★

Quill didn't wake up to a clean, antiseptic hospital room; she woke up in a tomb and she shrieked with terror. Then she was violently sick to her stomach.

She lay still after she'd vomited and tried to breathe slowly and quietly.

Doreen. Doreen's life was at stake. She had to get out of here. But where was "here"?

As time passed, she began to distinguish between the waves of dizziness and the disorientation of the dark. Because it was dark. Pitch black. She might have been in a sensory deprivation tank, for all she could see. She was glad she wasn't claustrophobic.

She raised her hand to her head and struck a rough, wiry ceiling. Or a lid, she thought with a sudden upsurge of panic. Was she in a coffin? She wiggled her toes. They struck a solid obstacle.

She decided she might be claustrophobic after all, so she shrieked again, which made her feel a lot better.

She moved her hands outward from her sides. Space, there at least. So if she were in a coffin, it was an extra-extra-large one. But the floor beneath her was wet, and made of dirt. They didn't put dirt in leaky coffins unless you were a vampire. If she was very careful, she could roll sideways. She rolled over once, twice, and then had to stop. Her head swam. Her head hurt. And she was very angry. Who'd put her here?

And why? The last thing she remembered was garlic. And Doreen. Something was going to happen to Doreen.

And then she slept.

When she woke up again, she was cold, and the last thing she remembered was big, mean lips. And the lips were attached to Donna Olafson's perfectly preserved face. And Donna was going to kill Doreen for three thousand three hundred and thirty pieces of silver. Quill wanted more than anything to go to sleep. Her eyes closed. A welcome tide of forgetfulness swept over her.

Doreen. Unconscious after the anesthetic. Hooked to an IV for a few vulnerable hours until she woke up completely. Alone in the recovery room.

Quill fought sleep as she'd never fought anything before. She bit her lip. She pounded her knuckles into the ground until she could feel the blood. And she forced herself to roll over and over again until she hit the opposite side of whatever she was in. She put her hands on her hips, little fingers on her hipbones, and extended her hands until the thumbs touched in the middle. Her hand span was about six inches; so if she was twelve inches wide, and counted as she rolled, she could figure out how long the space was. It was about six feet six inches long, because she could touch the opposing walls with the tips of her fingers when her arms were extended and her toes.

She rolled back, counting one, two, three, four. And froze. Something underneath her chirped. A rat? She shrieked a third time.

Not a rat. A rat didn't chirp; it squeaked. This was a chirp like a chipmunk.

Or a cell phone.

EPILOGUE

"A toast," Myles said, "to resolution." He raised his wineglass.

"None for you, Quill," Andy warned. "Not that you don't have resolution — you do. Anyone that had the presence of mind to figure out they were buried in a barn foundation by literally rolling out the dimensions has a great deal of resolution. I meant no liquor for a week, at least."

Quill adjusted the bandage at the back of her head and raised her water glass. Her hands were sore and already starting to scab over. It was Tuesday, one day after Myles and David had pulled her from the half-basement under Donna's new barn, one day after Doreen's successful operation. They all sat at a big round table in the dining room overlooking the Falls. Doreen and Stoke, John and Trish, Meg and Andy, Dina and Davey Kiddermeister. All the people she loved, in one room at one table, eating Meg's sun-dried tomato pasta and watching the sunset like a bronze-colored peacock settling into a great blue nest. She sighed happily.

Myles smiled at her. "Feeling sentimental?"

"Feeling glad to be alive." She clicked Doreen's wineglass with her own. "Feeling glad that no more people will die before their time in Hemlock Falls. Feeling ecstatic that Doreen's bouncing around like a rubber ball after her operation. Doreen, I have forgiven you for giving away five hundred dollars to that snake Carol Ann Spinoza."

Doreen's lower lip jutted out. She was a little woozy still, but she snapped the head off anyone who suggested that she remain in bed for a few days.

"Forgiven me? You should be givin' me a bonus." Her gray hair rose up like an affronted chicken's feathers. "If Carol Ann hadn't sent in that contest entry, how would we of caught the Inn saboteur? That's worth five hundred bucks, easy."

"It'd be worth more than five hundred bucks if Carol Ann went to jail," Meg muttered. "I can't believe she took that money. I can't believe we can't prove she tried to foment an employee revolution."

"She made a lot of sense," Dina said a little defiantly. "She may be the meanest person in Tompkins County, but she has a soft spot in her heart for the workingman."

"Stop," Quill said. Dina rolled her eyes and took a huge bite of Meg's Gorgonzola salad. "It does seem hard that she not only gets off, she gets off with our five hundred dollars."

Myles shrugged. "She didn't really break any laws, Quill. The only actual evidence we had linking her to the false WhyNots was the one she sent to Dave here."

Davey nodded. "At best, it's malicious mischief, according to Mr. Murchison. And of course, it turned out to be not so malicious after all, since Hackmeyer was dangerous. It was possible that someone would have died at the Battle of Hemlock Falls." He tugged at his mustache. "As a matter of fact, she's put the mayor up to giving her a Good Citizen Award."

Meg shrieked, *"Phuut!"*

It was time to change the subject. "Now *he's* going to jail, isn't he?" Quill asked. "Hackmeyer, I mean."

"He was arraigned yesterday," Myles said. "We'll see. At this point, it's in the hands of the lawyers, and he has a pretty determined defense team. But I'd say the odds are very good that he'll spend some time in jail."

For Myles, who was reluctant to predict any judicial outcome, this was tantamount to certainty.

"And what about Donna Olafson?" Andy took a drink of his red wine and set the glass down with a reflective air. "We wouldn't have been able to prove that she injected air bubbles into the IVs, you know. We could only surmise. And she hasn't confessed. If she hadn't tried to kill you, Quill, twice, we might not have been able to get her off the streets at all."

300

"I don't think she tried to kill me either time," Quill said. "She just wanted any evidence I had that she'd been handing out hand cream to those poor patients of Andy's eliminated. And the guys were coming to put the barn up a week from today, by which time I would have been too." Quill stopped in midsentence. She was scaring herself again. "Anyway. She killed Derwent Peterson, Nadine Nickerson, and Freddie Bellini. She assaulted me. Will she go to jail for the murders, Myles?"

"She'll go to jail for assault to commit grievous bodily harm. As for the murders, the forensic evidence is scanty, at best," Myles said. "But the circumstantial evidence is very strong. And her paranoia's obvious."

Andy said thoughtfully, "The preliminary diagnosis is narcissistic personality disorder with paranoid overtones. I'm starting to wonder if I should ask for psychological evaluations on some of our other staff."

"So," Quill said, "it's just as well that I went into the basement."

Andy looked startled.

"She doesn't mean she's glad Donna tried to bury her in the foundation of that barn," Meg said. "She means that she's feeling stupid that she hadn't cracked the case before she went to see Donna. She just walked into a murderer's arms."

"Which is another good reason why you ought to keep your darn nose out of these things," Doreen said. "What kind of detective work did you do here, anyways?"

"It was pretty lame detective work," Quill agreed meekly. "I would have figured it out in time, though. Heck, I *did* figure it out. So I forgive you again, Doreen."

"Have you forgiven her for throwing Azalea and Ralph out of the Inn?" Dina asked.

"You did what?" Myles said.

"It was that dopey contest," Quill said. "The employees all voted on who they wanted kicked out, and it was Azalea and Ralph, by a landslide." She reacted to Myles's expression by adding defensively, "I couldn't help it. I was stuck in that darn foundation. Doreen talked it up in the kitchen while everyone was at the banquet and they voted and Doreen marched right in, grabbed that awful film they were about to show, and boom." Quill threw her hands in the air.

"Boom?" Myles said. "It seems a little precipitate, Quill. What was so awful about the film?"

Quill, Meg, and Dina looked at one another. Doreen opened her mouth and closed it.

"Nothing," Quill said. "Never mind."

"It might have been better that you handled it," Myles said thoughtfully. "On the other hand, maybe not."

"You didn't find me until yesterday morning. Believe me, I would far rather have dealt with Azalea than spend the evening asleep in my would-be grave."

Myles nodded. "There is that." His hand brushed her own. Then he took it and cradled it gently.

Andy looked at Doreen with lively interest. "What happened exactly? How did you get them out of the Inn?"

Dina shook her head admiringly. "Doreen hollered at them awhile then called Mike to pack up their bags, and he escorted them right out of here. I have to say you did it with style, Doreen. You told them exactly what we think of stuck-up arty snobs that think they're better than anyone else."

"Oh, dear," Quill said. "Well, it could have been worse."

"Oh, it could have," Myles said. "As a matter of fact, it might anyway."

"How?" Quill said in indignant defense of her recovering cancer patient.

"It's all part of the new government cooperation between agencies. Those two were after Hackmeyer. We couldn't have tracked the financial end of the armament sales without them."

Quill stared at him. "You mean they were undercover for the FBI? They were agents? We've kicked undercover agents for the FBI out of the Inn? After insulting them six ways from Sunday?"

Quill had a sudden vision of Ralph, smirking at her outside the Inn: *Lot of cash in this business. It's a gold mine. Bet a lot doesn't get reported. Right, Quill?*

"Some FBI agent," Quill scoffed.

"They aren't FBI agents," Myles said reassuringly. "And they are genuine filmmakers."

"Thank goodness." Quill took a deep, relieved breath.

"I think I mentioned that we've entered into a new era of cooperation with other government agencies, Quill. They're filmmakers, because it's a heck of a good cover.

"They work for the IRS."

RECIPE

Meg's Gorgonzola salad is easy to make and delicious. She suggests you have it as a main course for lunch, or as a side for a dinner with pasta.

GORGONZOLA VICTORY SALAD

1 pound bacon, diced
1 medium Mayan onion, diced
3 heads fresh Romaine lettuce, well chilled
2 pints grape tomatoes, freshly picked
1 pint Kalamata olives
1 pint Gorgonzola cheese, well crumbled
quarter-cup sweet, pure olive oil

Sauté the bacon until limp; add the onion; sauté until the bacon is crisp.

While the bacon is crisping, break the lettuce into small pieces and place into a large wooden bowl. Add the tomatoes, olives, and Gorgonzola cheese.

Do not drain the bacon fat; it is part of the dressing. Add the olive oil to the hot bacon, stir the mixture with a wooden spoon, pour over the salad greens, and serve immediately.

ABOUT THE AUTHOR

Claudia Bishop is the author of eleven Hemlock Falls novels. She is at work on the twelfth. She is the senior editor of the mystery anthologies *Death Dines at 8:30* and the forthcoming anthology *Death Dines In*. As Mary Stanton, she is the author of eleven middle-grade books and two adult novels.

She can be reached at mstanton@red suspenders.com or claudiabishop.com. She divides her time between a cattle ranch in upstate New York and West Palm Beach.

The employees of Thorndike Press hope you have enjoyed this Large Print book. All our Thorndike and Wheeler Large Print titles are designed for easy reading, and all our books are made to last. Other Thorndike Press Large Print books are available at your library, through selected bookstores, or directly from us.

For information about titles, please call:

(800) 223-1244

or visit our Web site at:

www.gale.com/thorndike
www.gale.com/wheeler

To share your comments, please write:

Publisher
Thorndike Press
295 Kennedy Memorial Drive
Waterville, ME 04901